ROMANCING
the
BILLIONAIRE

JESSICA CLARE

BERKLEY SENSATION, NEW YORK

THE BERKLEY PUBLISHING GROUP
Published by the Penguin Group
Penguin Group (USA) LLC
375 Hudson Street, New York, New York 10014

USA • Canada • UK • Ireland • Australia • New Zealand • India • South Africa • China

penguin.com

A Penguin Random House Company

ROMANCING THE BILLIONAIRE

A Berkley Book / published by arrangement with the author

Berkley Books are published by The Berkley Publishing Group.
BERKLEY® is a registered trademark of Penguin Group (USA) LLC.
The "B" design is a trademark of Penguin Group (USA) LLC.

For information, address: The Berkley Publishing Group,
a division of Penguin Group (USA) LLC,
375 Hudson Street, New York, New York 10014.

ISBN: 978-0-425-27578-8

PUBLISHING HISTORY
Berkley mass-market edition / November 2014

PRINTED IN THE UNITED STATES OF AMERICA

10 9 8 7 6 5 4 3 2 1

Cover photo of "jewelry" © sbayram/Getty Images.
Cover design by Sarah Oberrender.
Interior text design by Laura K. Corless.

AUTHOR'S NOTE

In this book, I've taken liberties with a few minor things for purpose of the story, most notably the depth of the Thames River at a certain location. I hope no one finds it too jarring.

ONE

Violet DeWitt held the envelope marked "To Be Opened by My Daughter Upon My Death" and ran her fingers along the edges.

"Well?" the solicitor asked, clearly curious. "Aren't you going to open it?"

But Violet only eyed the calligraphic writing in her father's hand, reminiscent of medieval illuminations. She studied the ornate wax seal. It was such an unnecessary thing on a modern envelope. So very much something her father would do.

She carefully placed the envelope in her lap and gave the man across the desk from her a polite smile. "No, I'm not."

The man's broad forehead wrinkled, and he looked disappointed. "But it's your father's last wish, Ms. DeWitt. Don't you want to honor it?"

"I'm fairly certain I know what it says already, Mr. Penning," Violet said, keeping her voice brisk and cheerful as she tucked the envelope under her hands. "Now, is there anything else involved with my father's estate that you need me for?"

He cast her another puzzled look before turning to the stack of papers on his desk and flipping through them. She understood the look he was giving her. Most people that the solicitor saw were probably grieving or concerned about money they would inherit; Violet was not interested in anything of the sort. She just wanted to leave.

"Your father was a great man," Mr. Penning commented as he pulled out another piece of paper and peered at it through his bifocals.

"Yes."

"His work was so very respected. I've read three of his books, and even though I'm only an armchair enthusiast, I couldn't help but be fascinated. What an exciting life the man led. Really, just a great man."

"So I am told."

Now, Mr. Penning looked surprised. "Did you not know your father, Ms. DeWitt? I was under the impression—"

"I knew him," she corrected, wishing the conversation wasn't heading in this direction. The estate solicitor probably didn't want to hear about her workaholic father's long absences, his abandonment of her mother, and Dr. DeWitt's own callous treatment of Violet. Everyone just assumed that the legendary archaeologist Dr. Phineas DeWitt was as lovable and endearing to his family as he was to the documentary cameras. *Not the case,* Violet thought to herself. *Not the case at all.* But she put a patient smile on her face and leaned forward, as if interested in what the paper Mr. Penning was clutching read. "His estate is all handled, right?"

"Oh." He adjusted his glasses, refocusing back on the paperwork in front of him. "Yes, actually, I believe that envelope is the last item outstanding. Your father, I'm sorry to say, racked up quite a bit of debt prior to his death. It seemed he was privately funding a few personal expeditions and ran up several mortgages on his house, which was taken by the bank three weeks prior to his death."

Violet made a sympathetic murmur in her throat. She

didn't care about the money or the house, and she hadn't expected anything. She just wanted to leave.

"Luckily, there was an anonymous third-party donor who has paid off all of your father's outstanding debts."

"Very lucky," Violet agreed, her fist clenching. She had an idea who that donor was, and she hated the jerk. Anonymous, indeed. Now he'd expect her to be grateful and throw herself at him with gratitude. Not in this lifetime.

"I think that's everything, then." The solicitor gave her one last expectant look, his gaze sliding to the envelope in her lap. When she made no move to open it, he sighed and handed her a paper to sign. She did, and he stood and extended his hand.

"Thank you, Mr. Penning. Call me if I can be of any further assistance," she told him, all business. Then she shook his hand and left the law office, the unopened envelope clutched in hand.

When she got out to her car, Violet started the engine, tossed the envelope into the passenger seat, and then paused. She rubbed her forehead, willing the headache behind her eyes to go away. Envelopes were an old favorite of the late Phineas DeWitt. When she was eight, her father had given her an envelope for her birthday. Inside was a clue that, if followed, would lead her to a trail of additional clues. She'd been so excited at the time, and after a series of envelope clues, each one more complex than the last, she arrived at her present.

It was a copy of *The Encyclopedia on the Study of Ancient Hieroglyphics*. Used. The inscription inside said: *To Phineas, thanks for being a great teacher.*

Granted, it was an interesting book, but her eight-year-old self had wanted a Barbie.

Phineas paid no attention to Violet's other birthdays until she turned sixteen. She'd received another envelope in the mail and had been excited despite initial trepidation. At the end of the chase, however, her present had been a copy of a doctoral thesis written by one of her father's students on

Minoan frescoes. He'd tacked a note to it that read: *Pay attention, Violet. This is the sort of thing you'll need to write if you want to work for your father!*

Again, not something she'd particularly wanted. But Phineas DeWitt believed in two things—knowledge and adventure. All else was foolishness.

She'd tossed the photocopied thesis into the garbage and tried to forget about her father's terrible ideas for birthday gifts. When she was eighteen, she fell for it one more time, and was just as disappointed. The end of that envelope chase led to an ugly copper ring that turned her finger green and looked like something out of a tourist shop. That was after a week of frantic searching to find what her father had left her, hoping against hope that he'd remembered what she liked, her fears and hopes and dreams, and that he'd give her a present that showed he really, truly did understand his daughter.

Not so much. Phineas DeWitt gave presents, but in the end, it was still all about him. Just like everything else with her father's games, she knew that her initial excitement would lead to inevitable disappointment. The envelopes and the challenge were to mask the fact that Phineas put no thought or effort into her presents . . . just like he'd put no thought or effort into being her father.

And she knew what—and who—this last envelope game would lead to without even having to look.

Oh, Father. I know what you're up to. This is just one more little game, and I've no intention of playing this time. Nothing you say or do can make me want to talk to Jonathan Lyons ever again.

Violet didn't think she was a hard, unforgiving type. She was nice, darn it, and understanding. But when a guy gave you pretty words, got you pregnant, and abandoned you? That wasn't so easy to forgive, or forget, no matter what her father wanted.

Some things you just couldn't let go.

———————

"This is her classroom," Principal Esparza said to Jonathan Lyons, gesturing at the door ahead. "You're sure Ms. DeWitt is expecting you? She didn't indicate to me that she was anticipating a visitor, and this is a closed campus." The principal sounded disapproving, but she hadn't kicked him out. It was amazing what you could do if you showed up in an expensive suit with your personal bodyguard. Of course, being famous—or infamous—in the right circles certainly helped.

"She's expecting me," Jonathan said, adjusting the front of his suit jacket. "Perhaps she simply forgot to notify you. Violet is an old family friend of the Lyonses."

"Well," Ms. Esparza said with a happy smile. "I'm a big fan of your cars, though I certainly can't afford one!" She gave a girlish giggle at odds with her advanced age.

He gave her his best rakish grin, adopting the part of the flirty playboy billionaire. "Shall I have one sent to you?"

"Oh, no." Esparza giggled again, and tucked a gray-streaked lock of hair into her bun. "It's against school policy. But you're sweet to offer." She moved forward and knocked on the cheerfully lettered *Fifth Grade Social Studies* door.

Jonathan swallowed the knot in his throat and shifted on his feet. It was pathetic to be nervous. He'd rappelled off of cliffs in Nepal, snorkeled with sharks, been in God knew how many cave-ins, and once ended up on a ship attacked by Somali pirates. He'd never been nervous in all those situations. Adrenaline-fueled? Absolutely. Nervous? Hell no.

But standing outside of a fifth-grade classroom, waiting for a woman that he hadn't seen in ten years? His palms were sweating.

What would Violet look like? His memories of her were of certain things instead of the entire package. He remembered a short girl, no higher than his shoulder, with long, dark braids streaked with wild pink, a wicked smile, a lean figure, and a tramp stamp that said *Carpe Diem* across her lower back. He remembered the scent of her skin, the way she made soft little gasping cries when she came, and the tight suction of her mouth on his dick.

Just thinking about her brought a wealth of memories and regrets surging back to the forefront. There wasn't a day that went by that he didn't regret that last night, the last hour, the last minute they'd spent together.

She'd wanted to get married. Wanted their little summer fling in Greece to turn into something real. She'd insisted on returning to the States and settling down. And Jonathan had been nineteen, taking a semester off of college, and was dazzled by the dynamic Dr. Phineas DeWitt, who seemed daily on the verge of yet another important archaeological discovery. They'd both been participating in DeWitt's latest dig for the summer, and it was the most exciting thing Jonathan had ever done. Growing up, Jonathan was the younger son of a businessman in desperate need of a miracle. Jonathan had watched, year after year, as his father poured every hour of his time and every dollar in his wallet into making Lyons Motors a viable company, all without success. Jonathan hadn't been jealous of his father's obsession with his car business; it simply was something that one had to shrug and ignore.

In Dr. DeWitt, however, he'd found a mentor and a father figure who cared what Jonathan thought. Suddenly, he was important, and it was intoxicating.

But Violet had a quick and decisive change of heart. She didn't want a life of archaeological digs and adventure. She wanted home and a family, in that order. No more adventure, no more college, all at the age of nineteen. And she'd suggested that last night together that he give it all up and settle down with her.

Jonathan had laughed in her face, being a young asshole full of himself.

She'd slapped him, burst into tears, and stormed out of his life.

That was the night he'd lost her, and it didn't take long before he regretted his cruelty. Greece without Violet at his side just wasn't the same. In fact, nothing was the same. He began to miss her with the same intensity with which he'd loved the archaeological expedition, and confessed to Professor DeWitt, whom he viewed as a mentor and friend, of his longing. He was thinking about going after Violet. Apologizing. Trying again.

But her father told him it was a mistake. According to him, Violet had been stateside for all of a week before she'd shacked up with an ex-boyfriend. And he'd handed Jonathan a stack of field notes to bury his sorrow. Devastated, Jonathan threw himself into work.

A few weeks later, Dr. DeWitt had told a moping, despondent Jonathan that Violet had married and it was time to move on. Did Jonathan want to accompany him to an unearthing of a new tomb in the Valley of the Kings?

He did. He had. And he'd sunk himself into adventuring, archaeology, extreme sports—whatever it took to distract himself from the fact that he'd fucked up and lost Violet. When his father died and his older brother declared he didn't want the family albatross of Lyons Motors, Jonathan had taken over, determined to make a success of things. Ten years later, with hard work, ingenuity, and help from the Brotherhood—the secret society of businessmen he was part of—he'd turned it into a billion-dollar company. Between work and his excursions around the world, Jonathan kept a hectic, jet-setting lifestyle.

It never quite succeeded in distracting him from what he'd lost, though. Ten years later, he was still mooning over Violet DeWitt and how different things would have been if he'd settled down with her after all.

Footsteps clicked on the linoleum flooring of the school, bringing him back to the present. An endless moment later, the classroom door opened. Jonathan lifted his head.

There she was, standing next to the heavy wooden

classroom door, a faint, disappointed frown on her face, as if she'd expected to see him but had hoped otherwise.

Just like that, his palms began to sweat again.

She was different than he remembered. That was to be expected—he wasn't the skinny nineteen-year-old boy with questionable skin and a lack of chest hair anymore. If anything, though, Violet had grown more beautiful than the last time he'd seen her . . . and more sedate. Gone was the wild, devilish look he'd loved so much, and the waist-length, streaked braids. This Violet was still tiny, but her lean figure had softened to lush curves, outlined by a demure black skirt and cream-colored blouse with a bow at the neck and long, billowing sleeves. She had plain black kitten heels on, no jewelry, and the long hair he remembered was cut into an asymmetrical black bob that was tucked behind one small ear and swung at her chin.

This was his wild Violet? It looked like her . . . and yet, not. Married life suited her, that was clear. She was as gorgeous as when he'd last seen her, and the thought of another man in her life made him ache inside. It should have been *him* at her side, but he'd been a selfish ass.

"Jonathan," she said in a flat, polite voice. "What a lovely surprise." Her voice indicated that it was neither a surprise nor lovely.

"Just a reminder, Ms. DeWitt, that visitors need to be checked in to the office in the future," Principal Esparza said, casting another friendly smile in Jonathan's direction.

"Of course. My apologies," Violet said, ever so polite. "Won't you come in, Jonathan?" She gestured at the classroom.

He gave a nod to his security guard, who turned to stand at the doorway in an alert pose. Not that Jonathan was expecting trouble at Neptune Middle School, of course, but he had found out a long time ago that looking important got you as many places—and sometimes more—than greasing palms did.

Violet's little heels clacked as she returned to sit at her

oversized desk at the front of the room. He noticed she didn't offer him a seat, and eyed the rickety student desks lined up in neat rows. Her classroom was colorful and bold, pictures of exotic locations and maps of the world covering the walls, along with charts and flags. Despite the surroundings, the school was old and dark, the wood paneling warped with age, and he was pretty sure the tiles in the ceiling were going to fall down due to water damage. "Nice place. Where are your students?"

"It's three thirty," she said in that too-smooth, too-controlled voice. "Class is over. This is detention."

He turned to look over at her, grinning in what he hoped was his best flirty smile that had never failed to melt her in the past. "Guess I've been naughty."

Violet clasped her hands on her desk. "Mr. Lyons, I think we both know why you're here."

"Jonathan."

"Mr. Lyons," she echoed, her even gaze almost daring him to contradict her. She stared him down for a moment longer, then reached into her desk drawer and pulled out an envelope and held it out to him.

He approached, taking the familiar envelope from her, noting that the seal on the back was still intact. "You didn't open it?"

"I'm quite familiar with my father's little games. I don't need to open it to know I'm not going to play along. This is all a ploy of his for some purpose I haven't yet figured out, nor do I care to."

Jonathan wondered at her icy demeanor. Violet was being downright chilly to him, and he hadn't done a thing. "You still holding a grudge from the past?"

Her eyes narrowed.

That would be a yes. "Look, Violet. I was a kid, you were a kid. We were young. We did stupid things, made stupid mistakes. Can't we get past that and work together?"

"Work together? On what?"

He pulled his own envelope out of an inner pocket in his Fioravanti suit jacket and held it out to her.

She simply gazed at him, arching an eyebrow.

All right, he was going to have to do this the hard way. He flicked the envelope open, pulled out the paper inside, and read it to her. The first line was the middle school's address. The second line said: "My daughter Violet holds the key." He looked over at her to see her reaction to the cryptic statement.

Violet rolled her eyes.

"Well? What do you think?"

"I think my late father missed his calling as a dramatic actor," Violet said. "If there's a key to be found, it's probably in my envelope. You can have it." She nudged it toward him and took a stack of papers off the corner of her desk and pulled them in front of her. Then, she picked up a red pen and began to grade, as if he wasn't there.

Jonathan stared at her for what seemed like forever. She truly wasn't curious? She didn't want to know? "Aren't you the slightest bit interested in what your father was hiding?"

"No." She didn't look up, just kept on grading.

"Would you be surprised to hear that upon his death, not only were all his journals missing, but there was rumor that he'd stolen something important from his latest dig?"

"I would not be surprised," Violet said, still not looking up. She scribbled a note in red on a test, flipped it over, and went on to the next one. "If it could create drama and tension for my father, he'd do it."

"That was *my* dig," Jonathan said. "Your father stole from me."

She ignored him.

"Don't you care?"

At that, Violet looked up and gave him another cool look. "Should I care? I'm told that upon my father's death, an anonymous third party settled all of his debts and that they were not to be a concern of mine. I was also told to be thankful." Her mouth puckered on the last part, as if she'd bit down on a lemon. "I consider this one of those handled debts."

So she knew he'd taken care of things and wasn't pleased. It didn't deter him. "I want those journals. More than that, I want the stele he stole from my dig. It's irreplaceable."

She looked back down at her test again, and nudged the envelope with her other hand, easing it toward him a bit more.

"Goddamn it, Violet. Talk to me, here."

"I am talking," she said in that same even voice.

"I want to work together on this. I need those journals and what he stole."

"I told you. You're free to take my envelope."

Irritated, he snatched it off her desk and tore it open. There was nothing but a symbol inside, one completely unfamiliar to him. "I don't know what this means."

"That's really not my problem." She smiled faintly at him and pointed at the door, as if to suggest he should leave.

It was clear that she was done with him, just as it was clear to Jonathan that if he was going to get anywhere, he'd need Violet's help. Violet would have access to information about the late Dr. DeWitt that he wouldn't. Memories. Insider knowledge.

"I'll pay you a million dollars if you'll assist me with this."

She looked up from her paperwork, her eyes going wide with surprise. "You're serious?"

"I'm a billionaire now, or didn't you hear? I took over Lyons Motors."

"Hooray for you." Her face was impassive.

"So. One million dollars for you to agree to be my employee until we figure out whatever this means." He waved the letter in the air.

Violet thumped her pen on the papers, as if thinking. Then, she shook her head. "No."

"You're a schoolteacher. I'm sure you need the money."

"I am a schoolteacher," she agreed. "And it's the middle of the school year. I can't leave. That would put the school district under terrible distress."

"It's an adventure," he cajoled, remembering how her eyes used to light up at the thought of something like that. His Violet used to love a thrill as much as he did.

This time, the gaze she turned to him was steely. "No, Jonathan."

"Why?" He clenched his fist around the paper, dangerously close to losing his temper and storming out of the room.

"I don't happen to care about my father's little ploy to get the two of us together again."

He inhaled sharply. So she thought her father was deliberately throwing her at him? No wonder she thought he was the worst kind of scum, here to hit on a married woman. "Look, Violet, while it's great to see you—"

"I'm afraid I don't share the sentiment—"

"—I'm not here to fuck with your marriage," he continued, his heart aching. He wasn't sure what he'd hoped for from her. Maybe a bit of affection? Wistfulness over old memories? Wishing over what once might have been between the two of them? It was clear that whatever had been was dead and buried, and Violet didn't want anything to do with him. She was married, anyhow. No sense in mooning after a happily married woman. "I just want an old friend to help me with something important to me, all right?"

She looked up and tilted her head, frowning slightly, and tucked a lock of black hair behind her ear in a motion that brought back a wealth of memories. He remembered that thoughtful expression, and desire and longing came flooding back through him.

Ten years, and he was still insanely in love with Violet DeWitt, ice princess act and all. No wonder she wanted to scare him off.

"What did you say?"

He toyed with the front of his suit jacket, thankful that it was buttoned up so it would hide any hint of the erection he'd just gotten at that small gesture of hers. "I said, I'm not here to mess up your life, all right?"

She got to her feet, smoothed her skirt, and then came around to his side. She extended her hand. "Let me see that letter."

Finally, he was getting somewhere. Eager, Jonathan held both of them out to her.

Violet skimmed the letters, and then cast him another puzzled look.

"What is it?" he asked.

"Where did you get that I was married?"

Now it was his turn to be confused. "Excuse me?"

"I said, I'm not married. Wherever did you get that idea?"

The blood began to roar in Jonathan's ears. He watched, entranced, as she pushed a lock of hair behind her other ear. It made both of her ears stick out—which he remembered that she hated—but he found adorable. *His* Violet.

He'd given up on her so long ago because she'd married someone only days after she'd left his bed, and he'd regretted it ever since.

"You—" He coughed, irritated at how hoarse his voice was. He felt like all the blood had rushed to his face . . . well, that and one other extremity. Clearing his throat, he tried again. "You called off the wedding?"

Again, she gave him a curious look. "What wedding?"

"Your father said that when you left . . . you married someone else. Right away."

She raised both eyebrows at him, as if to say *really?* "And you believed him? Jonathan, your family was funding all of his digs at the time. He'd have told you cows flew on the moon if it was what it took to keep you at his side."

Well, goddamn it all. He'd known that Phineas was a sly old dog, but he'd had no idea he'd been taken for a ride on something so important. "You're . . . not married?"

"I don't see why it's any of your business—" She yelped as he grabbed her hand in his. It was just as soft as he remembered, her nails bitten short. It was a habit she'd never been able to break. There was no ring on any finger.

He'd been lied to.

He should have been furious. Filled with anger and hate and loathing that ten years had been wasted, ten years that had kept them apart.

But Jonathan didn't see any of that. All he saw was Violet—his Violet—standing so close to him that he could reach out and touch her again for the first time in so long that his entire being ached. Violet, with her hand in his. Never mind that she was trying to draw it out of his grasp.

His Violet was here, in front of him, and she'd never married. He'd be damned if he'd let opportunity slip through his fingers again.

Grabbing her shoulders, Jonathan turned her toward him fully, leaned down, and pressed his mouth firmly to hers. He kissed her with all the fierce passion of ten long, lonely years. She wasn't responding, but that was okay. He had enough need and love for both of them. She'd come around. He'd show her just how much he missed her. He'd never let her go again. He—

Violet's knee went between his legs, and connected with his groin.

———

By the time Violet left work, went to the grocery store, went to the gym, got home, and cleaned her tiny condo, she was still pissed. In fact, she was furious.

How dare Jonathan Lyons stroll back into her life just because her father died? How dare he think that she would drop everything—her life, her career—to help him out on some wild-goose chase that her father had bestowed like some sort of archaeological version of Willy Wonka?

How dare Jonathan think that he could just grab her and kiss her? Simply because she wasn't married?

A lack of a wedding ring didn't mean she was up for grabs; it didn't mean she didn't hate him with every fiber of her being. Fuming, Violet threw her groceries in the fridge, and then cussed when her carton of milk tipped over and spilled all over her carton of freshly washed spinach. Damn it! Swearing a blue streak, Violet grabbed paper towels and cleaned her fridge, and when she went to wash her hands, she noticed they were still shaking.

She was still trembling with fury, hours later, her nails bitten down to the quick.

She didn't want to deal with this. Any of this. Her life was nice and compartmentalized. If it wasn't exciting, it was safe and secure and there were no surprises. Violet didn't like surprises. They always ended up being disappointments.

So she took a shower, changed into flannel pajamas, read a mystery novel in bed, and went to sleep. Or tried to, anyhow. Her entire body was a locked mass of angry nerves, and she stared up at the ceiling, just brimming with frustration.

Jonathan Lyons had kissed her.

He'd waltzed back into her life like he hadn't abandoned her ten years ago, when she'd needed him the most. Still selfish after all these years. Some people never changed. She thought of the look on his face as she'd kneed him in the balls. It hadn't even been satisfying, really. She'd been so damn angry, and he'd looked so shocked and utterly surprised.

And hurt.

Like he couldn't believe that *his* Violet would harm him.

And that just made her crazier with anger. Like *she* was the unreasonable one. Twitching with frustration, Violet threw back the covers and stormed across the bedroom and into the living room. Her messy condo was tiny, but she didn't require a lot. She just needed a work area and a bed. Heading to her shelves full of books, she went to the section where she kept personal photo albums. Her mother's albums filled up most of the shelf, but there was one tiny album she pulled from the end and blew the dust off of.

The cover was decorated with a Greek key design, and she'd written AKROTIRI 2004 on it in bold, stylized letters. Returning to her bedroom, she curled up in the blankets and began to flip through the photos.

Her first—and only—trip to assist her errant father. Her mother had been against it, but Violet had been so excited to go, so very dazzled at the thought of spending the summer with her intelligent, famous father that she'd looked forward to it for what felt like forever. People joked that her dad was something like Jacques Cousteau for archaeology. She supposed that would be apt, if Jacques had neglected his family for two decades and driven his wife to drinking.

Violet flipped through the photos, thinking of that summer. Here was a picture of herself and her father near the excavation, pointing at a portion of a wall and smiling. Both of their faces were browned from the summer, and her hair was in two long, dark braids streaked with wild color. She was wearing a hideous pair of sunglasses and a tank top. Behind her in the picture, his hand at her waist, was Jonathan Lyons.

God, she'd been so in love with him. So incredibly stupid, but in love. As soon as she'd gotten to Santorini to spend the time with her father, she'd discovered that he'd invited a whole host of his students to his summer expedition as well. She'd been hurt, initially, having thought that she'd be special in her father's eyes, but her hurt soon turned to interest when she met Jonathan Lyons. Lyons Motors was famous—or infamous—for a line of cars that was rapidly becoming a joke, and he wasn't interested in the family business at all. Thin, a little geeky, and utterly enthusiastic about everything in the world, she'd thought Jonathan was cute.

There was something so incredibly exuberant and earnest about Jonathan that she'd loved. Whereas every move her father made seemed to be completely calculated, Jonathan appeared to live in the moment, and she adored that. His excitement for the dig was unquestionable. He'd been the first on site every morning and the last to leave. If something needed to be researched, Jonathan threw himself headlong into it.

He was a hundred percent intensity, bundled into an attractive nineteen-year-old college boy.

He'd been irresistible to her.

By the end of the first week, they were spending a lot of time together. By the second week, he'd kissed her and she'd flung him down on her bed and they'd screwed like rabbits. By the time a month had passed, she was in love.

By the time the second month had passed? She was pregnant with his baby.

It wasn't that they weren't careful. They were. They used condoms every time, but even condoms aren't infallible, and they'd been full of youth and enthusiasm, and sometimes he stroked in her a few times before putting on a condom, just because it felt so damn good for both of them. Jonathan had approached sex with the same intensity that he approached life—he was voracious and insatiable.

She had to admit, staring down at his photo, that he'd pretty much ruined her for other men. No other sexual experience had even come close.

Which sucked.

At nineteen, she hadn't even been upset that she'd become pregnant. She was utterly in love with Jonathan, and mentally linking their last names together and picking out names for the baby. If it was a boy, she'd call it Theseus DeWitt-Lyons, and a girl would be Ariadne DeWitt-Lyons, based on the myths of the labyrinth of Crete. She'd dreamed of marrying Jonathan and returning stateside to finish her college education and raise her family. It was clear that her father looked at her not as a daughter but as just another student on his dig, and she craved a family—a *real* family. She'd never had a functioning family, and the dream of a happy home was an intoxicating one. Instead of fantasizing about archaeological finds, Violet's head was filled with nurseries and starter homes. A husband and a wife and a child that was doted on and adored by both parents.

That was her new dream, and she couldn't wait to get started with Jonathan.

But she didn't want Jonathan to marry her just for the baby. She wanted him to marry her because he loved her and because he *wanted* to marry her. That was part of the fantasy, after all. She'd seen what it was like, firsthand, when parents married for the baby instead of for love. His family had money, and she wanted it to be his idea for them to get married, not hers, or it'd seem like she was simply digging for his fortune. In reality, Violet didn't give two craps about whatever car empire the Lyons family had. Her perfect life involved a homey cottage somewhere, family dinners with both children and husband, and kissing her spouse as he went off to work for the day. Some women dreamed of careers; Violet dreamed of a nuclear, close-knit family. It was all she'd ever wanted after a childhood of her mother's depression and miserable hidden drinking binges, and her father's long absences. She just wanted to be surrounded by *love*.

She'd been such a naive idiot back then.

Irritated, Violet flipped to the next photo in her book. Another of Jonathan, their cheeks pressed together as they stood on the Santorini beach. She remembered that night. That was the night before everything changed. They'd had a weekend furlough, and they'd decided to spend it together. They'd enjoyed a romantic dinner and spent the night at a hotel in Fira, and in bed, Violet had confessed her hopes to him. That she wanted nothing more than to start a family.

"It's not a bad idea . . . for the future," Jonathan had told her absently, playing with her long hair.

That hadn't been what nineteen-year-old-and-pregnant Violet had wanted to hear. She'd turned to him in bed. "What are you going to do after we leave this dig? What happens to us?"

"What do you mean?" he'd asked.

She hadn't been happy that she had to spell it out. "When we leave here, what are your plans?"

He'd shrugged. "Go back to classes. Start the next semester. Wait for Dr. DeWitt's next invite."

That . . . hadn't been what she'd wanted to hear. "And what about me?"

He'd given her that heartbreaking smile. "In a few years, maybe we'll both be working at the same university."

In a few years? A few *years*? At nineteen, a few years seemed like a lifetime. "But . . . I want us to be *together*."

"I want that, too." He'd looked sad.

No, he wasn't getting it. She'd clutched at his arm. "I want us to be together when we leave here. I want us to start a family. Together." She'd emphasized the last two words, hoping he'd realize what she was asking for and jump in with enthusiasm.

Start a family with you, Violet? God, I want nothing more. Let's do it!

I'd love to have babies with you, Violet.

I never want to leave your side, Violet.

Instead, he'd just furrowed his brow at her as if she were saying ridiculous things. "Start a family? Now?"

"Yes, *now*."

He'd laughed. Laughed! And rattled off a million things he had going on. He needed to return to Dartmouth. He'd told Dr. DeWitt he wanted to go on his next dig, no questions asked. Then he had family members waiting for him to take an apprenticeship with his brother, the heir. It would be years before Jonathan could settle down and even think about family, and he was too young to consider it.

Every word had broken Violet's heart a bit more.

Betrayed, she'd slapped his face and ran. She'd stormed out of their room and left him in Fira and returned to the dig. Then, she'd cried herself to sleep that night because she'd wanted the white picket fence and Prince Charming had other plans.

He'd tried calling her the next day, over and over again. Tried seeing her, but she avoided him. Instead, she poured all of her heartache into a letter. She hadn't wanted to tell him about the baby and use it as a tool to force him to her side, but she had no choice. She still remembered the last paragraph of the letter, down to the way it'd looked on paper.

> *If you love me, Jonathan, please come home with me. I want us to raise our baby together. If you care at all about being a father, please come with me. Please, please. I love you so much.*

She'd more or less begged him to pick *her*, and he hadn't even bothered to respond. A sour taste filled Violet's mouth as she stared at the picture, and she slammed the photo album shut and tossed it across the room.

Fairy tales were bullshit. Prince Charming had ignored her letter. She'd gone home, cried for two weeks, and lost the baby a month later. Which made her cry harder.

And then she'd picked herself up, returned to college, and vowed that her happiness would never be contingent on anyone else's plans ever again.

In her mind's eye, she kept picturing Jonathan's look of pleasure earlier that day. *You called off the wedding? You're not married?*

Violet thumped her fist into her pillow angrily, then flopped down on the bed, determined to sleep at some point that night. Jonathan had been shocked to hear that she wasn't married. So the saintly Dr. DeWitt had lied to his favorite protégé? Gee, there was a shock. Her father would have sold the shirt off his dead mother's back if it meant getting funding for a project. Violet had known that all her life. How could Jonathan not have realized that?

Briefly, she wondered if he'd ever gotten her letter.

It didn't matter in the end. Playing the baby card had been the only chip she'd had, and she'd lost that bargaining chip a month later. Jonathan wouldn't have stayed at her side regardless. Not when he had *other plans*.

She supposed things worked out for the best, after all. If Jonathan hadn't turned her down, she might have ended up in a miserable marriage to the bastard, and he would have been trapped in a marriage because of a baby he didn't want. She'd seen his true selfishness.

Yep, life always worked out the way it was supposed to, she told herself as she settled down into bed again.

But she still had trouble sleeping that night.

TWO

⌒

The next morning, Violet woke up five minutes before her alarm was scheduled to go off, bleary-eyed and miserable. She stared at her phone, buzzing on her bedside with a text, and picked it up.

Staff mtg @ 7 am in cafeteria. MANDATORY. Be there!

Groaning, Violet fell back in the pillows. Who the hell scheduled an impromptu staff meeting at seven in the morning? It was going to be an especially miserable day considering she'd only gotten about two hours of sleep. Ugh. Hauling herself out of bed, Violet took a quick shower and began to get ready for work.

Forty minutes later, she pulled into the school parking lot with an extra-large coffee in hand and a throbbing headache. The parking lot was already full, which meant all of the staff was in for this early meeting. Oh, goody. Hurrying inside the school, she noticed there was a Lyons convertible parked in the fire lane in the front.

Surely that was coincidence, wasn't it? Lots of rich guys drove Lyons. Owning one of the flashy roadsters had turned into a status symbol a few years ago when they'd been featured in one of those high-octane car movies. After that, Lyons Motors had turned from joke to success. Not that she followed how his company was doing. At any rate, there were Lyons cars all over the roads. It didn't mean that asshole was still here, did it?

Eyes narrowed, Violet clenched her coffee in hand and headed to the cafeteria for the staff meeting.

Despite the early hour, the tables had been unfolded and teachers filled the seats. Esparza's portable little podium was at the front of the room, and behind her, a row of seats was filled.

Jonathan sat in one of the seats.

Violet's hand clenched violently, and her coffee spewed out of the paper cup, slopping all over her hand, her white sleeve, and the floor.

With a hiss, she dropped the cup and shook her hand to expel the stinging hot coffee, even as her friend Kirsten raced up with a stack of paper towels. "You okay?"

"Just peachy," Violet told her, squatting in her heels and skirt to clean up her mess. "What's going on? What's with the meeting?"

"Something about funding," Kirsten murmured, helping Violet mop up the coffee. "You know the school district's been in the red for a while."

Oh, no. If it wasn't for the presence of that swanky car at the curb, Violet would have thought this was a layoff of some kind or an announcement of more programs being cut. But the fact that Jonathan—Daddy Warbucks himself—was sitting at the front of the room in one of his expensive suits?

It gave her a bad feeling. A real bad feeling.

She sat down at the back of the room, noticing that Jonathan's intense blue-eyed gaze was fixed in her direction. Goddamn it. He'd probably seen her spill her coffee everywhere. She wanted to seem cool and unaffected by his presence. Too late for that. Fine then. He wanted to eyeball her from afar? Violet leaned in close to the coach seated next to her. "Know what this is about?"

Coach Trammel shook his head. He was good looking, but he already had a boyfriend, and was a longtime friend of Violet's. "Not a clue. You?"

"Nothing," she said, making sure to smile and laugh in his direction. When she looked back over at Jonathan, his face was stark with anger and possessiveness. *Good. Let me know how it feels, Johnny-boy. You gave up your claim ten years ago.*

"Is everyone here?" Esparza called into the microphone, then beamed at the assembled teachers. "This won't take long, but I wanted to get all the teachers together to go over the good news."

Oh, no. Oh, no no no.

Esparza clasped her hands together, practically dancing with excitement from behind the tiny podium. "As you all know, Neptune School District has had issues with funding over the last few years. You are all aware that the repairs on the gymnasium cost quite a pretty penny, and we've been worried that we'd have to cut back on student enrichment programs in order to keep everyone employed, and that also means outdated textbooks for another year or two." Her smile grew brilliant. "But, I'm happy to announce that Mr. Jonathan Lyons of Lyons Motors has taken an interest in the Neptune School District and has made an extremely generous offer to pull us into the black and even allow us to purchase iPads for students in need."

There were several gasps out of the audience, and some of the teachers clapped with excitement. Neptune was one of the poorer school districts in their area, with a lot of low-income families, and it was no secret that they were struggling. Heck, Violet's own paycheck reflected that they were struggling. She hadn't had a raise since she'd started there three years ago. But it was what it was.

"We'll be meeting with the school board over the next

few days to determine the best way to allocate funds, but I just wanted you all to know how very excited we are about this." Esparza clapped so enthusiastically that for a moment, she looked like an eager seal waiting for a fish. "And in addition, we're putting forth a motion to have the school renamed the Jonathan Lyons Middle School."

Violet thought she might throw up in her mouth. The last thing she wanted was Jonathan's name everywhere she turned for the rest of her career. God, she'd have to switch school districts just to get away from reminders of him.

She looked over at Jonathan.

Still staring at her. Violet's eyes narrowed as the audience began to talk and excitedly clap again. Something wasn't adding up. Why was Jonathan taking such an interest in her school?

Her school, the day after she turned him down and told him there was no way she could accompany him?

No no no no.

The meeting ended with that. Violet surged to her feet as the rest of the staff did, hoping to blend in with the crowd.

"Ms. DeWitt," Principal Esparza called over the crackling microphone. "Could you please remain for a few minutes? I need to talk to you."

Violet practically snarled with anger. She could just *guess* what this was about.

Jonathan watched as Violet more or less stomped to Principal Esparza's side. Her arms were crossed over her breasts and he noticed that one of the pale white sleeves of her blouse was now stained with coffee. Her breasts were heaving magnificently over her arms, though, and he had to force himself not to stare at them like a schoolboy.

Instead, he thought of the way she'd leaned into the man she'd sat next to and smiled at him. Laughed at him. Was that her boyfriend? An ex-lover? A current lover? Jonathan's hand clenched at his side and a surge of jealousy roared through him. He wanted to be the only one who got her damn smiles.

Not that she was smiling right now. She looked as if she wanted to shank him, actually. He grinned archly, knowing she was going to hate what came next. His Violet hated not being in control of things.

And she *would* be his again.

"Principal," Violet said in a crisp, almost cold voice. She refused to look over at Jonathan. "What can I do for you?"

"Well, it's a bit unorthodox," Esparza said, her voice becoming a little overly soothing and motherly. "But I hope you'll hear me out and listen without making judgment, of course."

"Let me guess," Violet said flatly. "He's handing out money in exchange for me traveling with him for the next few weeks."

Jonathan bit back a smile at Violet's astute observation, and at the way Esparza spluttered, clearly surprised that Violet had already figured things out. But his Violet had always been sharp.

"I assure you, Ms. DeWitt, it's all very aboveboard," Esparza began. "It's just that Mr. Lyons is looking for an expert on history, and what with the school being so tightly budgeted and all—"

He hated to see the poor woman get so flustered. Getting to his feet, Jonathan pushed his hands into his pockets and affected his "playboy billionaire pose," all smiles and leaning elegance. "What the lovely principal is trying to say, Violet, is that I requested the company of an old friend for traveling. You told me you couldn't possibly leave the school in a lurch and there was no money for substitutes. I ensured there was. It's the least I can do to spend some of my money in a philanthropic gesture."

Violet turned to him, her eyes practically stabbing daggers at him. "I presume if I don't go with you, none of this windfall of magical philanthropic money will ever make it to the school district, right?"

Actually, it would, but she didn't have to know that. "Nope," he lied. "And I have it on good authority that a few people will be let go at the end of the semester to keep the budget running. And no iPads or musical instruments for the children. Poor, poor children." He shook his head. "All deprived of a better education because of the self-centered needs of one teacher."

Violet's hands clenched at her sides. She looked ready to spit nails. Or attack him. He didn't care which. Either was better than the cold indifference she'd served him yesterday. He could take a fiery, feisty Violet who hated him. He couldn't do anything with a woman who pretended he didn't exist. "So basically I'm being blackmailed to go with you and chirp historical facts in your ear?"

"Yep," Jonathan said lazily. "You going to do it?"

"I don't have a choice, do I?" Violet ground out.

"You do. But think of all the children who would suffer if you chose selfishly."

"Mr. Lyons," Principal Esparza cut in, a frown on her lined face. "I really don't know that this is appropriate after all—"

"It's all right, Betty," Violet said, and her voice sounded tired. "I figured he was going to try something like this the moment I saw him this morning. I'll go with him. It's fine. Just be sure you get that money in writing, and make sure the contract's ironclad." She looked over at Jonathan, clearly seething. "When do we leave, oh, philanthropic one?"

He couldn't quite hide his triumphant grin. "Tomorrow."

That evening, Jonathan couldn't keep his mind off of a certain schoolteacher.

Tomorrow. Violet would be his again, starting tomorrow. He lounged in the backseat of the Lyons sedan as his driver headed to his hotel, a pleased smile on his face.

Oh, sure, she didn't *want* to be at his side, but she'd come around eventually. She'd always been prickly at first meetings. He remembered the first time she'd met him, back when she'd had those long, beautiful braids and a tart mouth. At nineteen, she'd had no patience for fools, and he'd definitely been a foolish boy, utterly giddy just to be in her presence. She'd been snippy to him then, too. It was clear that Violet wore a suit of armor around her heart, and she didn't let anyone get near.

She reminded him of one of his friends, Hunter, though he'd worn his scars on the outside. And so he'd decided to befriend Violet, because she was gorgeous and smart, and, hell, he'd been a horny nineteen-year-old. It had taken him about a week to get her to open up and let her defenses down, and then Violet had been a warm, teasing, delicious girl.

He remembered the way she smiled, as if she knew a secret no one else did.

She'd been giving that smile to another man earlier today, the one who sat next to her in the meeting. Jonathan's hand clenched his phone, fury bolting through him. Violet had said she wasn't married. That didn't mean she wasn't seeing someone. Jealousy snaked through him. If she wasn't married, she was still fair game. He'd simply have to seduce her back to softness, back to smiling at *him* like that.

He wanted her. Pure and simple. He'd always wanted Violet. He'd never stopped.

The car pulled up in front of the hotel and Jonathan got out, still lost in thought. To think that he was in Detroit several times a year for auto industry meetings, and had never known that his Violet was right under his nose, teaching at a local school.

Fate worked in mysterious ways.

Jonathan headed up to his familiar hotel room. He tended to be in Detroit a lot for business, and though it probably would have been fiscally wiser to purchase a residence here, he stayed in the Townsend because he couldn't be bothered with setting down roots. He didn't want a house. Not if it meant coming home and finding it empty and hollow.

As he entered the suite, he noticed things were set out the way he liked, without having to ask. He was here often enough that his assistant simply faxed his schedule to the manager of the hotel, who made sure that Jonathan's every need was met before he had to ask, and he was paid handsomely for it. Thus he had extra pillows, bottles of his favorite water at the bedside, and bath sheets instead of a robe.

He also had a hooker in his bed. As usual.

The woman sat up as he entered the room and tugged off his tie. Jonathan barely glanced at her. He didn't have to. He knew what she'd look like. All the girls he got had a profile: Short. Dark haired. Jonathan didn't like romantic entanglements. He hadn't had a girlfriend since, well, since Violet. It was so much easier to pay someone for a quick fuck and then have them leave.

She sauntered over to him, dressed in nothing but thigh-highs and a corset. Her tits were huge and probably fake, but she had a pretty face. "Hello there," she purred, coming over to help him unbutton his shirt. "My name is Sally," she told him in a low, sultry voice. "And my safe word is 'Kitty.' I'm open for anything you might want to do."

And she reached for his cock.

He stopped her, grasping her wrist. "I'm tired tonight, Sally."

She looked surprised, and then hurt. "Oh. Do you . . . um, do you want me to call the agency and ask them to send someone else?"

"I don't want anyone tonight," he said gently. Well, he did want a particular someone, but she was probably sticking pins into a voodoo doll of him at the moment. The thought of fucking Sally instead of Violet was displeasing, like wearing brown shoes with a black suit. There wouldn't be repercussions, but it just didn't *feel* right.

The girl in front of him bit her bright red lip. "Oh."

Sally still looked hurt, and he felt like an ass. He'd never turned down a girl before, and the agency had sent over just what he liked. She'd probably been filled with stories about how if she made him happy, he'd start asking for her on a regular basis, and he tipped well.

Jonathan guessed that Sally was probably more upset about the money than about not getting his dick. So he pulled out his wallet and began to flip hundred-dollar bills out of his money clip.

She put up a hand, trying to stop him. "Oh, Mr. Lyons, the agency pays me—"

"I know. And I want you to tell them that I was very pleased with your services tonight. *Very* pleased." He pulled a total of two grand out of his clip and offered it to her. "My driver's downstairs. Tell them at the front desk that you have his services for the rest of the evening. And I'd love for you to go shopping, on me. It's my way of apology." He waved the money at her.

Sally looked at it, then at him, and beamed with pleasure. "Thank you, Mr. Lyons." She took the money from him and grabbed her clothing from the neat stack on a nearby chair.

"Enjoy," he told her as she hauled her clothing on and left a moment later.

Then, he was alone. Thank God.

Shrugging his jacket off, he tossed it on the foot of the bed and sat down. He rubbed his jaw, thinking. Then, he pulled out his iPad and brought up a PDF of Violet's letter from her father. He did a reverse search for the image on the Internet, but it brought up nothing recognizable. Huh. Frustrated, he tossed the tablet aside and lay back, thinking of Violet.

The pillows on his bed smelled like Sally's perfume. It was a thick, musky fragrance, very different from Violet's own scent. She smelled like coffee and, well, paper. Funny how he'd found that arousing. He thought of Violet again, but this time, instead of her cold response to him yesterday, she was raging with anger, anger that melted into raging hunger when he touched her.

With Violet on his mind, he undid his trousers and began to jerk off.

The next morning, Violet looked out the window of her condominium to see a limo waiting outside. She rolled her eyes at the sight, but hefted her carry-on and her purse. *Here goes nothing.*

She'd festered with resentment all night at Jonathan's high-handedness, but today she was full of acceptance. She could fight this, or she could accept that he'd outmaneuvered her and was just being a jerk. She could go along with things, get it over with, and then go back to her life. So she would, and she'd smile through gritted teeth the entire time.

She locked her apartment and headed down the elevator and then out to the street. As she emerged from the building, a man got out of the driver's side of the limo and approached her. "Miss DeWitt?"

She sighed and handed him her bag. "Thank you."

He nodded and opened the back door of the limo for her, and she got in.

It wasn't surprising to her that Jonathan was in the back seat of the limo, waiting. Somehow she'd guessed that he'd be there to pester her every second of this trip. "Hello, Mr. Lyons," she said in a coolly polite voice. She noticed he was dressed rather casually this morning, a blue Superman T-shirt under his blazer, and jeans. His dark hair was slightly messy, as if he didn't care how he looked that day.

She didn't know what to make of that. Part of her was glad that she didn't have the super-expensive-suit-wearing Jonathan with his impeccable grooming and pricey wrist-watch and even more expensive shoes. But to just not give a shit about what he looked like when he was with her? Not even brushing his hair? Really? Didn't she warrant a little self-grooming?

"Morning, Violet," he said, and held out a lidded cup to her. "Three sugars, extra cream, right?"

Her eyes narrowed. He even remembered how she liked her coffee? Was this all so he could charm her back into his bed? Not a fucking chance. "Thanks." She took the cup from him but didn't drink.

He noticed that. "I didn't poison it, you know."

"Of course not. I imagine it's hard for even a billionaire to hide a body."

"That, and you're far more useful to me alive." He lifted his own cup to his lips. "We're heading straight for the airport, if you're ready."

"Ready?" She snorted. "You're the one kidnapping me."

"It's not a kidnapping, Violet. Your father stole a one-of-a-kind stele from one of my digs—"

"A stele?"

"Yes. You know, one of those stone tablets with a ceremonial inscription on it—"

"I know what a stele is, Jonathan!" Like she was uneducated. The nerve.

"Yes, well, then you know it's very important from me. You're the only person who might have known how to get it back."

"You keep saying he stole from you." Phineas DeWitt was a heartless prick, but he was a devotee of archaeology and a huge supporter of museums. Violet wasn't sure that she bought the whole "thievery" angle. "Why?"

"That's the question, isn't it? It's important mostly because of where it's from—Cadiz. Here." He pulled out a laptop and began to type. A moment later, he flicked the camera on and dialed a call. "Are you there, Sergio?"

A rattle of Spanish came through the speakers of the laptop, mixed with feedback. The picture on the screen swung back and forth. Violet winced and rubbed her ear as Jonathan adjusted the volume.

"Sergio, I have Ms. DeWitt in the car with me," Jonathan yelled at the camera. "Can you show her where the missing stele came from?"

"In the hole?" Sergio yelled, accent thick. The camera bounced around dizzily, as if someone was walking.

"Yes, in the hole!"

"In the hole?" Sergio repeated, clearly missing Jonathan's commands.

"In the damn hole!"

Violet's lips twitched with amusement. "So much yelling about holes. Should I leave you two alone for a private moment?"

Jonathan shot her a quelling look.

"Okay, in the hole," Sergio said, and he barked something in Spanish to someone, then changed to English again to address Jonathan. "I'll put on the headgear."

"Thank you," Jonathan said tersely.

The camera shifted again, and Violet caught a glimpse of a golden-skinned man with amber eyes and a curly mop of black hair before it swiveled around. "Camera is on. Can you hear me?"

Jonathan looked over at Violet and then nodded. "We can hear you."

Curious, Violet leaned forward to watch the picture on the laptop as it bounced with every step. Even though it was morning where she was at, the sun was late afternoon bright in the picture. Pixels bounced around as Sergio maneuvered through a busy encampment.

"Where is he?" Violet asked, her voice pitched low so the computer's microphone wouldn't pick it up. She found herself interested in spite of her irritation at Jonathan.

"A dig I'm jointly sponsoring with a friend of mine. We're looking for what might be the ruins of Atlantis."

"In Spain?"

"Yes. Recent data has shown that there was a very large civilization on a coastal plain that was wiped out due to a tsunami at the right time. We're looking for anything that would link it to Atlantis instead of, say, Tarshish, which is the current theory. Your father was supervising the dig last year, until he got too sick to continue."

"Mmm," Violet said noncommittally. Was that supposed to be a jab at her? She hadn't known that her father had cancer until it was too late. She'd barely spoken to him in the last ten years and only found out his situation after he'd died. Then, she'd resented the fact that he'd prevented her from seeing him one last time. She'd always suspected that family wasn't important to Phineas DeWitt, but denying his daughter her final good-bye to her erstwhile father? That made her irrationally upset, and when she was upset, she locked her emotions down and went cold.

Kind of like she was doing right now.

So she watched the camera jounce around and said nothing until the picture bobbed and she was looking down into a tight, dark crawlspace. "What's that?"

"That is the hole," Jonathan said. "It leads to a cave we found what we believe was used for oracular purposes and worship. The entrance is buried under several tons of rock and mud, but we were able to dig down several feet and break in from above."

"Going in," Sergio called. There was a minor scuffle, and then the camera stared at the rocky wall as Sergio climbed down on a creaky metal ladder into a narrow, dark tunnel.

"Brave man," Violet commented. "You must be paying him well."

"Actually, Sergio is a volunteer from the university," Jonathan said.

"And he's willing to jump into a hole like that?"

"Of course. That's what archaeology is about." Jonathan

grinned at her. "I seem to recall a girl who had 'carpe diem' tattooed on her lower back. Where's your sense of adventure?"

"It was long beaten out of me," Violet said in a disapproving voice. "I've had enough adventure for one life."

"I am at the bottom," Sergio called, and the picture bobbed again. "Heading into the atrium." More scuffling, and then in the darkness, a light flared on. "At the site," Sergio called, and the camera shifted. "Can you see?"

Violet looked over at Jonathan, one eyebrow raised inquiringly.

Jonathan pointed at the computer screen. "Do you see that painting on the wall? You can barely make out a mural, but it's mostly destroyed." His finger skimmed the screen. "This is a bull, and this person is a festival dancer here. Quit moving, Sergio."

"Sorry," came the tinny voice, and the camera stilled.

"I'll take your word for it," Violet said. "What does this have to do with me?"

"Below the mural," Jonathan said, and his finger pointed at a slightly darker line, "we found two inscripted stone slabs—two stelae. One was hand-sized and one was larger. The larger was written in hieratic, and mentioned a great festival. The second one was in Etruscan and a variant we'd never seen before. It was commemorating something that one of our men interpreted to be a great flood or a disaster with water."

"Mmm."

"Atlantis."

She rolled her eyes. What did he want her to say?

Jonathan continued to watch her. "Your father took the smaller stone to have it carbon-dated and catalogued, and no one has seen it since. Nor has anyone recorded it being taken to a lab for carbon dating." He turned back to the computer, tapped the screen, and then frowned to himself. "Thank you, Sergio. That is all I needed."

"Anytime," Sergio called back, his voice garbled. He said

something else, but the connection disrupted and the call went dead.

Jonathan shut his laptop and gave Violet a scrutinizing look. "Well?"

"That was a lovely bedtime story, but what does this have to do with me?"

"Do you know anything about your father stealing artifacts?"

"I barely talked to my father in the last ten years. How would I know anything?" Her lips curled with derision. "You're the one who was so in love with him. You should be the one to know."

"I think he stole it because he knew I'd want it." Jonathan gave her a curious look. "And I think he expects me to come after you and ask questions."

"Well, if this was part of his master plan, it's a pitiful one. I want nothing to do with him. Or you, for that matter."

"Nevertheless, here we are." Jonathan's intense gaze made her shiver. "You said you'd help me find my stele and his journals."

"You didn't give me much of a choice," she retorted back.

"He's not my father," Jonathan said.

He might as well have been. Violet sure hadn't been close to Dr. DeWitt. She drummed her fingers. "Let's just get this over with, all right?"

"Like I said, we're heading straight to the airport. I don't want to waste time, either. Every day that passes without that stele, the trail goes colder."

"I have my passport." She kept her voice even, and kept her gaze off of him.

He nodded. "All right. Can I ask where we're going?"

She frowned and looked over at him. "Why are you asking *me* where we're going? This is your little trip!"

"You're the one who's meant to understand the symbol your father left." He pulled out a tablet and began tapping on it, then offered the tablet to her. There, scanned in, was a copy of the symbol on one of the letters.

Right. This was all a little game her father had designed to keep her in Jonathan's eyes so he'd continue to fund Phineas DeWitt's pet projects even after death. "Yes, I know where that is."

"Care to share?"

She hesitated. "When I was growing up, I was very into Ancient Roman studies. One of the superstitions the Romans had were curse tablets. They believed that if you wanted to curse someone, you wrote the curse on a tablet and then hid it in a place that no one could find. When I was nine, I wrote a curse on my Etch A Sketch and buried it in the backyard of my childhood home. And because I wanted to find it later, I carved that symbol onto the tree." She pointed at the symbol on the paper.

He took the tablet back from her and squinted at it. "I thought it was a hieroglyph."

"It's a devil."

He turned the tablet, still staring at it. "Are you sure? There are five limbs and three eyes. Maybe it's a bug of some kind?"

"I know what I drew," Violet snapped at him. "And I wasn't very good at carving, all right?"

His lips twitched in amusement. "So, who did you curse?"

"My father. He'd left my mother again and she was depressed." He'd left her mother a lot in those days.

"What did you curse him with?"

This time, Violet's mouth curled in a wry smile, remembering her childhood anger. "I believe I demanded that his peepee fall off."

"I have an incredible urge to cross my legs and slide farther away from you."

"You're lucky there's not an Etch A Sketch handy."

He laughed, his smile so utterly brilliant that it lit up his entire face. In that moment, he wasn't Billionaire Jonathan Lyons, daredevil and mogul. He was just nineteen-year-old Jonathan who'd made her heart flutter.

Like it was fluttering right now.

She took a big gulp of the coffee and turned to stare out the window, not caring that her mouth burned on the heat of the drink. The last thing she wanted was to get cozy with Jonathan again. "At any rate," she said, turning her voice back to that cool diffidence, "we need to head to Alamagordo, New Mexico."

"Is that where you grew up?"

"Yes."

"Is the Etch A Sketch still there?"

"No. My mother made me dig it up and then told my father about it when he returned a few months later. He didn't care. In fact, I seem to recall that he corrected me on my curse and said that the Romans would have never marked such a spot, as it defeated the purpose of the curse."

"So he turned it into a lesson?"

"It isn't a lesson if you're already aware of the facts."

"So you marked it on purpose? Did you want him to find it?"

She had. She'd wanted her father to realize how furious and hurt she was that he'd left, and that Mommy spent all day in bed, crying and nursing a bottle of rum. She'd had no outlet for her anger, so she'd carved that symbol angrily into the tree, hoping that her father would return home the next day and ask about the symbol. *What's this, Violet?* And then she could show him.

But he hadn't returned home until months later, and he'd never noticed the tree. It had been her mother, giddy with excitement that her husband was home and paying a bit of attention to her, who had brought up Violet's curse. *Isn't that precious of our Violet?*

That was pretty much how her entire childhood had gone. Her father would leave. Her mother would drink. Violet would rage. Her father would return. Her mother would smother him with affection. Then he would leave again. All through this, Violet built resentment for her brilliant, flawed father.

"Violet?" Jonathan asked in a low voice. "You okay?"

"Alamagordo," she said flatly. "I agreed to be your guide, not your entertainment."

He sighed with resignation, and she felt a bit like an asshole.

THREE

～

Violet was rather alarmed to see that the limo didn't head to Detroit Metro Airport, but instead went to a smaller airfield. "Where are we going?"

He gave her that cocky look that made her nerves grate. "The airport."

She gritted her teeth. "What airport is this?"

"A private one."

Clearly. She peered out the window at the small hangar. "We're not taking a commercial flight?" She'd been hoping for a multitude of passengers and some in-flight magazines to distract her from her company.

"Since we're just heading to New Mexico, I figured I'd fly us there."

Fear made her eyes widen. "What? We're not going to have a real pilot?"

He turned that intense, cocky look on her. "I *am* a real pilot, Violet. I fly my planes all the time."

"Yes, but . . ." She trailed off. It seemed rather impolite to say *I don't want to leave my life in your hands*. But what choice did she have? She could refuse and turn around and leave . . . and then everyone in the school district would resent her.

Yeah, like that was a choice. Violet sighed. "If you crash, I'm going to be furious."

"I'll take that into consideration."

She gave him a sharp look to see if he was joking, but . . . he didn't seem to be. With a sigh, she continued to stare out the window and bit back any comments or concerns she had about taking a small plane.

A half hour later, when she saw the actual plane itself, Violet gave a moan of distress. "You're kidding me, right? It's so small."

"Not that small. This is one of the bigger in its class," Jonathan said, staring up at it with what looked like affection. "Socata TBM 850. Turboprop. We'll have enough fuel to make it to New Mexico without having to stop and refuel."

Violet stared at it, then at Jonathan. "And you're the pilot."

"I'm the pilot."

She shook her head as he pulled out the tiny staircase for her to get on board. The plane was red and white, and she counted three windows going down the body. As she climbed on, she couldn't suppress another moan of horror. The interior was about the size of her hatchback, all beige leather, and seemed barely big enough for the bucket seats inside. "I can't believe we're flying in this thing."

"I won't let anything happen to you," Jonathan said. "Just get in already."

Reluctantly, she did so, heading for one of the back seats.

"In the front," Jonathan said. "I'm going to need company to keep me awake while I fly."

"I hope you're joking," she snapped. When he only winked at her, she sighed and headed to the front, squeezing into the passenger seat. She wasn't relieved to see the massive control panel at the front or the twin sets of steering-wheel thingies. It only made her more upset. What if

Jonathan couldn't fly and she had to take over? They'd die for sure; she had no idea how to fly a plane.

"Can't you have a private jet like every other billionaire?" she grumbled while he slid into the front next to her.

"It's more fun to fly your own toys," he told her with a grin, buckling in. "You get to really appreciate them."

"*Appreciate* is not the word I'm thinking of," Violet muttered, and made sure her seat belt was on tightly. Then, she closed her eyes and began to bite her nails, praying that the flight would be over soon.

——————

The weather was great all the way across several states, and the flight itself was a breeze. Jonathan tried talking to Violet at first, but when it became clear that she was surly with anxiety, he left her alone and she fell asleep. So instead, he just watched her as she dozed, slumped over in the copilot's seat.

She was still incredibly lovely. For all her prickly demeanor, he could spend every minute of the rest of his life with Violet and not grow tired of her. He was fascinated with the thick fringe of her dark eyelashes, for one. They hid those lovely dark brown eyes he couldn't forget. The stubborn curve of her jaw was just as he remembered it, though, and he remembered pressing kisses there.

Not that she'd let him do that now. She loathed him.

Jonathan was disappointed she'd clearly nurtured hatred toward him over the years. Sure, they'd had a messy breakup, but time had passed and they were both adults. He didn't hold a grudge for her running home and leaving him. He didn't hold a grudge because she'd changed her mind on what she wanted overnight and demanded that they start a family, and when he hadn't liked that idea, run off back home to her mother. He figured they were both young and stupid at the time, and now they could be adults. Friends, if nothing else. But she acted like he was her mortal enemy, and he didn't understand it.

He'd just have to win her over again.

He'd won her once, back when she was a closed-up teen-ager. He'd talked and smiled and flirted and made an utter fool of himself until she'd broken down and started respond-ing. He could do the same with a stiff, angry Violet. Just keep talking and bothering her until she exploded and told him what was pissing her off so bad, so he could fix it.

Fuck, he'd do *anything* to fix it. He'd never wanted any-one but Violet. She was everything to him. He didn't care what it took.

As if she could hear the turn of his thoughts, Violet shifted in her seat, snuggling down farther against the leather, her cheek cradled against the seat belt that separated her still-magnificent breasts. "Mmm, Jonathan."

He froze, staring at the instrument panel. He no longer saw the gauges in front of him, or the sky that filled the windows. His mind was on Violet's sleepy moan.

Obviously she was dreaming. Obviously. He repeated this in his mind, but it wasn't sticking. His dick had gotten hard as a rock within seconds. What was she dreaming about? What was she imagining that he was doing? His hands grasped the yoke tightly, the dual sticks reminding him of gripping his cock, of all things. Fuck. Fuck. Like he needed to be thinking about jerking off at the moment? Just because she'd moaned his name in her sleep?

"Mmm," Violet said again sleepily, and he glanced over at her sharply. Was she just fucking with him? But she didn't stir. Against the thin fabric of her proper blouse, her nipples were stiff.

Oh, Jesus.

Jonathan began to sweat. He wasn't going to ogle her while she was sleeping. He was going to ignore it. Ignore the fact that those delicious nipples were poking against the filmy blouse, just begging to be touched. He remembered how much she'd loved to have her breasts played with, how she'd cried out and thrashed when he'd tugged on her nipples with his lips . . . He wiped his brow, surprised that it wasn't coated with sweat. Violet always talked in her sleep, he remembered. No big deal. She was just dreaming.

Hear that, dick? She's just dreaming. Now go fuck off. She still hates us when she's awake.

Of course, his dick was listening about as well as Violet was. The cockpit of the Socata was small. Too small, he thought. His traitorous mind was telling him to reach over and put a hand on her thigh, slide it up her skirt and see if she was wet . . .

And then she'd really fucking hate him, wouldn't she? Jonathan scrubbed a hand over his face and then returned it to the yoke, staring grimly ahead. He'd just have to ignore her. So he concentrated on things that would make his rearing dick go back down to normal. Things like his wrinkled old housekeeper who worked in his NYC town house. Spotting the paparazzi waiting outside of a hotel he was staying at. His new lineup of sportscars rolling out as lemons. Jumping out of a plane and his parachute cord not responding.

After a few minutes, he was under control again. Good.

She shifted in her seat again, her skirt riding higher up her thighs. "Mmm, oh, yes—"

"Violet," he barked. Jesus. A man could only take so much.

She jerked awake with a small snort, limbs flailing a bit. Then she looked around, eyes glazed and narrow with sleep. "Huh?"

"Wake up," he said gruffly.

She raised a hand and rubbed her face. "I was trying to sleep, you know."

"Yeah, but I want company," he lied. She'd flip out on him if she knew the real reason he'd woken her up. "Talk to me."

"Grow up," she muttered, straightening in her seat. "I can't believe you woke me up because you were bored."

He glanced over at her, noticing that she crossed her arms over those erect nipples to hide them, and her cheeks were flushed. Was she aware she was having dirty dreams about him? Sounded like they both needed a distraction. "Tell me, why is it you never opened the letter your father sent?"

She stared out the window to her right, avoiding his gaze. "You're kidding me, right? You should know more than most people that my father and I were never exactly on good terms."

"You never saw eye to eye. I remember that."

"Understatement," she said flatly.

"Still, he must have loved you quite a bit to put in all the work to set up some sort of scavenger hunt after his death. I assume we're not going to find what we're looking for at your childhood home?"

"Nope," she drawled out the word. "It's going to lead us to a clue, which is going to lead us to another clue, which is going to lead us, ultimately, to disappointment. Trust me on that one."

"I'm not so sure about that." Dr. DeWitt had put a lot of effort into this while sick and dying. It didn't strike Jonathan as a whim. As long as this trip had his stele at the end of it, and Violet's company during it, it would be a win in Jonathan's book.

"I'm sure," Violet said flatly. "This is my father we're talking about. Everything was always a disappointment with him."

"Yes, but for him to send both of us letters, it's clearly intimating that it's something we should work on together."

"Or, it's all part of my father's plan to keep you funding his projects after he dies. He dangles me under your nose, and you keep throwing money into the things that mattered to him."

"You don't know that's true."

"He sent you a list, didn't he? Of foundations and projects he wants continued after he's gone?"

Jonathan's mouth quirked slightly at that, though he bit back the smile that threatened. She knew the old man well. Dr. DeWitt had, in fact, sent Jonathan a laundry list of causes dear to his heart that he wished to continue to see supported after his death. But the old man knew he didn't have to throw Violet in Jonathan's path to get Jonathan to support him. "I've already handled his wishes."

"Of course you have," she said flatly. "You've always been his little puppet, haven't you?"

Irritation flicked in Jonathan's mind. He ignored her needling words. Violet could lash out at him, but he wouldn't respond in kind.

So he only said, "We'll be landing shortly."

———

Violet was silent as they rode in the back of the sedan through the streets of Alamagordo. It wasn't an elite sort of city—Alamagordo was anything but—so she'd been surprised to see that Jonathan had a chauffeur waiting for them when they landed at the tiny private airport. Apparently he had really efficient assistants.

She hated to say it, but she was feeling . . . guilty. Just a bit. She could tell she'd hurt Jonathan's feelings by lashing out at him in the plane, calling him her father's puppet. It wasn't fair, she knew that. Her father had been the most manipulative man she'd ever met. He was friendly and pleasant and dynamic to be around precisely because he knew it got him what he wanted. You didn't realize he was trampling all over your own wishes until much, much later. Most people didn't mind that Phineas had been a manipulative old goat, but then, Violet wasn't most people. For Jonathan to be completely swept up in the old man's charm was understandable.

So, yeah, she felt a bit like a jerk for being so short with him on the plane.

It was just that . . . she'd been having the most disturbing dream. Violet absently bit her nails, remembering. One of the things she held against Jonathan—one of the many, many things—was that he'd been incredible in bed. He practically vibrated intensity at all times, and to have that intensity focused on her pleasure had been a multi-orgasmic experience each time. Post-Jonathan? She'd been dissatisfied with quite a few of her lovers, simply because they hadn't put in the time or care to make sure she got off until her brains were mush. Not like Jonathan had. That was another thing that irritated her—that she'd peaked sexually with an asshole who dumped her.

And apparently her body recalled just how good he'd been in bed, because it was reminding her as she slept. She'd been having the most erotic dream about him. Images of Jonathan's body poised over her own still filled her mind. Of him drilling into her from behind until she was screaming with pleasure. Of her begging for him to flip her over and eat her pussy until she couldn't stand it any longer.

Of him pushing her onto her back and doing just that.

She cleared her throat and crossed her arms over her breasts, staring mutely out the window. Her stupid nipples were responding again, and she knew her panties were wet, all from that dream. She hated that. Her loins needed to remember how badly he'd treated her in the past.

"We're almost there," the driver said, turning in to an old subdivision.

"Thank you," Jonathan replied. He looked over at Violet. "Shall I take the lead?"

Like she wanted to be in charge. "Be my guest."

He nodded and seemed to visibly tense as they approached her old house. An old memory of Jonathan rose in her mind. He was an extremely focused person, but when given a task he was excited about, he seemed to grow in intensity. She remembered that, and the determined set of his shoulders was bringing back a wealth of memories that she wanted to forget.

They pulled up in front of the house and Violet stared at her childhood home. It seemed smaller and much older than she remembered. The house had been blue when she'd lived there and was now a cheery yellow with ruffled curtains in the windows. The tree she remembered in the front yard was nothing but a stump.

"Let's go," Jonathan said, opening his door and getting out of the car before the driver could get out to open the door for him.

Violet hesitated, but when Jonathan moved to her side and opened the door, she followed him. Memories were just that—memories. No need for her to be upset over them. Still, it was hard not to see her childhood home and imagine her mother inside, sobbing out of depression and unhappiness. And when she wasn't crying, she'd been drinking. Violet couldn't remember which one was worse.

Jonathan offered her his arm, as if they were heading to a social event.

She gazed blankly at him and ignored it. "Let's just go, all right?"

He shrugged and headed to the front door. "I'll do the talking."

That was fine with her. She walked up with him and stood quietly as he knocked on the front door. This was, well, it was just odd to her to walk up to her childhood home and knock, waiting for a stranger to open the door. "What are we going to do if no one's home?"

He considered for a moment. "Break into the backyard and bribe the police if we get caught?"

She stared at him. Was he joking? It was hard to tell with Jonathan. Sometimes he was deadly serious about the strangest things. "I wouldn't answer the door if I saw us here. We look like we're trying to sell someone something."

He flashed a grin at her. "I'll sell the owner a sports car for a dollar if they let me in that backyard."

"Of course you would," she muttered.

They both fell silent as they heard the sound of the chain and turned back to the door.

A wrinkled little old woman in a floral muumuu and with her hair in rollers answered the door and gave them a sweet smile. "May I help you?" Her gaze went from Violet to Jonathan, then seemed to linger there. "Are you . . . ?"

He extended his hand. "Jonathan Lyons, ma'am. Have you heard of me?"

The woman giggled and placed her fingers in Jonathan's hand. "Oh, my. You're that man with the cars, aren't you?"

"That's me."

"Is this for television?" She peered around them, looking for cameras, and seemed disappointed to see none.

Jonathan grinned. "No, ma'am. I need to ask a favor of you. May we come in?"

Two minutes later, they were in Violet's childhood home while Jonathan talked to the owner and explained to her why they were visiting. Violet stared at her surroundings uncomfortably. Her memories of this house were dark floors, tightly drawn drapes, and sadness. This house was just as cute inside as it was outside. Light, airy colors and open windows filled the living room with sunlight and cast shadows on the knickknacks that filled dainty shelves along the wall. A small table with Queen Anne chairs sat under one of the windows, and a rag rug decorated the retiled kitchen floor.

"So you want to dig up a tree in the backyard?" She peered at Jonathan curiously, and then her face lit up. "You're with that nice man who came here last year, aren't you?"

Violet turned at that. "Last year?" Had her father planned things that far back?

The woman nodded. "A gentleman asked me if he could bury something under one of the trees in the backyard. Told me a lovely story about it meaning something to his daughter." She shrugged. "I thought he was a little cuckoo but harmless."

A reluctant smile spread across Violet's face. "Cuckoo was a good description for my father." She wasn't so sure about harmless.

"He told me to expect you in the future. Lovely man." She gave Violet a sweet smile. "Spoke so nicely about his pretty daughter, too." Before Violet could scoff at that, the woman continued. "Well, come on, then. I don't mind. Do what you like, just don't touch my daylilies."

"We won't," Jonathan assured her.

They made their way out to the backyard, and it, too, was transformed from Violet's memories. For a heart-stopping moment, she worried that the tree would be gone. Not that she cared, of course, but she didn't put it past Jonathan to come up with another sort of scheme to keep her at his side while they tried to figure out where the next lead would take them. But Violet counted trees and realized that the slim cottonwood she'd staked out as a child was, in fact, still there, just thicker and taller.

Drawn to it, Violet headed forward, looking for the mark she'd made when she was young. Jonathan followed behind her, and when she got to the tree, she ran her fingers along the upraised ridges of the bark. There, faintly among the ridges, was her drawing. It did look like a squashed bug. Just a bit. Violet smiled to herself. Huh. "This is the tree."

"Mind if we dig at the base?" Jonathan asked the owner.

"Go right ahead," the woman said with a tittering laugh. "You're sure this isn't for TV?"

"I'm sure," Jonathan said with a chuckle. "Got a shovel?"

Violet waited as Jonathan got a few gardening implements from the owner, and then he returned to the tree.

"Dig here," Violet told him, pointing at the front of the tree. That had been where she'd hidden her Etch A Sketch back when she was a child, between two upraised roots. She stepped back and watched as Jonathan dug, all of his casual friendliness gone once more in the face of his focused intensity.

He didn't have to dig far. Violet figured as much. After all, her father had wanted it found. A few shovelfuls of dirt in, Jonathan clanged against something, and all three of them paused and bent over to see what he'd uncovered. He leaned down and brushed the dirt away from a small metal box, then pulled it out and held it out to Violet. "Do you want to do the honors?"

She waved him away with a hand. Violet would never admit that she was a little curious, herself. "This is your party. You go ahead."

He examined the box for a moment, holding it up. To Violet's eyes it looked like a plain lockbox. She half-wondered if they'd find an Etch A Sketch inside, and her heart twanged painfully.

But when he opened the box, Jonathan reached inside and pulled out two thick cream envelopes with her father's familiar red wax seal. "One has my name on it, and one has yours."

Violet stared at the envelope with her name on it. She was surprised her hand didn't tremble when she reached forward and plucked it from his grip. She didn't open it. Not yet. Instead, she waited as Jonathan tore his open, his eyes that dark, sharp intense stare that made her shiver and remember her dreams from earlier.

He flipped the paper open, scanned it, and was almost disappointed. "Just one word. GLIRASTES. I'm not sure what that's referring to." He showed her the paper, his gaze turning to her. "What's yours say?"

Reluctant, Violet flipped hers over and gently eased the seal open. Her heart thumped as she saw her father's familiar, crabbed cursive writing with certain letters bolded. There were eight lines of it, and she scanned it and then began to read.

"I met a traveller from an antique land
Who said: "Two vast and trunkless legs of stone
Stand in the desert. Near them, on the sand,
Half sunk, a shattered visage lies, whose frown
And wrinkled lip and sneer of cold command
Tell that its sculptor well those passions read
Which yet survive, stamped on these lifeless things,
The hand that mocked them and the heart that fed."

Violet frowned down at the paper. "Poetry? Really? You got a made-up word and I got poetry? Was my dad on crack in his last days?"

She looked up and to her surprise, Jonathan's face was lit up with recognition.

"What?" she asked warily.

"'And on the pedestal these words appear,'" Jonathan murmured, getting to his feet and dusting off his jeans. His intense gaze held hers. "'My name is Ozymandias, King of Kings: look on my works, ye mighty, and despair!'"

Her eyebrow went up. "Ozymandias?"

"Shelley," he said excitedly, and his hands gripped her arms and he pulled her into his arms. "It's Shelley!"

She was going to ask him to explain when he grabbed her and pulled her against him in a quick, brisk kiss of excitement. Before she could chastise him, he pulled away from her, grinning, and turned and grabbed the elderly woman and gave her a big smacking kiss on the cheek. "Shelley!" he pronounced again.

The elderly woman tittered.

Violet didn't laugh. It was a nothing kiss. Just excitement.

Still, Violet's cheeks flushed as she remembered her dream from earlier, and Jonathan's mouth between her legs. She forced herself to remain outwardly indifferent. "Do you mind explaining what you mean by 'Shelley'?"

Jonathan turned back and gave her a brilliant smile, his solemn face lighting up in a way that made him impossible to look away from. "Percy Bysshe Shelley," he explained. "He wrote the poem 'Ozymandias' when he saw a statue of Ramses the Great in London."

"So," she said thoughtfully, tapping the paper on her hand. "Knowing my father, we're either to follow the rabbit trail after Shelley himself and go to London, or research Ramses the Great. What does your clue have to do with any of this?"

"No idea," Jonathan said, that boyish smile still on his face. "But I'm positive there's a connection somewhere. We just have to figure it out."

"Mmmhmm." Violet nodded, staring at the paper. She traced her finger over the lettering. "Some of these characters are darker than others. That must be part of the clue." She folded up the letter; she'd figure it out later. Right now, she couldn't stop thinking about that brief press of his mouth against hers. Damn it, what was wrong with her? One day in his company and she was salivating over him just because he ate a good pussy? Jesus. Did she have no morals? He *abandoned* her when she was nineteen and pregnant. Why did she care if his eyes lit up when he was excited about something, or if he'd been a great kisser? None of that mattered if he was a terrible person, and he was.

He was just like her father, using people for his own means.

She glared icily at him when he smiled back at her, determined not to be swayed by his charm. "So now you're going to drag me off to London, I take it?"

His exuberant expression died slowly, his face smoothing. "Unless you think we should start with Egypt?"

Violet shrugged. "I'm just the hired help. You're the one calling the shots."

He nodded, lost in thought, and tucked his letter into his jacket. He turned back to the owner of the house and gave her another charming smile. "I cannot thank you enough, madam."

"You could give me one of those fancy cars you sell," she told him, and then tittered behind a liver-spotted hand, her curlers jiggling.

He bowed over her hand as if responding to a command. "It's done. I'll have one delivered."

Her eyes widened into two circles. "I—Mr. Lyons, I didn't mean—I was just teasing—"

"I know," he said. "But I shall insist." He took her hand in his, kissed the back of it, and grinned. "Cherry red?"

She gave him an awestruck nod.

Again, Violet had to resist the urge to roll her eyes. If the man was going to give a car to every person he ran across, he'd be broke in days. That was no way to run a business, Violet thought grumpily.

They thanked the woman once more and Jonathan texted her information to his assistant, and then they headed back out to the waiting car.

Once they were inside, Jonathan grabbed her and dragged her across the seat toward him.

"Jonathan—"

His mouth covered hers, and he kissed her again. Shocked, Violet remained frozen as he pulled her against him and his lips coaxed hers apart. Memories blasted through her, along with his kiss. Memories of his excitement on the dig; he'd never been more turned on than when they had an breathtaking discovery. Adrenaline made him hard as a rock, whether it was from archaeology or something else. It appeared that adrenaline was pumping through him right now, and he'd forgotten that she hated him.

She tried to pull away, but his tongue slicked against hers, and she weakened. It coaxed into her mouth, firm, decisive thrusts that were just as intense as the man himself. His hand moved to her nape and he held her against him, groaning her name between hot, fevered kisses. "Violet. God, Violet."

The way he said her name made her nipples harden. Her mouth parted under his and she fell into his spell. The flavor of him was sweet against her mouth, tasting faintly of mint. His lips were firm against hers, as insistent as his grip on her. When his tongue thrust into her mouth and then curled along her own, she moaned. Oh, God, he'd always been such a good kisser. He knew just how to push her buttons—

Violet gasped, realizing what she was doing. She was kissing the man she hated above all other men. The man who had betrayed her and left her, without a care in the world.

She jerked away from him, hauling backward. "No, Jonathan!"

"Violet," he murmured, and the look in his eyes was sleepy with lust.

She slapped him across the face.

That got his attention. He pulled away, clearly surprised at her violent response. He released her and his hand went to his jaw. "My apologies. I didn't realize you were so unwilling."

"I will *always* be unwilling with you," she hissed. "You think you can just waltz back into my life and throw me into your bed like nothing has happened?"

The look in his eyes grew intense again. "If I could throw you into my bed this moment and know you would stay there? I would in a heartbeat, Violet."

"No," she cried furiously. "You don't get to touch me! Ever again!"

He raked a hand through his hair, clearly frustrated. "I realize we parted badly, Violet, but fuck. We were two stupid kids. Can't we be adults about this?"

"'Be adults about this'?" She laughed, the sound hysterical. "You're the one pawing me every chance you get."

"I love you, Violet," he said quietly, his tone deathly earnest. No loud crowing of affection for Jonathan; just quiet, solemn intensity. "I never stopped loving you. Ever. I want you back."

She trembled, her entire body shaking violently with the force of emotions swirling through her. "You lost my love when you abandoned me."

He shook his head. "I was nineteen, Violet. What nineteen-year-old wants to settle down and raise a family?"

"You should have thought about that before you got me pregnant!"

He stilled.

She sucked in a breath. The look on his face was terrible in its bleakness.

"What . . . did you say?" He could have been carved from granite, for all the emotion he showed.

"I was pregnant and you still abandoned me," Violet said softly, because screaming at him in the face of such stillness seemed . . . unnatural. "Don't pretend like you didn't know."

"I didn't." He sounded deflated.

"I told you I wanted to go home and start a family immediately. And when that wasn't clear enough, I left you a note."

"I never got a note."

She didn't know what to think of that response. "Well, you don't have to worry. I lost the baby a month later, so I'm not going to hit you up for child support." All her anger was exhausting her. She'd carried it for so long, and spewing it now just felt . . . lackluster. She shook her head. "Look. I just want you out of my life, all right? Whatever we had between us died ten years ago. I want this done so I never have to see you again."

He stared at her.

He kept staring at her for so long, utterly still, that she grew unnerved. "What?" she snapped.

"There was a baby?" The words were calm, flat.

"Don't start this game, Jonathan," she said wearily. "Just don't. You can't reverse ten years of hatred with a bit of pretending, okay? So don't even try."

As she watched him, he seemed to leach of color, the light, the intensity in his eyes that was so very Jonathan seeming to die in front of her. He sat back, looked at her for a moment more, and then turned to the driver—who, Violet was horrified to notice, had been listening to the entire conversation. "Hotel, please," Jonathan said hoarsely.

Violet sat back in the seat, her arms crossed, her mouth still bruised from his kiss, and stared out the window as they pulled away from her childhood home.

Why did she feel like the bad guy here? She was the wronged party, not Jonathan.

FOUR

⟿

Now he knew why she hated him.

Jonathan watched Violet march across the lobby of the hotel. He trailed behind her, just staring after her with longing as she checked in, flicked an angry glance his way, and then disappeared into the elevator.

Moving right back out of his life again, he thought bleakly.

He thought about heading up to his room and emptying the minibar. Just drinking away his misery. But the minibar didn't have enough to numb him. He headed to the hotel bar instead.

The bartender was young, pretty, and female, with a wealth of curly black hair. She gave him an appreciative look. "What can I get you, gorgeous?"

He sat down at the bar. "Scotch."

"On the rocks?"

"In the bottle." He tapped the front of the bar. "Just bring it."

"Bad day?" She gave him a sympathetic look and turned to get the bottle.

"One of the worst," he agreed. Second only to the day that Violet had left him. He took the glass she poured in front of him, slammed it, and waited for her to fill it again. He didn't normally drink to oblivion. He didn't like to have his senses dulled. But today? Today he just wanted to fucking forget.

There'd been a *baby*.

He rubbed his forehead. He should have known there was a baby. He should have fucking guessed. It made sense, now. Why his carefree, stubborn, independent Violet had gone from enjoying the summer to demanding that he abandon college with her and start a family right away. He'd been so goddamn dumb. So wrapped up in assisting Dr. DeWitt that he'd never even considered the reasons behind why Violet had been so upset and gung ho to leave Greece and return to the States.

She'd been pregnant. And she'd wanted it . . . and wanted him.

And he'd abandoned her. Hadn't even fucking chased her down to tell her that he wanted her. He'd thought she was married and out of his reach, but that had been a lie, a lie told to him by Violet's father.

Today, he'd lost everything.

He'd always thought of Dr. DeWitt as a mentor and a father figure. He knew the old man was a wily bastard, but he'd always admired his tenacity to get what he wanted. He'd trusted the man despite that, thinking that because Jonathan was one of his closest friends, there was a level of respect between them.

Turns out it was all bullshit. DeWitt had lied to him about Violet just to get him to stay and continue financing things, and he'd happily done so.

Meanwhile, he'd abandoned the woman he loved, who had been pregnant and afraid.

And she'd lost their baby and blamed him for it.

He threw back another glass of Scotch, then just grabbed the bottle from the bartender and started to drink.

Violet hated him. He'd been so fucking overjoyed to find out that she wasn't married, that she'd never been married, because it meant that somewhere, somehow, he could still make Violet his.

Now, that dream was gone. He couldn't fix this. He couldn't make her love him again, not with the shadow of a miscarriage—a miscarriage that was his fault—between them.

He'd lost her for good, and this time there was nothing he could do to fix it.

Jonathan chugged the Scotch. It tasted like shit, but what did it matter?

Nothing did. Nothing mattered anymore.

The Next Day

Violet flicked off the TV in her hotel room and glanced over at the phone. She debated for a minute, then called down to the front desk. "Hello. I'm looking for Mr. Lyons. Could you patch me through to his room?"

The operator connected her. The phone rang for several minutes, just as it had last night. No one picked up. He wasn't answering.

She was starting to get concerned. Not that Jonathan was pouting and ignoring her—she didn't care about that—but that he wasn't contacting her at all. She felt emotionally drained after her big confession, like a hollow shell of Violet DeWitt. She wasn't even angry anymore, just tired. So tired. More than anything, she just wanted to be done with him and go back to her nice, quiet life.

Weren't they supposed to be doing this stupid scavenger hunt together? Just sitting in a room in New Mexico felt like a huge waste of time, but what could she do? She was pretty sure that if she just up and went back home to Detroit, he'd withhold the money he'd dangled in front of the school and state that she'd reneged on her end of the deal. What would the school do if she cost them the money? They wouldn't be happy, that was for sure, especially the next time that budget cuts came around.

But seriously, exactly how long was she supposed to stay in her room and watch episodes of *House Hunters* while waiting on him?

She clicked off the remote a moment later and swung her legs over the edge of the bed. Fine. If he wasn't going to answer her phone calls, maybe he'd answer when she showed up at his door and explain to her what the hell was going on. Violet slipped on a pair of shoes and tossed a sweater over her T-shirt, then headed down to the lobby.

She approached the front desk and gave the woman there a polite smile. "Could you please tell me which room is Mr. Lyons's? I'm working with him on a project and can't seem to connect with him at the moment."

The girl at the front desk bit her lip.

"What?" Violet asked.

"I can tell you what room is his," she said quietly, "but he's not in it."

Alarm pounded in Violet's veins. "Where is he, then?"

"The bar."

The bar? That didn't sound like Jonathan. He wasn't much of a drinker except in social situations. That was one of the reasons she'd fallen for him originally; he was a refreshing change from her alcoholic mother. Violet glanced at the clock on the wall. It was ten in the morning. What on earth? "You're sure?"

The girl nodded. "He's been there since I started my shift late last night."

All day? Frowning, Violet thanked her and headed over to the hotel bar. The bar area was dark and atmospheric despite the early hour . . . and deserted. Chairs were flipped over on tables, and someone ran a vacuum over the carpets. Violet scanned the room and paused when she saw a booth in the far back still covered in half-drunk bottles. There was a pile of laundry on one corner of the table.

When the laundry moved, though, Violet realized that it was a person. Jonathan. Pursing her lips, Violet strode forward. She made a mental note of the empty bottles of vodka, the myriad glasses on the table with red stirring straws and residue on the rim, remnants of mixed drinks past. There were several near-empty bottles of Crown Royal, a few other liquors she didn't recognize, and in this sea of bottles, Jonathan appeared to be asleep, his head resting on the table. His jacket had been pulled over his face as if to hide it from sunlight. Her lip curled in disgust. There was nothing worse than a drunk.

She'd had a lot of experience with sloppy drunks. Her mother had been one, and Violet had spent her childhood making excuses for her mother's behavior. She hated seeing someone normally so vibrant and intelligent dulled by drink. It filled her with a helpless anger.

She reached over the bottles and snatched the jacket up. "Jonathan?"

He groaned and sat up with a jerk, peering at her. His eyes were red and bloodshot, his face was unshaven, and his hair was a mess. His suit was wrinkled, and it looked suspiciously like the one he was wearing when she'd last seen him. His gaze focused on her, and that stark expression returned to his face. "Ah, fuck. Violet."

"What's wrong with you?" she hissed, throwing his jacket at him.

His mouth twisted to the side. "The better question might be to ask, what *isn't* wrong with me?"

She ignored that. "Have you been drinking all night?"

"Dunno." He shrugged his shoulders and reached for one of the bottles with alcohol still in it. "Don't care."

"Well, I care."

He smiled thinly. "We both know that's a lie, Violet."

She bit her nails, thinking. "Aren't we supposed to be going on to Egypt and looking for your stele so we can continue this pointless little scavenger hunt?"

"Like you just said," he slurred. "It's pointless." He raised his glass to her and then chugged it.

She drummed her fingers on her arm. This wasn't like Jonathan. Getting excited over minor discoveries? Chasing down adventures? *That* was Jonathan. This miserable drunk in front of her who didn't care? That wasn't Jonathan. If anyone could accuse Jonathan Lyons of something, it was that he cared too much and tended to get too wrapped up.

She frowned to herself. Actually, that wasn't always true either. He'd abandoned her . . . hadn't he? That wasn't the action of a man who cared too much. Unless everything she'd thought had been a lie . . .

Either way, she was his partner until they were done, for better or for worse. "Jonathan, please. We need to continue this. Not because I particularly care what little scheme my father has cooked up, but because I have students to get back to, and I can't until you release me. You're holding me here."

"I wish I was holding you," he said, and there was such bleakness in his tone that it made her suck in a breath.

"Very funny, Jonathan," she said, hating that her voice shook. "You know what I meant. You have me here until we're finished with this, so let's get going."

But he didn't move. Instead, he traced a finger around the rim of a dirty glass and then gave her a morose, red-eyed stare. "No, Violet, I don't think I ever had you."

"If you're going to be like this, I'm going back up to my room," she warned.

He shrugged, poured himself another drink in the dirty glass, and raised it in a toast. "Bottom's up."

Violet stormed away, angry and confused. Why was he acting like this? What she'd told him had been no surprise . . . was it? Even if she asked him, could she trust that what he told her was the truth?

All of a sudden, she didn't know anymore.

———————

That night, she called down to the front desk again. "Is he still in the bar?"

"He is," the front desk clerk assured her. "We can't get him to leave. The bartender keeps slipping him glasses of water so he doesn't get alcohol poisoning, but we're starting to get concerned."

"I'll be down in a minute," Violet said. This had to stop. He was going to drink himself into kidney damage if he wasn't careful. She hung up the phone and headed down to the lobby, then made a beeline for the bar. Sure enough, Jonathan was still there in his regular spot. The liquor from earlier had been replaced by all new bottles. Now, it seemed, he was drinking tequila. He was upright—barely—a shot glass in one hand. The front of his Superman shirt was stained with alcohol.

He didn't even look up as she approached, just stared morosely at one of the bottles.

"Jonathan," Violet said, moving to stand by his table and crossing her arms over her chest. It was her very best Angry Schoolteacher pose and never failed to make her students pay attention. "This has got to stop." When he didn't respond, she reached over and grabbed his chin, forcing him to look at her. "Jonathan!"

Jonathan stared up at her, and his eyes were so wounded that she ached inside. "Violet."

"You need to stop this. Seriously."

His mouth drew slowly into a lazy smile. "Why?"

"Well, first of all, you're starting to smell like a bar. And second of all, this isn't healthy."

"Does it matter?"

"Please," she cajoled, changing her tone. Maybe if she

tried a different tactic, she could get through to him. "You're scaring me, Jonathan."

"What's it matter? You hate me, Violet." The look in his eyes was stark. "You've made that clear."

She felt a twinge of pity. "That doesn't mean I want to watch you drink yourself to death. Now, please. Come up to bed."

For a moment, his eyes lit up and he stood up from the table, his tall body weaving. "Your bed?"

"No!"

He sat back down again.

Violet gave him an exasperated look. "Really, Jonathan?"

He ignored her and began to pour another drink.

She reached over and grabbed the bottle out of his hand, and he glared at her. "You need to stop. This isn't like you."

Jonathan shook his head slowly, his messy hair sliding over his forehead. "How would you know, Violet? You haven't seen me in ten years. Maybe I decided to drink after you left me."

She carefully pried the glass out of his fingers. "You said it dulls the senses, and you don't like yours dulled. I remember that."

He shook his head, not looking at her. "I don't want to remember anything right now."

Another twinge of pity. Damn it. "Jonathan, just come on. Let's get you back to *your* room and get you into *your* bed, all right?"

He simply put his head down on the table and morosely stared at one of the bottles.

"Do you need help, ma'am?" One of the waitstaff came over. "I can help you take him up to his room, if you like."

"No, we're fine," she said with a small smile of appreciation. "Has he been like this the whole time?"

The man nodded. "When he's not crying."

"Crying?" Violet was horrified. She'd never seen Jonathan cry. She couldn't even imagine it. Even when they'd fought, he'd just stared at her with those grim, smoldering eyes.

"Yeah. We figured someone died. Keeps saying he lost her." The man shrugged. "You going to pay his bill? It's a big one."

Her heart twinged again. Someone *had* died. But Jonathan hadn't cared about the baby . . . had he? She shook the thought off. "No, I'm going to get him out of here. He can pay his own bill. The girl at the front desk can add it to his room." She pulled money out of her pocket and offered it to him as a tip. "Thank you for your help, though."

The man nodded and took the twenty. "Let me know if you need anything else."

He left as she knelt down next to Jonathan's table. She studied him for a long moment, thinking about the man's words. *Crying as if he'd lost someone.* Lost *her.* She reached out and stroked his arm with her hand, and her voice was softer this time. "Jonathan. Come on. Let's get you up to your room, all right?"

Jonathan turned to her, propping his head up on his arm as he gazed in her direction. "You know I loved you, Violet?" His voice was soft.

"I know. But that was a long time ago."

He shook his head, just a little. "Never changed for me," he said, his words slurred thickly. "Never stopped. Too late now, though."

Keeps saying he lost her.

Now *she* wanted to cry. She couldn't bury ten years of festering hatred in a night, but she could pity a man who was clearly miserable. "If you love me, won't you come up to your room?"

"Doesn't matter if I love you or not," he murmured. "Lost you anyhow."

Violet thought for a moment. "If you go up to your room and get to bed, I'll kiss you."

Slowly, he sat up, and she felt the urge to laugh. So she'd

found the carrot that would entice the donkey, had she? "But you hate me, Violet."

"I hate you being drunk here more. The offer stands." She got to her feet and extended him a hand. "You go up to your room and I'll kiss you. If you don't, you can just stay here with your bottles."

Jonathan got up from the table so quickly he nearly knocked it over, the glassware rattling noisily. He wove unsteadily on his feet, but his intense gaze was back on her. "Come kiss me, then."

"Uh uh," she told him. "Up to your room, first." When he started to slouch again, she put an arm around his waist and got a good whiff of his breath. "Up to your room, and after you have some mouthwash, that is."

That got a drunk chuckle from him, and he wrapped his arms around her, dragging her against his front. He inhaled deeply, burying his nose in her hair. "Forgot how good you smell." His words were almost a moan of pure joy, and it sent a shock wave through her body.

"You're drunk," she reminded him with a pat on the arm. "Now, let go and we'll get you upstairs, okay?"

He leaned on her heavily as they made their way—slowly—toward the lobby elevator. The girl at the front desk gave her a grateful look as Violet passed by, and held the elevator open for them as Violet and her handsy, drunken companion continued to grab her and exclaim how wonderful her hair smelled. Eventually, though, she got him up to his room and managed to get the keycard out of his wallet and in the door.

"Almost there," she encouraged.

"Almost to kissing?"

She stifled a laugh at the tipsy hope in his voice. "Almost."

They wobbled their way across his suite to his bed, and he collapsed into it, flopping onto his back with a groan. Violet pulled back just in time before he dragged her down with him, though her chin-length hair went flying. "Ooof."

"In bed," he said, as proud as if he'd accomplished

something. He raised his arms, clearly expecting her to leap into them.

She snorted. "Fat chance." She glanced down at his legs and then gestured at his feet. "Let's get those shoes off of you, okay?" Violet leaned in and bent over to untie his laces. For a billionaire with tons of money, he sure did have some grubby sneakers on.

"I don't mind when you're angry at me, you know."

She continued to work on a knot in the laces. "That's a good thing, then, because I'm angry at you a lot."

"It's when you ignore me I can't stand it. When you give up on me and cut me out. It's like you're gone again, and I hate it."

Damn it, she needed to stop feeling sorry for the man. Pulling viciously on his shoe, she managed to tug it off and tossed it to the floor. His sock followed a moment later. "Other foot now."

"Miss you," he said softly.

She ignored him, prying off his other shoe, then jerked off his sock. "There we go. You should probably take off your jacket, too. And that shirt is filthy. Come on."

He sat up slowly, and she helped him remove his clothing. When his shirt came off, he groaned and fell back on the bed, scratching his chest. "Man, that's good."

She gazed down at his chest in surprise. She remembered a tall, lanky Jonathan with a lean, boyish chest and nary a chest hair. He'd filled out. His arms were tanned and brawny, ripped with muscle. His pectorals were furred with a light sprinkling of dark chest hair, and there was a trail down his abdomen that just begged to be followed. Violet felt the oddest urge to run her fingers along the cords of his muscles and see if they felt as hard as they looked. Oh, Jesus. He even had a super flat abdomen and little taut ridges down at his hips. Oh, that was sexy.

God, that wasn't fair. Ten years had passed. He should be gross and balding, not hotter than she'd ever seen him.

And he was gazing up at her with that dopey, drunken

smile on his face while she was lusting over his tanned, tight abs. She saw an ugly black tattoo of skulls and money on his upper arm. "Drunken night in Rio?"

"Nope." And he just smiled at her. "Do I get my kiss now?"

"Boy, you sure did fixate on that, didn't you?" Violet muttered, but she considered him for a long moment. At least he was out of the damn bar. "Brush your teeth first."

"Yes, ma'am."

"That's yes, Ms. DeWitt," she corrected in a sassy voice, then wanted to slap herself for flirting with her drunken ex-lover. *Terrible idea, Violet.* This man was bad news. She just needed to keep reminding herself that. "Go on." She wiggled her fingers in the direction of the bathroom. "Brush up."

He bounded up from the bed—and nearly cracked his head open, running into the wall. She smothered a giggle and sat down on the edge of the bed as he wove his way, stumbling, to the bathroom and began to vigorously brush his teeth. He kept glancing back to her as if checking to make sure she was still on the bed and hadn't escaped.

If it had been anyone but Jonathan, she would have been amused.

But since it was Jonathan, she was just . . . confused. He'd been so upset over their fight that he'd taken to drinking, and now that she was with him, he was acting like a giddy—albeit drunken—schoolboy. It didn't make sense, really.

Unless everything she'd thought about him was a lie.

Maybe he really hadn't known about the baby. She wanted to ask him about it, to get a real, straight, honest answer out of him, but he was drunk. There was no point in questioning a drunk man. It would have to wait. She clasped her hands and watched as he rinsed his mouth, then used mouthwash with great gusto, swishing away to ensure his mouth would be clean enough for their kiss.

Then, he wobbled back into the room and gave her a

slit-eyed smile, his eyes practically closed out of a mix of exhaustion and alcohol. "Kiss me now?"

"Lay down," she commanded, getting up off the bed and patting one pillow.

He more or less staggered into the bed and then looked over at her, waiting. She leaned in, and then at the last moment, kissed him on the forehead.

"Cheat," he murmured, eyes closed.

"You're too drunk to appreciate anything more," she told him.

He made a sound that might have been affirmation, and before she'd even pulled the blankets up over him, he was asleep.

She stared down at him, thinking. She didn't know what to do with him. Or what to think. Jonathan still drove her crazier than crazy in every possible way. Why was it that ten years apart felt like an eternity . . . and yet it felt like yesterday at the same time?

He rolled over in the bed and hugged the pillow, exposing his backside and the wallet sticking out of his pocket. Oh, right. She reached over and pulled it out of his jeans so it wouldn't disturb him while he slept, intending to put it on the nightstand. Instead, she stared at it for a moment and then snuck another peek at him. Still fast asleep.

So she opened his wallet, unable to resist her nosiness a moment longer.

It was full of money. That was no surprise to her; he was a billionaire. That interested her less than what else was in the wallet. Was it stuffed full of condoms? Pictures of other women? She dug around, knowing it was a shitty thing to do and not caring. Behind several platinum and black credit cards, she found a picture tucked away. Aha.

But when she pulled it out, it was her own face staring back at her.

The picture was creased, the edges worn, and it was obvious that it had been carried in this wallet—or others like it—for a long, long time. The photo was of Santorini, her and Jonathan standing in front of the Akrotiri ruins, both of them wearing hats and stripes of white zinc on their noses. They looked like dorks.

They looked so happy.

Nineteen-year-old Violet's braids were hanging over her shoulders and she was gazing up at a smiling Jonathan with an adoring look. Violet felt a weird little lurch in her stomach at the sight of that. Once upon a time, she'd adored him. And judging from this photo, that was how he'd wanted to remember her.

She carefully put the folded photo back into his wallet and looked for any other photos of women. There was nothing, just the photo of her. Frowning, she closed his wallet and put it on his bedside table.

At her side, Jonathan moaned in his sleep.

She stiffened, listening and watching him. To her horror, a harsh sob racked his body. "Violet," he moaned.

He sounded so tortured. Heart aching, she reached out and touched his arm. "I'm here, Jonathan. Go back to sleep."

Immediately, his sobs died down and his breathing calmed, and he returned to sleep.

Violet stared down at the man she thought she knew.

She didn't know what to do. For a long, painful moment, she wanted to turn and run right out of his room, out of the hotel, and keep running all the way back to Detroit. Pick up her nice, safe, quiet little life again and forget all about the billionaire who'd used her and hung her out to dry. Running away was sometimes a lot easier than staying and facing things, and she was a big fan of running.

But she didn't leave. Instead, she reached over and brushed the curls off of Jonathan's brow and then sighed when he didn't wake up. Well, shit.

She spotted his phone on the other nightstand and got up, heading for it. It was a smartphone, and she slid her thumb across the button, wondering if it was password coded. Nope. Her heart thumping, she went to his list of recent contacts. Several businesses scrolled past the screen, and then she found a name. Cade.

Chewing on her lip, she considered it for a moment, and then dialed.

It took a few rings before someone answered. Then, a man's cheerful voice came on the line. "Hey man, what's up?"

"I— Is this Cade?" Violet tried to keep her voice calm. "Are you a friend of Jonathan's?"

The man's tone immediately became more guarded. "Who's this?"

"My name is Violet—"

"Oh, damn. Violet, huh?"

She frowned. "Yes. Why?"

"*That* Violet?"

"That Violet what?" she snapped at him, growing irritated. What did this man think he knew?

"From a long time ago? The one who broke his heart?"

She felt her cheeks heating. "That's personal."

"That's also not a no." The man's voice grew kind. "What can I do for you, Violet? And why are you calling me on Jon's phone?"

She glanced over at the man sleeping in the bed, his brow furrowed as if his dreams still tormented him. "I think I broke him again," she whispered.

———

Cade agreed to head to New Mexico, but he couldn't get away for another day. In the meantime, Jonathan woke up, surly and dark, and headed right back to the bar. The front desk called Violet again—as if she could stop him!—and through more cajoling of a drunk man, she managed to get him back to his room to sleep it off again.

She didn't know if she could keep doing this. It was too hard on her heart. Her mother had drank herself into a stupor so many times that Violet felt herself mentally distancing every time someone picked up a bottle. Now, Jonathan was doing the same thing, and it made Violet's soul ache. Jonathan was being impossible and refused to listen to reason when she tried to talk to him. It was like he was trying to shut everything and everyone out, and the bottle was the only way he could do so.

Which was why she was ridiculously relieved when she got a text from Cade on her phone. I'm here. Shall we meet?

Violet raced down to the lobby. She hoped desperately that Cade would know what to do with Jonathan, because she was running out of ideas—and he was starting to get frustrated with her bribes of chaste forehead kisses.

The man waiting in the lobby for her was dressed in an elegant gray suit and had to be just about the prettiest man Violet had ever seen. He was angelic looking, from his blond hair to his shining blue eyes and his perfectly tanned skin. Good lord. "Um, Cade?"

He strolled forward, extending his hand. "Cade Archer."

She shook it, giving him a nervous smile. "Violet DeWitt."

"You look just as Jonathan described you."

She blinked in surprise. "He described me to you?"

"In glowing terms," Cade said, tucking her arm into the crook of his and leading her toward the hotel's elevator. Then he gave her a wry grin. "He was also drunk as a skunk."

She wanted to laugh, but it only made her feel a bit bitter. "So he only brings me up when he's drunk?"

"That's the only time Jonathan ever opens up," Cade agreed. "The rest of the time, he's locked down tighter than Fort Knox. If you want to go cliff diving, he's your man. If you want to talk about feelings, he's the last person you'd head to."

Violet chewed on her lip as she considered this. "Does he have a drinking problem, then? I can't seem to get him to stop."

Cade shook his head. "I've known him to drink all of twice in the time I've known him. The other time was at his father's funeral. He was beside himself with grief. Got drunk, talked a ton about you, and then clammed up and refused to speak of anything again afterward."

Well, that didn't make her feel much better. "I don't know what to do to get him to stop drinking right now. I . . . We fought and I said some harsh things. I guess I hurt him worse than I imagined."

He gave her a friendly smile. "I find that hard to believe."

He also hadn't seen Jonathan the last few days. Violet shrugged. "He's in a funk. We're supposed to be searching for a message left for us from my father, but Jonathan won't get out of bed. Or if he does, he heads to the bar. I'm trapped until we finish this."

"Trapped?" Cade looked curious.

"Trapped," she agreed flatly. "He's basically bribing people to keep me at his side, all under the guise of being charitable."

"That . . . also doesn't sound like Jonathan."

"Is that so," Violet said politely. "Perhaps you and I should compare Jonathans and see which one is the real one. Because he and I seem to be having a hell of a time together."

"Well," Cade said as they strolled across the lobby. "The Jonathan I know is extremely loyal. Very passionate about his work, and willing to do anything to win someone over to his cause. He's a bit single-minded but a good man. Very intense. Very determined. And a bit of an adrenaline junkie."

Okay, so that did sound like him. "Don't forget the part about not being able to keep his hands off of women."

That time, Cade gave her a curious look. "Really? I've never known Jonathan to act like that. He's been groping women in front of you? The Jonathan I know keeps himself closed off. I don't ever recall him having a steady girlfriend."

Her cheeks pinked. He'd been groping *her*, not other women. She thought of the photo in his wallet. No condom, no other women's phone numbers or pictures stuffed into his billfold. Just a picture of her with zinc on her nose. "Like I said," she fidgeted. "I guess we're seeing two different men."

"Strange," Cade murmured, but he didn't argue with her.

They went up to the bar. It was busier due to the time of night, but Violet still had no trouble finding Jonathan's table. She just looked for the one with the most bottles in the darkest corner. Yep, there he was. Violet sighed and pointed. "At the table in the back. He's busy trying to drink himself into a stupor again."

"Damn." Cade rubbed his jaw and looked over at Violet curiously. "What exactly did you say to him?"

"It's . . . personal. So you'll handle him from here?"

"You don't want to stick around?" He looked surprised.

Her smile was bittersweet. "I don't think he wants me around at the moment. I'm sorry." Violet gave Cade an apologetic look and hustled off before he could ask further questions.

It was cowardly of her to run, but she couldn't handle things at the moment. Her mind was spinning. She didn't know who—or what—to believe anymore.

FIVE

Jonathan barely glanced up from his bottle of Scotch as someone sat down at his table. To his surprise, it looked like his friend, Cade. He closed his eyes, and then rubbed them. "Damn. I think I'm drinking too much."

"What's on the menu?" Cade asked, picking up a bottle and sniffing it. He winced. "Jesus, man. Did you buy up all the decent brands already?"

He shrugged. "Alcohol is alcohol."

"And you're not one to drink." Cade waved someone over. "Can I get a glass, please? And two waters." He turned back to Jonathan. "So, you want to say what's bothering you?"

Jonathan poured himself another drink and slugged it down. "My life is fucking rotten, that's what."

"Odd thing to hear from a man who seems to love mountain climbing and chasing down lost cities."

"All dumb shit to pass the time," Jonathan said. "It's all bullshit that doesn't fucking matter." Nothing mattered because ten years ago, he'd had Violet and she was carrying his child . . . and he'd pissed it all away to go gallivanting around the world with a man who lied to his face while pretending to be his friend and mentor.

Christ, he was a fucking idiot. He'd given up Violet. His Violet. Jonathan rubbed his face again and moaned as the reality of it came crashing down again. "Cade, I'm such a fool."

"Is this about that lovely woman who just ran off?" Cade sipped his drink, his expression friendly and understanding. Of course Cade wouldn't judge him. Cade never judged anyone. If ever there was a man who deserved to be sainted, it was Cade Archer. Jonathan couldn't even hate him for it.

Instead, he craned his neck, hoping for another glimpse of Violet. "Did she leave?"

"Couldn't get out of here fast enough."

He stared down into his glass, thinking of Violet's wary brown eyes, her smooth hair, her lush figure that had only ripened with age. "She is beautiful, isn't she? She makes my heart hurt just to look at her. I see her face, and I see everything I could have had." He shook his head and wanted to bang it on the table in frustration. "But I don't have any of it. I have nothing."

"That's a bit dramatic, don't you think?" Cade squinted at him, analyzing him. "You've turned your family's fortunes around. You're one of the wealthiest men on the planet. You're a benefactor for dozens of charities. You're never cruel, you're generous with your money, and you have some really kick-ass friends." He grinned at the last part. "It can't be all bad, can it?"

"But none of it matters because she hates me," Jonathan snarled. His hand gripped his tumbler so tightly Cade thought it might shatter. "I'd give it all up in a heartbeat to know she loved me again."

"I don't think she hates you," Cade said quietly. "She wouldn't be this unsettled if she did."

"What do you know? You've never lost anyone you loved. You have a perfect life."

"Perfect," Cade echoed, and his smile twisted a little, looking surprisingly brittle. "Are we confessing our sins, then? All right." He leaned forward and poured himself a bigger drink, not looking at Jonathan. "I've loved and lost, too."

"Who?" Jonathan didn't believe him. Cade was just spouting shit to make Jonathan feel better.

The blond man took a long swig of his drink and considered it for a time before looking up at Jonathan again. "Daphne Petty," he said slowly.

Didn't ring a bell. Sounded familiar, but Jonathan's brain was skunked at the moment. "Am I supposed to know who that is?"

Cade's expression was rueful. "You might be the only one in the world that doesn't. Audrey's sister. Reese's Audrey." When Jonathan's expression remained bland, Cade continued. "Reese Durham? Your buddy in the Brotherhood? Ladies' man? His wife's twin sister is Daphne. She's a singer. The one with the purple wig and the plastic bikinis and the tattoos?"

A memory sparked. "Was she in a men's magazine last month?"

"Probably."

"Yeah, I think I jerked off to her." He hadn't, not really. Violet was the only one who got his dick hard. He just wanted to wipe that cheerful look off of Cade's face.

"Asshole."

"So you're in love with her?" If he was thinking of the right girl, she was wild and more than a little badly behaved. Didn't seem like Cade's type at all. "The singer?"

"I was in love, yeah. Back in the day." Cade considered his glass. "She got famous and she changed. She's not the same girl anymore, and I don't know what to think. All I know is that I feel like she's the one that got away." He gave Jonathan a thin smile. "So. You're not alone in the heartbreak corner."

He was surprised to hear all of that coming from Cade. "Yeah, but you didn't destroy her life, did you?"

"No, she seems to be doing that well enough on her own," Cade said flatly.

"Well, I destroyed Violet." Jonathan thought of the pain in her eyes. A baby. There had been a baby and he'd never known. She'd lost it after she'd gone home. Had it been because she was so stressed and unhappy to be abandoned? Probably. He could lay the blame for that at his own feet, as well. It just made him hate himself more. "I've dreamed of her for ten years, Cade. Missed her with every waking moment. And now I find out that she hates me and she'll always hate me. It's like a knife in my gut." Despair threatened to overwhelm him. "I'll never get her back now. Ever."

"Maybe it's time for both of you to start over," Cade said. "It's been ten years. You're both different people than you were before."

Maybe. He just didn't know if Violet would ever give him that chance. He'd fucked it all up ten years ago. There might never be a chance to fix it now.

Someone knocked at Violet's hotel room door a few hours later, just before she was about to go to sleep. Curious, she pulled on a robe and peered through the peephole. Cade. Violet unlatched the door and opened it a crack. "Is everything okay?"

Cade flashed her a brief smile. "Well, he's drunk again."

"This isn't surprising. He's been drunk for the last few days. I'm pretty sure he's spent more time drunk than sober since we've been together."

"He's pretty miserable at the moment," Cade said, glancing down the hallway. Violet craned her neck out the door and caught sight of a man sprawled in a chair at the end of the hall, a bottle tucked under his arm.

"Yes, he looks *quite* miserable," she said in a droll voice. "I'm sure he's quick to blame me for all of this."

"Actually, no. He blames himself." Cade glanced at her, then down the hall. "He's pretty sure he's destroyed his own life and ruined yours, and places responsibility for his actions squarely on his own doorstep."

She felt a twinge of pity at that. "Well, you can assure him I'm just fine."

"I would if I could get a word in edgewise."

"What do you mean?"

"I mean he's constantly quoting poetry at me. Watch." Cade stepped into the hall a few paces. "Jonathan? Ready to go upstairs?"

"'I was a child and she was a child,'" singsonged the drunk voice down the hall. "'In this kingdom by the sea. But we loved with a love that was more than love—I and my Annabel Lee!'"

Someone in the next room banged on the wall in response.

Violet pressed her fingertips to her mouth to keep from laughing. It wasn't funny. It wasn't. "Is that Edgar Allan Poe?"

"Is that what it is?" Cade grimaced. "It's godawful."

"I think so. I took some poetry classes in college and it sounds familiar." She'd been majorly into poetry back when she'd started college. She hadn't known that Jonathan knew poetry. Was this another facet of him that had cropped up in the last ten years, or had it always been there and she'd never noticed? "So you couldn't get him to stop drinking?"

"He was already wrecked, so I figured it wouldn't hurt to get a few more details out of him before I implement my plan."

She tilted her head at him, curious. "Your plan?"

"Yes." He grinned and rubbed his hands together, looking so utterly boyish that she wanted to smile back. "Phase one—glean information. Phase two—strategy. Phase three—execution."

"It all sounds very corporate."

"It does, doesn't it?" He seemed rather pleased with himself.

Down the hall, Jonathan began to drunkenly ramble again, voice singsonging another poem that he was slurring too much for her to make out.

She glanced down the hall at him, and played with the high neck of her robe. "Should you, um, stop him?"

"Nah. I'm going to let him get it all out of his system. As of tomorrow morning, he's not going to want another drink."

"You sound very confident."

"Trust me. I know what makes Jonathan tick. I just need your word that you'll go along with everything I throw at you."

"Me? What's my part in this?"

"Just that. I'll come get you for breakfast, and anything I suggest to you, just agree with it. We'll get Jonathan out of his funk and back on the road with you in a heartbeat."

She wasn't sure if that was the case, but Cade seemed awfully confident. "If you say so."

"Great. See you then. I'll get that one off to bed." He gestured at Jonathan, then walked away.

"Wait!" When he turned, Violet couldn't help but ask, "So what did he tell you?"

Cade smiled mysteriously, but his words were blunt. "That he's still madly in love with you and regrets that he's lost you forever."

For some reason, those words made her feel a sharp, unhappy little stab in her heart. *He's lost you forever.* Of course she knew that was what this was about, right? Still, hearing the words spoken aloud made her feel anxious and a little unhappy. She wasn't sure she wanted to be lost forever. "I'm fine with being friends with him," she confessed. "I just can't trust him with more."

"I understand," Cade said. "And I'm not judging. See you in the morning, Violet." He gave her a nod and walked away.

A moment later, she heard him moving to Jonathan's side, encouraging the drunk man to get out of his chair and back to his room.

As she shut the door on them, Violet caught a few more lines of Jonathan's drunken poetry spouting. "'And this maiden,'" he rambled, "'she lived with no other thought than to love and be loved by me.'"

"Come on," Cade murmured, and then they were silent.

But Violet had the words ringing through her head for a long time afterward. *She lived with no other thought than to love and be loved by me.*

The "Annabel Lee" poem had a wretched ending, if she remembered correctly.

The next morning, promptly at nine, someone knocked at Violet's door.

She answered it, her brain full of whirling, uneasy questions. She'd had a sleepless night, filled with more dreams of Jonathan and lovemaking, and it made her restless. There was a rational reason she kept dreaming about his mouth on her skin, she told herself. She hadn't had sex in well over a year, and now she was hanging out with an ex-lover. It made plenty of sense.

Sensible explanation or not, she was still waking up aching and full of need every morning, and today was no different.

She'd dressed conservatively, though, since she didn't know what Cade's great plan was to get Jonathan out of his funk. She'd worn slacks and flats, along with a plain black boatneck sweater. It would be serviceable clothing for just about any situation. Still, when she answered the door and saw Cade standing there in another impeccable gray suit, she wondered if she was underdressed.

"Violet," he greeted her cheerfully. "You look lovely this morning."

"Thank you," she murmured, stepping out of her room and making sure the door was locked behind her. She didn't see Jonathan, and strangely enough, she was disappointed. "Are we alone?"

"No—" Cade began.

"Why? Did you want to be?" From around the corner, Jonathan walked slowly toward them, sunglasses covering his eyes. He scowled at Cade, who only gave her an oblivious smile.

"Why, no," Violet said, surprised. "I was just curious. What crawled up your ass and died?"

"Everything, if my brain is any judge of things," Jonathan said bluntly. "My head is fucking killing me."

"That's your own fault." She couldn't stop staring at his hair. It was an absolute disaster, and several days' worth of beard growth was lining his jaw. He looked like a mess. A deeply, deeply hungover mess. So she increased the volume of her voice. "I'm *starving*. Shall we go down and eat?"

Cade offered her his arm with a smile, and she took it.

Jonathan just scowled at both of them.

When they got to the hotel dining room, Cade insisted on pulling her chair out for her so she could sit down. That earned him a sharp word from Jonathan. What was Cade's game? He seemed unruffled by Jonathan's increasingly sour mood, but it had to be an act of some kind. She spread her napkin on her lap, curious, and watched the men.

Jonathan more or less slumped in his chair and put a hand to his forehead. It was clear he was feeling his drinks. Cade, however, seemed cheerful and alert.

When the waitress came over, Jonathan ordered whiskey.

"Um, I'm n-not sure we s-serve it this early," the girl stammered, looking at him with alarm.

Cade frowned at him. "Are you sure you want to do that? We need you sober."

"Fuck off," Jonathan told him and then pointed at the

waitress. "Whiskey. Hundred-dollar tip for you if you bring it in the next two minutes."

"Yes, sir," said, flushing. "Can I get anyone else a drink?"

"Orange juice," Cade told her.

"Same," Violet said, opening her menu.

"Now, Violet, remember, breakfast is on me," Cade told her, and reached over to pat her arm. He smiled at her and clasped her hand, giving it an encouraging squeeze.

Jonathan frowned at the two of them. He ripped his sunglasses off and glared at her over her menu, his eyes bloodshot. Then, he stared at Cade. "Why is breakfast on *you*?"

This was a good question, but Violet was going to play along with it. "Thank you, Cade. I appreciate it." She pulled her hand from his and pretended to consider the menu.

But Cade remained cheerful. "I told Violet that since I was taking the reins on this project, I'd also handle her expenses."

Jonathan's eyes narrowed even as the waitress brought his drink over and placed it carefully in front of him. He ignored her, his eyes still fixed on Cade. "What do you mean, you're taking over this project?"

And now she understood Cade's plan. He was going to make Jonathan jealous.

Part of her wanted to throw her napkin on the table and smack both of the men silly for acting like this. After all, she wasn't an object for them to fight over, and making Jonathan jealous wouldn't establish anything other than prodding an already irritated bull. And what did it accomplish, really? So he was jealous? So what? It wasn't like she was going to launch herself at Cade *or* Jonathan. She just wanted to go home and pick up the reins of her quiet little life.

But she couldn't help but peek through her lashes at Jonathan to see how he'd react. And she couldn't help the weird, excited little flutter in her belly when he glared at Cade as if he wanted to rip the man's head off.

Which was ridiculous. Why did she care that it bothered Jonathan?

Perhaps there was some sort of girly bone in her body that enjoyed seeing a guy go all alpha-male caveman on her. But she couldn't resist prodding the situation. So she pretended to consider her menu a bit longer, and then gave Cade a brilliant smile. "You're so sweet."

"Why," Jonathan growled, his voice gravel in his throat, "the fuck is *he* sweet? What's he doing?"

"Violet told me about her situation," Cade said, smiling at the waitress when she set orange juice down in front of him. "That she wants to return to her school but she's obligated to remain at your side until the mystery is solved. And since you're indisposed and determined to remain here, I thought I'd step in and assist her."

That got a response from Jonathan. The whites of his eyes showed, and his nostrils flared. "Cade," he gritted. "Back. Off."

"Why?" Cade wouldn't be deterred. He gestured at Jonathan's drink. "It's clear what your plans are."

"Back. Off," Jonathan repeated, clearly furious.

"He's just trying to help me out, Jonathan," Violet interjected, unable to resist rubbing salt in the wound. "I asked him to come. You've been impossible to talk to the last few days." To her horror, a knot formed in her throat and she had to blink repeatedly to keep from weeping like an idiot. She hadn't realized how stressed she was until she said it aloud. "I didn't know what to do. All you do is drink and yell at me."

The look Jonathan gave her was utterly tortured. "Violet, please—"

"No," she said, and her voice wobbled. She got to her feet. "I can't do this, all right? I can't stay here forever, not when I'm needed at the school. And I can't sit here and watch you drink yourself into a coma like my mother did. You forced me to do this stupid scavenger hunt when all I wanted to do was forget that my father existed. So now I'm here, and you need to decide what it is *you* want, because either we finish this or I get to go home." She threw her napkin down on the table, her appetite gone. "I'll be in my room."

As she stormed away, she heard Jonathan's low voice behind her. "Damn you, Cade."

A half hour later, Violet had neatly repacked her luggage and brushed her teeth again, and now sat in her room, waiting for the phone to ring so someone could tell her what was going on. When a knock came at the door, she was relieved; being in limbo was emotionally exhausting.

When she opened the door, though, Jonathan was standing there. He leaned heavily against the doorjamb as if it were the only thing keeping him upright. If it was even possible, his hair looked worse than before. He gazed at her solemnly.

She considered him for a long moment. "Hi."

"Can we talk?" he asked.

"Sure."

He pushed off of the doorjamb and headed into her room without waiting for an invite. When he sat on the edge of her bed, she put her foot down. "Don't sit there." For some reason, having Jonathan on her bed in any sort of manner felt entirely too personal.

Without missing a beat, he slid forward and thumped onto the carpet, legs sprawled out in front of him, his back resting against the bed. "This better?"

"I suppose." Violet glanced through the doorway but there was no sign of Cade. "Is your friend coming?"

Jonathan snorted. "Some friend. I told him to go fuck off. He just laughed in my face." He shook his head and rubbed his brow. "Fucker knows he's right about everything, too. I'm glad you called him here."

Violet shut the door and tentatively stepped toward Jonathan. Okay, this was a good sign. She sat on the foot of the bed, and then, after a moment's indecision, slid until she was sitting on the carpet next to him. "So," she said softly. "Let's talk."

"Can we start over?" He extended his hand to her. "Hi. I'm Jonathan Lyons. I make cars and have pissloads of money and I'm apparently pretty shitty at reading people."

Her mouth quirked with amusement and she placed her hand in his. "Violet DeWitt. Schoolteacher and known to hold a grudge—no matter how petty—for a very long time."

He gave her a soulful look with those dark eyes of his. "I don't think you're being petty, Violet."

"I know. And I don't think we can start over fresh. There's just too much between us to ever clear the waters." She looked down at her hand in his, but he was still holding it. It occurred to her that she should really pull away.

But she didn't.

"Violet," he said in a low voice, gazing down at their joined hands. "When I lost you ten years ago, I lost my best friend. All romantic entanglements aside, I really, really miss her."

That stupid knot was back in her throat. "I know how you feel."

"*Can* we start over, then? As friends? Whatever we had in the past can't be forgotten, but I know that you've moved on and you're not interested in me. As much as that hurts, I can live with that. But I'd really like to be your friend again, Violet. Please. You can't imagine how much I've missed you."

Can't I? she thought, but didn't say it aloud. Instead, she mulled over his offer. Friendship, nothing more. Partners in solving the mystery of her father's envelopes, and then she'd go back to her life minus one really big chip on her shoulder.

Could she do it?

She could.

Ever since she'd lashed out at Jonathan and sent him to

his drinking binge, she felt . . . not exactly cleansed, but the wound she'd let fester inside her for so long had been cauterized with the confession. Seeing his response had made her realize that perhaps he wasn't the evil, horrible villain she'd made him out to be. That Jonathan was just as human as she was after all this time.

And she couldn't hate him anymore.

So she squeezed his hand, still locked in hers. "Friends. I think I can do that."

The smile he gave her was brilliant, intense, and so Jonathan that it made her ache all over again. "I don't suppose friends carry headache meds for my hangover?"

Violet gave him a smile. "You only get it if you promise not to drink anymore." Her smile faded and she squeezed his hand again. "You really had me worried, you know. Just because I've been angry at you doesn't mean I wanted to see you hurt yourself."

"I know," he said, staring down at their joined hands. He reached out with his free hand and traced a finger along the back of her hand, gliding over her knuckles. "I just . . . didn't want to think for a while. It hurt too much."

His fingertip brushed over her skin, sending tickling sensations through her body. She knew she should drag her hand away, but she couldn't seem to make herself do it. So she squeezed his hand again. "You weren't the only one hurt, you know."

Again, he gave her that wounded-animal look that seemed to gut her. "I know, Violet. God, I know. That's part of what's eating me up inside."

And what could she say to that? She pulled her hand from his—trying not to think about the feel of his fingertips on her skin, grazing delicate patterns there—and gestured at her suitcase. "So . . . are we going to start our madcap little journey again?"

"I'm ready if you are."

"Um." She considered his disheveled, hungover

appearance. "Please tell me you're going to let someone else fly the plane this time?"

He laughed. "For you, I can do that."

She smiled.

———

A few hours later, they were buckling themselves into seats inside the private jet that Jonathan had chartered. Violet had taken one of the seats in the back of the plane, and Cade, Jonathan saw, took a seat in the front, most likely so he could give Jonathan and Violet some privacy to chat.

He decided maybe he wouldn't kill Cade after all.

Jonathan slid into a seat across from Violet, pleased when she didn't flinch or frown as he did so. Instead, she gave him a tentative smile and he returned it.

It was a fresh start. He was so fucking relieved that they were trying again that he didn't even care that they'd vowed to be just friends. He'd take any piece of Violet he could get in his life. If he was friend-zoned permanently, then he'd live with that, just as long as she wasn't glaring at him with hatred any longer.

Violet fastened her seat belt and tightened it. "Can I just say how happy I am that you're not flying this plane?"

He tried not to gaze overlong at the way she smoothed her clothes and tucked a strand of hair behind her ear. He didn't want to make her uncomfortable. Instead, he pulled out his phone and pretended to read something on the screen. "I've had hundreds of hours in the cockpit, Violet. I'm a good pilot."

"Yes, but it feels weird to me to have someone I know driving it. You're more fallible than a nameless, faceless expert."

He smiled faintly. More fallible? "Because I'm human in your eyes?"

She looked startled, her gaze flicking to his. "I . . . guess so."

Judging from the look on her face and the blush staining

her cheeks, she didn't like to think of him as human. He supposed it was easier for her to think of him as a monster, a jerk who'd left her and their baby high and dry. His gut clenched at the thought, and he felt the urge to vomit.

She had every right to think of him as the world's biggest asshole. Now he just had to prove to her that he was a regular man. A regular man who needed to hide the fact that he was still madly, ferociously in love with a woman who wanted nothing more than a tentative friendship.

But he'd do any amount of playacting to keep Violet at his side.

"So where are we going now?" Violet asked him, her hands clasped in her lap, her gaze focusing on him again. "You haven't said."

He drank in the sight of her, admiring her lush form, the way her dark hair brushed against her jaw until she tucked it back behind one of those ears that stuck out a little more than she liked. Her lovely dark brown eyes with the long lashes. Her small frame that seemed to be composed entirely of rounded curves that he could stare at for hours on end and never grow tired of.

"Jonathan?" She snapped her fingers at him. "Hello?"

He blinked. "Sorry. Hangover's killing my ability to think," he lied. Far better for her to think of him as a mess due to the alcohol instead of the truth—that he was still endlessly fascinated by everything about her.

"That's why I didn't want you to fly," she said with a pert nod. "Now, where are we going?"

"New York City first," he said. "We need to drop Cade off and I have a meeting to attend tonight that I can't miss." It was Brotherhood night, something he'd almost forgotten in his drunken stupor, but since they were taking Cade to the city, he might as well take a few hours out of his schedule and put in his time as well.

"New York City?" She frowned. "First, you're drunk for days and days, and now you're going to make me sit and wait on you while you attend a business meeting? When are we going to hunt down this 'Glirastes'?"

"Very soon," Jonathan vowed. "I promise. If I could get out of this, I would. It's something that's been scheduled weeks in advance."

She rolled her eyes, but there was no anger in her face. "So your schedule is more important than mine?"

"Trust me when I say that nothing is more important to me right now than you." God, it nearly choked him trying to keep those words light and easy so she wouldn't get skittish on him. "I'm asking you to humor me . . . as a friend." Another word that choked him—friend.

But it worked. She nodded. "All right."

It was progress.

———

When the limo pulled up to the club, Jonathan watched as Violet wrinkled her nose. "Your business is in a nightclub?"

"It is," he agreed.

Sitting across from them, Cade gave Violet an easy smile. "I know it looks strange, but I assure you, we're not going to pick up women."

"I wasn't thinking that. Just . . . no more drinking, all right?" Her brows knitted with worry and she looked over at Jonathan.

"I won't drink again," he vowed, and he meant it. He must have caused her a lot more concern than she let on. His Violet carried steel-plated armor around her heart because she'd been hurt so many times by the people she loved. And he'd hurt her again, it seemed. For that, he wanted to kick himself. The thought of drinking more alcohol while knowing it would upset her? That was the furthest thing on his mind.

She nodded, clearly uneasy.

He reached out to touch her hand on the seat, unable to

help himself. "We'll be a few hours. I want you to wait with the car . . . for me." He could call and get her a hotel so she could relax comfortably, but the thought of releasing Violet into New York made him anxious. He worried that if he turned his back, he'd find her gone.

"Stay in the car?" She clearly wasn't a fan of the idea and pulled her hand away from his. "How long are you going to be?"

"I don't know." He pulled out his wallet and unfurled several bills, stuffing them into her grasp before she could protest. "Go shopping. Spend money. Something. Just stay with the limo, and I'll be back as soon as I can. I promise."

She watched him for a moment, then nodded, smoothing the money he'd handed her. "I'll be here."

"Thank you." He wanted to reach over and kiss her again, but he didn't dare. Clenching a fist to keep himself from grabbing her, he nodded. "Wait for me."

Then, he followed Cade into the club.

Every week for years on end, the Brotherhood had met in the basement of the dingy club. Their secret society had been formed in college and continued on ever since. If at all possible, each man tried not to miss a meeting, as it inconvenienced his brothers. Jonathan was pretty sure he missed more meetings than most, given his proclivity for rushing off to the far ends of the earth on another mission.

Tonight, he wished he'd done the same. He was twitchy even as he and Cade pushed through the busy, noisy club and headed to the back, then down the long hall toward the basement. Hunter's bodyguard was already there, standing to guard the door, and out of habit, Jonathan gave him the signal: he touched two fingers onto his shoulder and slid them over his arm down to where his tattoo was. Cade made the same gesture, and the man nodded and stepped aside.

Then, they headed into the smoky basement, the smell of cigars wafting through the air. As Jonathan stepped down the stairs behind Cade, he could hear one loud female voice above the murmur of the others. "Come on, flush! Momma needs a destination wedding!"

"That'd be Gretchen," Cade said. "Again."

Jonathan said nothing. Truth be told, he'd hated when Hunter started dragging his fiancée to all of their supposedly private meetings. It rather ruined the spirit of secrecy, but Hunter wouldn't be deterred; if he was there, Gretchen would be there. The other men's fiancées and wives knew about the club but didn't show up like Gretchen did.

Used to be, he hated seeing Gretchen's face across the poker table from him. Now? Now that Violet was back in his life? He got it. He understood that ravenous sort of possessiveness that made a man want to haul his woman to his side and never let her leave. Hell, he was practically itching to go and drag Violet out of the limo upstairs and bring her with him, but that would cause more questions than it would answer.

As they entered the room, Reese pulled his cigar from his mouth and gestured with it. "Well, well, if it isn't the missing pair. We were starting to wonder if you two would show up."

"We had business," Cade said easily, heading toward his regular seat.

Jonathan said nothing, heading to his own chair and taking the chips offered him. Already at the table sat the inner circle of New York's business elite. There was Logan Hawkings, billionaire conglomerate owner, who was currently staring at his cards with an impassive expression. There was Hunter Buchanan, a real-estate king who owned half of the eastern seaboard. His red-haired, disheveled fiancée Gretchen was currently perched in his lap, giggling gleefully over her cards as Hunter watched her with hungry fascination.

Across the table from them was Griffin Verdi, a European viscount with an aristocratic pedigree and Jonathan's frequent co-funder on archaeological digs. He was simply shaking his head at Gretchen's antics. Next to him was Reese Durham, recently married playboy who'd also recently acquired a series of cruise lines.

It seemed like over the last year, they'd all gone from bachelors to either married or heading in that direction. All except him and Cade, of course. He thought of Violet again, and a surge of intense longing buffeted through him. He'd gladly give up his bachelorhood for her.

"Looks like everyone's here," Logan said. "This meeting of the Brotherhood is officially called to order."

"Fratres in prosperitatum," they said in unison, raising their glasses. Jonathan raised an empty one for the toast. When Reese offered him a bottle of his favorite Scotch, he shook his head. Normally he had a glass just to be social, but the thought of it crossing his lips today seemed revolting. He wouldn't touch it, not with Violet waiting for him.

"So, boys, what's on the business menu tonight?" Gretchen picked up the deck of cards and began to shuffle, ignoring the looks the others sent her way. "World domination?"

No one said anything.

She sighed. "Eventually you guys are going to talk business in front of me. Eventually."

"Not tonight," Reese said, and only grinned when Gretchen flipped him the bird.

Impatiently, Jonathan tossed his ante into the pile. "So no business tonight?" Why had he come to the meeting, then? He thought of Violet, sitting out in his car, and he longed to be beside her, just drinking in her presence.

"Down, boy," Cade murmured. "It'll do you good to give her a breather."

Jonathan glared at him.

"Give who a breather?" Griffin asked, turning to them.

"No one," Jonathan said before Cade could respond. His relationship with Violet was . . . private. Private and rather tangled.

Cade nodded in Griffin's direction. "How's that lovely Southern belle of yours? She still adjusting to being the next Viscountess Montagne Verdi?"

Count on Cade to say the right thing to distract the man. Jonathan bit back a smile as Griffin grimaced, swiping his cards off the table.

"We are having visitors this week," Griffin said, tone clipped. "My town house is currently infested with 'Mama and them.' They're helping Maylee pick a location for the wedding."

"You trust them to do that?" Reese asked.

"Of course not. That's why I hired a wedding planner to be at Maylee's side at all times. My lovely Maylee is kindness itself, but she has appalling taste in clothing." For a moment, Griffin had a besotted look on his face, then shook his head and cleared his throat.

"Yeah, like you're marrying her for her taste," Gretchen said with a snort. "I mean, she said yes, so we know her taste in *men* sucks."

Griffin ignored Gretchen's jab. "I'm just bloody thrilled she's no longer trying to get her hound to be the ring bearer."

Reese nearly spit his whiskey on the table. The others laughed, and Cade reached over and slapped Reese on the shoulders when he began to cough. It was no secret amongst them that Griffin was the latest to become engaged, to his polar opposite—a redneck southern girl who was as friendly as Griffin was aristocratic and reserved.

Again, Jonathan thought of Violet and her wry, reserved smile. She wasn't open like Griffin's Maylee. Maybe she had been, once, but the Violet waiting in the limo was guarded. Like she was just waiting for the next blow to fall, and she was positive it was coming.

He hated that he'd done that to her. What had happened to the wild girl with *Carpe Diem* tattooed just above her backside?

But he knew that answer now. She'd been abandoned

while pregnant and then lost the baby. It had changed her, and he'd lost her for good.

"You in?"

Jonathan stared at his cards without seeing them, his mind still on Violet. He'd give anything to make things right with her. Maybe being friends was a step in the right direction after all. Or maybe it was selfish of him and he needed to take himself out of her life again, cut out like a cancer. What was best for her? He didn't know, but whatever it was, he'd do it. Violet and her happiness was the only thing that mattered to him. Maybe someday he'd be able to show her that.

A rough elbow gouged his arm. "Hello? Earth to Johnny-boy." Reese shoved his elbow at Jonathan again. "You in or not?"

He blinked at Reese's grin without seeing it, then stared at his cards. A pair of kings. "I fold."

After all, folding would give him more time to think about Violet.

SIX

⟿

A few hours later, Gretchen's first yawn cracked. Jonathan used that to excuse himself from the group. "I have a plane to catch, boys. I'll see everyone next week." He cashed out his chips and murmured his good-byes, still distracted. The night had been interminably long, but it was over now, and he could get back to his Violet. Practically bounding up the stairs, he headed out of the cellar and down the hall, back into the club that was still pounding with a wild beat.

He fished his phone out of his pocket, ready to text the limo driver to bring Violet back, but as soon as he hit the street, he was surprised to see it parked nearby. Had they been waiting there the entire time? Why did the thought of Violet waiting for him fill him with such unholy joy? He headed to the limo and knocked on the window.

It rolled down a crack and Violet looked up at him with sleepy eyes. "All done?"

"All done," he said.

She opened the door and scooted over as he got in. As

soon as he shut the door, he was surprised when she offered him a coffee cup. "This one is yours. Still take it black?"

He didn't, but he would for her. "Thank you." The cup was still warm through the cardboard. "You . . . went and got coffee?"

"Several rounds of coffee, actually." She gave him a rueful grimace. "I drank the first one and we went back again, and even took a trip into the restroom. I wanted something to drink to pass the time."

"You didn't go shopping?"

She made a face. "Of course not. Here's your money back, minus the cost of the coffee, of course." She held the money out to him.

He took it, strangely pleased at the thought of Violet waiting for him, even thinking of him enough to get him a coffee. "I'm sorry that took so long."

She waved a hand. "I did some research on my phone while you were in your meeting. I figured I could work while you were there, since this is what you hired me for."

"What did you find out?"

"Well." Violet put her coffee cup down in a nearby holder and lifted her phone, dragging her thumb across the screen. He was fascinated by that small action, by her dainty fingers as they moved across the face of her smartphone, typing. "I started with 'Ozymandias,' of course, since that was on my note. But the more I read about fallen empires and tragic pasts, the more I wonder if it's some sort of veiled daughter-shaming. Knowing my father, that could be part of the reason he gave *me* the poem." She cast him a sidelong look. "Which pissed me off, so I tried a different route. So I focused on 'Glirastes.' It didn't take much to find out what the connection was."

Anticipation unfurled in his belly. "And what is it?"

Her eyes sparkled as she grinned up at him. "A dormouse lover."

"A what?" She giggled at his expression, and he was

fascinated by the sound, by the way she smiled. God, her happiness alone was making his dick hard as a rock. He longed to touch her, to feel that soft skin under his fingers. Instead, he only gripped his coffee cup harder.

"A dormouse lover," she repeated, still smiling. "It seems that Shelley's nickname for his wife was 'dormouse,' and so he picked 'Glirastes' as pen name for an inside joke. It means dormouse lover."

"It's an interesting tidbit, but why would your father point that out?"

"Well." Violet tilted her head and began to scroll through her phone again. "Remember that my letter had certain parts of words written in a bolder hand than the others. If I take all the bolded letters, it spells out 'thirteen steps underneath.'"

"Yes, but underneath what? Where do we start looking?"

She held up a finger again. "I'm getting there. So, 'dormouse' was apparently a nickname that Percy gave to Mary during their time in a city called Marlow, which is on the Thames River. And Marlow is best known for an old suspension bridge. This bridge." She pulled up a picture on her cell phone and held it out to him.

Jonathan took it from her. For a moment he was distracted by the warmth left from her grip, and he had to force himself to focus on the photo of the bridge. "You think it's here?"

"It's as good a place to start as any," she told him. "But 'Ozymandias' was first published under the name 'Glirastes,' and Glirastes came in to play because of the time they spent in Marlow. I figure we can check under the bridge. I mean, if it's thirteen steps under a house, I'd rather not tear up anyone's basement without trying all of our options first."

He looked over at her, so lovely in the shadows of the car. "*Our* options?" That tiny change in her thinking stuck out at him. For so long, she hadn't wanted to be part of this chase. She'd all but planted her feet every time he suggested anything.

And now Violet was researching on her own time? Talking about searching together?

She leaned over and nudged him with her elbow, the gesture similar to one that Reese had given him earlier. Except this time he reacted completely different. Violet's soft body next to his played havoc with his senses, the faint scent of her perfume filling his nostrils, and his body immediately responded to her touch, his cock hardening.

"I figure we're in this together," she told him. "Whatever my father wants us to find out, he wants us to find it out together."

"Together," he agreed. He liked the sound of that.

Violet fidgeted and shifted in her chair, trying to get comfortable. Despite the late hour and the relative poshness of the leather chaises in the private jet, she couldn't relax. Maybe it was the three cups of coffee she'd gulped down while sitting in the limo. Maybe it was the fact that they were on their way to London for the next part of the scavenger hunt, and she was feeling excited despite herself.

She suspected it was all those things, but throw in a very sexy, intense Jonathan Lyons sitting across from her? Sleep was impossible. He was wearing another blazer over a T-shirt and jeans, and the effect was overtly masculine and confidently casual at the same time.

Sad to say, she was still affected by his presence. Their sexual relationship was ten years in the past, but the way her nipples seemed to react, you'd think it was just yesterday that he'd had his mouth on them. Of course, she couldn't blame her nipples—not when the rest of her body wasn't playing fair, either. There was an ache between her legs that wouldn't go away, and her skin prickled with awareness whenever he drew close enough for her to smell his aftershave.

Her mind was the most traitorous of all, because every

time Violet closed her eyes, she saw Jonathan's body moving over hers. It wasn't the nineteen-year-old Jonathan, either. It was the man seated across from her, hard with muscle, eyes world-weary and intense all at once. He'd been sexy as a college boy, but he was utterly devastating as an adult man.

And it was making her antsy as hell.

She shifted in her chair again.

"Can't sleep?" Jonathan asked, and his foot nudged her leg from across the aisle.

Well, no sense in pretending any longer. She straightened up and propped her chin on her hand. "Something tells me that all that Starbucks earlier was a bad call." *Your proximity isn't helping.* She didn't say that aloud, though. Not while they were on neutral ground. But still, the man should have guessed that his sitting directly across from her in a plane with at least a dozen other empty seats would rattle her, right? Or he should have known that when he sat with his legs open and sprawled as if he owned the place, it would make her body break out in goose bumps.

Heck, he probably *did* own the place. "Too much coffee," she muttered when a new round of goose bumps pricked her arms and she rubbed them.

The smile he gave her was slow, gorgeous, his gaze utterly focused on her. "You'll wind down in a bit."

For some reason, she felt nervous and fluttery under that intense stare. "I suppose." Now that they'd vowed to just be friends, it seemed her body—stupid, stupid body—was fixated on other, non-friend-like things.

"Can I ask you a question?"

Her heart started thumping faster, and her gaze went to his sensual mouth. She tried to play it casual, though. "Oh, um . . . question? Sure?"

"How many do you think there will be?"

For the life of her, she couldn't figure out what he was talking about. "How many what?"

"Letters? Clues to follow?"

"Oh!" Her mind had been anywhere but on their actual business together. "Usually there were about four."

"Mmm. So we're looking at two more." He rubbed his chin thoughtfully.

Violet found herself staring at his long fingers as he rubbed. She flexed her own. *Down, girl. It's still Jonathan, jerk at heart.* Except she wasn't so sure she believed that anymore. "Don't get too excited," she blurted. "I've found every single one of these chases to be a disappointment at the end."

"Even so." He continued to rub his chin idly, and she had to hold back the urge to snatch his hand away from his jaw. That slow, thoughtful rubbing was driving her to distraction. "There has to be a point to this little postmortem game of his. Even if we discount the fact that he hid his journals, it's not like Dr. DeWitt to steal from an excavation site."

"I told you the point already," Violet said, her irritation ratcheting up a notch. "He wants to get me back in your life so you'll continue to fund all of his projects. My face in front of yours will be a nice little reminder of what he wants. This is all just more maneuvering from him."

"Mmm. You sound angry. He wasn't a very good father to you, was he?"

She sighed. "Are we going to talk about this now?"

"What's wrong with now? Was I keeping you from your sleep?" Damn it, now he was aiming that lethal smile at her again, as if they were sharing a secret.

"No," she snapped, her tone a little more brusque than it should have been. Violet straightened in her chair again. "But of the two of us, you're the only one who seems to have pleasant memories of him."

"I don't recall you hating him that summer—"

"That was a fluke," she interrupted. She knew exactly how she felt about her father, and didn't need anyone else reminding her. "That was back when I still thought I could get him to care about me. I learned my lesson and didn't make that mistake again."

"I find it hard to believe he didn't care about you at all," Jonathan said in a quiet voice. "In fact, I find it almost impossible to conceive of anyone willfully disliking you."

She squirmed in her seat. Surely she'd mistaken the heat in his tone. It was her own imagination running away from her. "My father cared about one person and one person alone. Himself. Everything he did was to further his own ambitions. He destroyed my mother with his neglect."

Jonathan tilted his head, regarding her. "Dr. DeWitt never talked about your mother."

"That doesn't surprise me."

"Why?"

"Well, what's there to talk about?" Violet rested her head against the back of the chair and tried to think of her mother without tears in her eyes. It was surprisingly difficult; all her lingering memories of Connie DeWitt involved her depression, her drinking, and how it had affected Violet. "She married him when she was twenty and he was fifty. My mom was one of his students, back when he still taught at the university. She was young and pretty and totally in love with him. He was, well . . . He was an old perv."

Jonathan didn't laugh.

Violet shrugged and went on. "They had me a few years later, and pretty much after that, my dad grew more and more famous, and the more famous he got, the less he came home. He drove my mother to depression, and when the drugs didn't work, she drank herself into a stupor. She cried over everything." Her throat went dry and she thought of her lonely childhood, full of dark rooms and tiptoeing quietly through the living room because Mom was passed out drunk on the couch. At least when Mom was asleep, she wasn't weeping. The weeping was worse than anything. "My father would show up a few months later and everything would be great for about a day or two. Then they'd start fighting, my mother would cry and get depressed all over again, and then my father would leave as soon as he could get out the door."

"I'm guessing that's why it's so hard for you to trust people."

She gave him a sharp look, her hands twisting in her lap. But there was no judgment in Jonathan's gaze, no reproach, just that wicked intensity she found so enthralling. Like she was a puzzle he'd put aside for ten years and had decided to solve again. Except she didn't need solving, or saving. She was doing just fine on her own. "I'm sure my father seemed like a paragon to you, but he was only good to people who could get him what he wanted. The rest of us, he just didn't give a crap about."

"I never knew," he said softly.

"That's because I never let anyone know that it bothered me," Violet confessed, and was surprised to hear those words coming out of her own mouth. How many years of therapy had it taken for her to get there? Violet knew she wasn't good at sharing. Hell, she sucked at it. She expected everyone around her to come after her with an agenda.

No wonder she'd assumed the worst about Jonathan.

You don't know that it's not true, she chided herself. Still, she kept thinking about his days-long drinking binge and how upset he'd been when she'd attacked him. Drinking yourself into a stupor wasn't the action of a happy person. She knew that from experience with her mother. You drank to forget the world.

Maybe she'd withheld too much of herself from him once upon a time.

Maybe it wasn't entirely Jonathan's fault that he hadn't come after her. Maybe she hadn't made her feelings clear enough. Hell, maybe she hadn't been clear enough about the baby. At nineteen, dancing around the topic of marriage and family and then sending a note had seemed obvious. Ten years later, it just seemed childish. Maybe she hadn't let him in long enough to have him see the real girl underneath all the armor, the scared, lonely pregnant teenager who just wanted a family of her own that wouldn't drink or disappear on her.

She bit her lip. God, she hated thinking about the past. Violet glanced back at Jonathan. "So . . . how have the last ten years treated you?"

"They've been lonely."

She knew why. He said he'd missed her. It made her . . . uncomfortable. And also breathless and excited, even though she knew she shouldn't be. And angry at herself for being breathless and excited. Violet waved a hand. "Other than that, I mean."

"I've been busy with projects. The first two years after I got out of college, I spent getting the car company back on its feet. It mostly took some shuffling of management and some new ideas."

"Now you're being modest," she told him. She'd read the *Time* magazine articles about how his creative ideas and smart investments had turned Lyons Motors around and made them a force to be reckoned with.

He shrugged. "It's just work. It's not where my heart is. As soon as Lyons Motors could run itself, I started traveling."

"Traveling?" she asked, a touch wistful. Once upon a time, she'd wanted to travel as much as he had. "Where did you go?"

A flash of real pleasure crossed his face, and her body reacted to see that. "Where haven't I gone?" Jonathan said, and to her surprise, he got up out of his chair and sat down on the seat next to her own. She started to protest until he pulled out his tablet computer and began to show her photos of his travels.

And then, she was just fascinated.

"You went to Macchu Picchu?" She grabbed his hand, stopping him on the current photo before he could scroll past it. His fingers locked and twined with hers, something she tried not to notice.

"I've been twice," Jonathan told her. "It's fascinating but not quite as untouched as the Galapagos or even Easter Island."

Her breath caught in her throat. "You've been to Easter Island?"

He nodded and looked over at her, and his thumb rubbed against one of her fingers still tangled with his. An accident, she told herself. "Want to see pictures?"

She nodded.

He pulled his hand from hers—almost reluctantly—and began to swipe through the photos again.

For the next couple of hours, Jonathan showed her photos and told her stories of his travels. While she'd been struggling through college and working shit jobs to make ends meet, he'd been traveling up one side of the world and down the other. There were photos of Antarctica, Tibet, the Great Wall, the Australian Outback, water caves in Thailand, Mongolian steppes, and more incredible locations. Each place had a story with it, and Jonathan filled her in on the details. How crisp the water tasted in Iceland, how you couldn't toss any of your waste—even human waste—in the Antarctic. How nomadic peoples still crossed the steppes in Asia. How Tokyo seemed to be lit up like Christmas at every hour of the day.

It was all wonderful, and the way he described it with such enthusiasm made her imagine she was right there with him, snorkeling off the Great Barrier Reef, skydiving over the Grand Canyon, marathoning in the Antarctic. She snuggled against his shoulder and peered at the pictures as he talked, and dreamed of being there with him, living life to its fullest.

Eventually, though, her head began to nod and she yawned.

Jonathan put the tablet away but didn't get up. "Get some sleep, Violet. We have a long flight tonight."

"Mm, I should. The chair's uncomfortable though. It's not made for short people." She'd curled her legs up under her now that she could lean on Jonathan, but as soon as he got up, she'd be without a prop to snuggle up against.

"You can use my arm as a pillow. I don't mind." His voice was low and soft and seemed just as sleepy as her own.

It occurred to Violet that she should protest and lean against the window or something. But Jonathan was warm and smelled good and he was right there already. She didn't even have to move, really. Just close her eyes and doze off and let Jonathan's strong arms handle things.

She shouldn't lean against him, but she didn't move. She didn't want to. As she drifted off to sleep, it occurred to her that she never got to ask Jonathan the things she'd really wanted to ask him about the last ten years. Things like if he'd had a girlfriend, or a wife, or any children. Important things.

But then she fell asleep, and it didn't matter.

Jonathan didn't move a muscle as Violet curled against him and slept, as trusting as a kitten. Her dark hair lay against her cheek, so shiny and soft that he longed to touch it. But he wouldn't move, lest she wake up, realize how close she'd tucked her body against his, and come to her senses.

He just savored the moment instead. The warm feel of her smaller form against his. Her soft skin where it brushed against his hand. The even breaths she took, even the tiny little snore she emitted when her head tilted back a bit. He loved all of it.

He thought about their conversations tonight. It had been rough on him to see the longing in her eyes as he showed her pictures of his travels. He'd avoided showing her pictures of the trips he'd taken with her father, unwilling to sour her mood. He'd showed her his personal trips instead, trips all over the world with friends, family, and sometimes by himself. To her, they represented adventures. To him, they were just distractions—another diversion to try to stop him from dwelling on his aching loneliness and the longing he had for Violet.

But he wasn't lonely any longer. She was here, and she was curled up at his side. His heart felt so full that he might explode from the sheer joy of it.

He thought about DeWitt and his envelopes. Four rounds of these. Five, if he was lucky. That wasn't enough time. There'd never be enough time. He'd have to figure out some way to stretch things out, to make his time with Violet last for as long as possible . . . without raising her suspicions, of course.

In her sleep, she sighed and burrowed against his arm, mumbling something under her breath.

Greatly daring, Jonathan reached with his free hand and gently brushed a lock of dark hair off of her forehead. She didn't stir, just continued sleeping.

If there was a way to extend this to keep Violet at his side, he'd do it. He'd do anything.

SEVEN

This is Higginson Park," Violet said, reading the tourism site she'd found online. Her fingers brushed over the tablet's surface. "I think it's where we need to be."

"Sounds good," Jonathan said, motioning to the cab driver. He offered the man money as they pulled over on High Street. "Wait here and we'll be back shortly."

They exited the cab and headed to the park together. Violet was practically trembling with excitement. It seemed stupid to get worked up over one of her father's letters, but she was here in the United Kingdom, about to search under a two-hundred-year-old bridge for a clue that her father had left behind, after his death. She'd have to be a statue not to get a little antsy over that.

Couple it with the fact that she'd had more erotic dreams about Jonathan on the plane ride and had woken up to find her hand on his thigh? Well. That didn't help her nerves any.

Violet smoothed her hair behind one ear and decided to ignore Jonathan and concentrate on her surroundings. There were trees, flowers, and greenery everywhere. It was early in the morning, and the skies were overcast and gray. A light fog hovered over the grounds, and along one of the paths she could see a decorative sign that read *Thames Footpath*. She pointed to it and Jonathan nodded. There were a few vendors just setting up down the road, and Violet suppressed a yawn. Maybe after they found her father's envelope, they could head to a nearby coffee shop and get something to wake her up.

As they approached the river, several ducks began to swim toward them, quacking. "Oh, dear," Violet said with a laugh as the ducks continued to follow them as they walked. "I think they're expecting a handout."

"Unless they want a stick of gum, I don't have anything for them."

She laughed again, tucking another lock of hair behind her ears. The laugh died when she saw the intense, almost hungry look Jonathan cast in her direction. God, how had she ever thought that they could hang out together as friends? Jonathan didn't know how to be friendly with a woman. All he knew how to do was devour her with his eyes.

Like he was doing right now.

Averting her gaze, she took another experimental step forward, and the ducks continued to swim alongside. "We should get something to distract them," she told him. *And you.* "Do you want to go to a nearby coffee shop and get something to eat?"

"I suppose I could," he said slowly. "Do you want something, too?"

"That'd be lovely," she told him, flashing him a smile. "Three sugars, extra cream?"

He nodded and jogged down the path, heading in the opposite direction from where she stood. She watched him go, admiring the lines of his shoulders in his jacket and the way his ass filled out the back of his jeans. *Damn you for not having a potbelly and a bald spot,* she thought with a self-deprecating grin. Then, she turned and marched toward the Marlow Bridge, tablet clutched tightly in hand.

Following the footpath, she soon came to the bridge and edged toward a plaque set amongst the bricks, curious despite herself. *Marlow Suspension Bridge*, it read, along with the name of the designer. She scanned it but there was no mention of "Ozymandias," no mention of Percy Shelley, and she felt a bit of doubt. What if they were grasping at straws? Surely her father hadn't meant for them to take thirteen steps underneath the bridge?

After all, thirteen steps underneath pretty much led right into the water. Violet gazed at the quacking ducks, who were eager for a handout.

Then, she shrugged and sat on the grassy bank, undoing the buckles on the ankle of her high heels. After her disorienting wake-up, she'd "armored" herself in her schoolteacher attire. In a knee-length wool skirt, a demure long-sleeved cardigan, and low, strappy heels, she felt like her normal self, her controlled, careful self. That was the woman she was now, she told herself. Not the girl who'd fallen in love with an intense, soulful-eyed college boy so long ago.

The fleet of ducks quacked and streamed away from Violet, and she looked up to see Jonathan returning, two coffees and a small brown bag in hand. He frowned down at her as she removed her first shoe. "What are you doing, Violet?"

"Getting ready to go into the water."

Nearby, a goose honked.

He gazed down at her, his expression intent. "It's cold. I should be the one doing it."

"It is cold," Violet agreed, her hands moving to her other shoe and working on the straps. "But, it's also my father who sent us on this chase, so I'm the one going in."

He was silent for a long moment, no doubt formulating a new argument, Violet figured. She was surprised when he capitulated. "Very well," Jonathan said. "Just be careful."

"I will," she told him, and tossed her other shoe on the bank. "You'll have to feed the ducks and keep them away from me," she said, and glanced up at him.

Her breath escaped her throat.

Jonathan's intense gaze had moved from her face to her legs, and his hands were clutching the coffees so tightly she could see the whites of his knuckles. The expression in his eyes was pure lust as he regarded her stocking-clad legs, which she'd thoughtlessly sprawled on the embankment. There was a prominent bulge in the crotch of his jeans.

Oh.

Violet turned away, her cheeks reddening, and she picked up a shoe and pretended to fiddle with one of the dainty buckles. Jonathan was aroused by the sight of her stripping off her shoes on the riverbank. She should be appalled. She really should be.

Instead, she felt an old, familiar ache start between her legs. Her breathing quickened, and she put the shoe down and did the worst thing imaginable.

She hitched up her nice, sweet, demure skirt to the tops of her thighs and began to slowly roll one thigh-high down her leg with great care. He wanted to watch, did he? She'd give him something to see.

Funny how the thought of him watching her undress made her breath catch.

Ever so slowly, she rolled the stocking down her thigh. Her fingers brushed her knee and she bit her lip, hesitated, and then continued downward, gently tugging the stocking down her calf. She arched her foot and pointed her toes as she lifted her leg into the air and carefully pulled the stocking off. "You don't mind if I'm the one who goes into the water, do you?" she asked him in a sultry voice, placing the stocking into the grass.

When he didn't answer, she looked over.

Jonathan's jaw was set, the lines of his mouth hard and flat. He might have looked angry if it weren't for the dark, smoky look in his eyes that she'd seen so many times before.

He was incredibly aroused.

And suddenly, Violet felt as if she were playing with fire. What was she doing? Why did she care if Jonathan was aroused by the sight of her stripping her stockings off? Jesus, was she insane? Violet suddenly wanted to kick herself. This was not the way to keep him in the friend zone. This was just her torturing him with what he couldn't have.

It was rather classless of her.

One of the geese honked again, as if to agree.

Angry with herself, Violet jerked at her other stocking, shoving it down her leg as unsexily as possible. When both of her legs were bare, she got to her feet and paused on the bank. She'd originally planned on taking off her cardigan so she could see how Jonathan reacted to her wearing nothing but a skimpy camisole underneath, but that suddenly seemed like an incredibly stupid idea. What was she *thinking*? Violet frowned to herself and buttoned her cardigan up higher. "Just hold my coffee until I get done, all right?"

"Of course," he said in that low, ardent voice.

Shivers rippled through her. She ignored them, ignored him. Brushing off her skirt, she headed to the edge of the water. "Thirteen steps in, right?"

"Thirteen," he agreed tensely. "Be careful."

"I'll be just fine," Violet assured him, glad for the distraction. She tiptoed to the edge. It was hard to tell how deep the water was from the bank, but there was a bridge, so that meant deep, right? Violet swung one foot over and dipped the other in, trying to determine how deep it was.

To her surprise, it only came up to her calf. "Wow. It's not all that deep. Maybe the river's low at the moment." She took another step in and let her hitched-up skirt drop, since it was clear that it wasn't going to get wet. Another step in and she turned around, glancing back at Jonathan. "Do you think that it's thirteen steps from the bridge, or thirteen steps into the water?"

"Your guess is as good as mine."

"Well," Violet said, and put her hands on her hips. "Nothing to do but wander around and hope I hit something with my feet, then."

"Be my guest," Jonathan said. "I'll just be here on shore with coffee and muffins."

"Beast," she teased, feeling a bit more at ease. It didn't sound like he was holding her little striptease against her, which was good. "If you break out those muffins, watch for the ducks. They'll chew off your arm to get to that bread, I suspect." Even now, they were hovering near him, ignoring her.

"I'll save my muffins for you," he said, and the amusement was back in his voice. Good. She was relieved to hear that.

Violet trudged along the muddy bottom of the river, moving slowly and feeling around with her toes. The water was cold but shallow, and she took her time, not wanting to step over something and miss it. It got deeper as she moved farther in, and she ended up hitching up her skirt a bit more. There was a little graveyard and a church across the river, and she wondered if she was starting from the wrong side. Did that have meaning? Was Shelley buried there and they were looking in the wrong place? Now that they were here, the clue seemed awfully vague.

"How's it going?" Jonathan called after a time.

"Nothing," she said, turning around and moving a step or two over, then heading back the way she came, toward the bank. She looked over at him with his coffee, sipping it as he watched her. "I'm starting to think I shouldn't have been so quick to volunteer. That coffee looks rather good."

"It is rather good," Jonathan said. "But I promise not to relish it an unfair amount."

She shook her head, grinning. "Do you suppose there's a box of some kind buried here? What if it got picked up by the current and went downstream? What do we do then?"

"Don't know," Jonathan said. "It might take us a few weeks to find it."

"That's a rather dismal thought."

"Is it?" He didn't sound as if he disliked the idea at all.

And that made her wonder. She kept her wondering to herself, though, and continued to trudge, up and down the riverbank. She tried thirteen steps out from the shore. She tried thirteen steps out from the base of the bridge. She tried small steps. She tried large steps. But all that was under her feet was silty river mud. She went back and forth over every inch of riverbank that the bridge covered, and when that all turned up nothing, she looked over at Jonathan again.

"I'm not getting anything," she told him. "There's nothing but mud. Should we try the opposite bank?"

"We can," he said, getting to his feet. "Want to go across the bridge?"

"Actually I'm pretty sure it's shallow enough," she began, heading toward the middle of the river, "for me to wade through—"

Her foot didn't connect, and her entire body went under the water.

For a brief, frightening second, Violet's world was nothing but water. She heard a male voice shout her name, the sound murky. Then her feet touched the ground, just a bit of a step down, and she pushed back up, gasping for breath.

Her head broke the surface and she pushed streaming water out of her eyes, spluttering in outrage.

A moment later, two strong hands grabbed her and she was hauled against a large male form. "Violet! Are you all right?"

She blinked river water out of her eyes, surprised to see Jonathan right in front of her. He'd waded right in to rescue her, his jeans were wet up to the knee, and she was pretty sure he was still wearing his shoes. "I . . . I think I'm okay," she said weakly. "Just surprised."

"Christ, you scared the shit out of me," he said in a ragged voice, his fingers tight on her arms. It was like he was trying to squeeze some of the water out of her sweater just by touching her. The mental image of that made her giggle. "It's not funny," Jonathan snapped.

"It's a little funny," she admitted, still giggling. She had to laugh at herself. It was funny. "Watch that next step. It's a doozy."

He snorted. "What did you trip on? Is it a lockbox?"

"It's nothing. I just stepped into a hole, that's all. Lost my footing and went under." Even now, she felt silly. The river wasn't all that deep, and she'd somehow managed to dunk herself. *Great going, Violet.* "No lockbox, unfortunately."

"Well, whatever it was, we're done looking for now." He hauled her against him, his arms going protectively around her as he began to pull her to the shore.

Though he was being a bit heavy-handed with things, Violet wasn't complaining. Her clothes were clinging to her body and now the morning had gone from slightly chilly to wickedly cold, and the only thing warm was Jonathan's big body pressed against hers. She ignored the wet adhesion of the fabric to her breasts. "I can walk on my own."

"Clearly, you can't."

"Jonathan—"

"Violet, don't make me carry you back to the shore," he warned.

"Oh, please. You couldn't if you tried."

He looked down at her and gave her a challenging look. "Is that a dare?"

"Just calling it like I see it."

Without a word, Jonathan leaned over and grabbed her behind her knees, hauling her into his arms. She gave a squeal of fright and clung to his shoulders as he pushed through the water. "We're going to fall!"

"I'm not going to drop you," he told her. "Stop wiggling."

She was streaming water everywhere, and she was

terrified Jonathan would drop her. She wasn't a dainty teen-ager any longer. She was solid now, with an adult's curves and an adult's addiction to Ben & Jerry's. But he wasn't putting her down, so she squeezed her eyes shut and hoped for the best.

A few moments later, she felt his steps change, and when she looked down, Jonathan had made it onto the bank. Water was sluicing down from his jeans and his sneakers squished with every step. He paused and gently set her feet down on the pavement, giving her a smug look. "You're not heavy, you know."

She just rolled her eyes. "You're not Prince Charming, you know."

The teasing look faded from his face, replaced by an expression of pain, quickly masked with politeness.

She felt like an ass. She'd meant the "Prince Charming" comment in a teasing way, referring to the way he'd carried her like a princess in need of her fainting couch. He'd apparently taken it the wrong way. So she just crossed her arms over her chest to hide her breasts and shivered on the bank. "What do we do now? Want to try the other side?"

"Take my jacket," he told her, stripping it off.

"You're not cold?"

"I'm fine," he said brusquely, pushing the blazer over her shoulders before she could protest.

He wasn't fine. That wasn't the tone of voice of a man who was "fine" but she didn't want to argue with him. She slipped her arms through the sleeves of his jacket, grateful she'd at least be able to hide her too-perky nipples. "Thanks."

"Let's go across the bridge and try the other side. This time I'll do the exploring."

She made a face at him but didn't protest. She hadn't been able to find anything herself. Maybe he'd have better luck than she did.

She gathered up her shoes and stockings and followed him. They picked up their coffee cups—the contents had spilled when Jonathan had plunged into the river after her—and Violet sniffed hers mournfully. The ducks had attacked the paper bag as soon as it had hit the ground, and there was nothing left of it but shreds and crumbs. "So much for breakfast," she said in a light voice, hoping to restore their easy mood from earlier.

Jonathan didn't reply, just put a hand at the small of her back and steered her toward the bridge.

Violet sighed to herself and let him guide her.

They had just stepped onto the footpath-designated area of the bridge when Jonathan stiffened at her side.

"What is it?" she asked him, curious.

He looked down at her, his eyes gleaming in a way that made her pulse race. "The letter said thirteen steps underneath, right?"

"It did."

"What if there was a comma?"

"A comma," she echoed, not following. She was too distracted by that roguish look in his eyes. Oh, God, did *that* look give her memories. It was the same one he'd given her just before he'd gone down on her. That *wait till you get a load of this* look that always promised—and delivered—such good things.

She really, *really* needed to stop thinking about sex around him.

"Thirteen steps," Jonathan said, "comma, underneath."

Realization dawned. Thirteen steps, underneath. She looked behind them at the start of the suspension bridge. "Thirteen steps from there, do you think?"

Jonathan was already racing back, and she watched him turn, and then began to count aloud. He passed her and paused. "Thirteen." Then, he dropped to his knees and stuck his head over the side of the bridge. A moment later, he leaned in and his entire torso moved over the edge.

"Jonathan, be careful," she warned as he twisted his

body farther over the side, reaching for something she couldn't see.

"Got it," he called up, and then held an envelope aloft a few moments later.

Violet squealed and danced in place; she couldn't help herself. "You did! You found it! Jonathan, you're a genius!"

He sat back on his haunches, just grinning up at her like he'd won an award, and Violet had to clench her fists to keep from going over and planting a big happy kiss on his face. She should have been grumpy that he was able to find it so easily, but she was simply excited that he'd found it. It felt like they were a team.

She sat down next to him on the walkway, ignoring the people who had to maneuver around them, and peered over his shoulder as he flipped the envelope in his hands. It was larger than she thought it would be, and sealed entirely in a thin layer of plastic. The exterior was plain, but she could see her name and Jonathan's written on the front in her father's handwriting.

The sight of it sent a pang of emotion through her. What was her father thinking when he placed it here? What was his goal? She stared down at the sealed envelope, wishing she'd understood her father just a little bit. But even in death, he was inscrutable to her.

Jonathan offered the envelope to her. "Do you want to do the honors?"

She shook her head. "You found it. You open it. It only seems fair."

He flashed her a grin and then tore at the plastic covering the envelope. He tugged it free and slipped a finger under the wax seal, and then reached inside.

EIGHT

Jonathan pulled out two familiar yellowed envelopes from the plastic covering, each one with its own seal. One had Violet's name on it, and the other, Jonathan's. He held the envelope with her name out to her, and when she hesitated, said gently, "Why don't you open yours first?"

She nodded and took a deep breath. This was just another clue. There was no reason to be nervous. It was just more of her father's games that would lead to yet another unsatisfying clue, and eventually an unsatisfying prize. Violet plucked the envelope from Jonathan's hand and tore open the wax seal, then pulled out the letter inside. She scanned the lines of text, and then began to read aloud.

"Turn, Fortune, turn thy wheel, and lower the proud;
Turn thy wild wheel thro' sunshine, storm, and cloud;
Thy wheel and thee we neither love nor hate.

Turn, Fortune, turn thy wheel with smile or frown;
With that wild wheel we go not up or down;
Our hoard is little, but our hearts are great.

Smile and we smile, the lords of many lands;
Frown and we smile, the lords of our own hands;
For man is man and master of his fate.

Turn, turn thy wheel above the staring crowd;
Thy wheel and thou are shadows in the cloud;
Thy wheel and thee we neither love nor hate."

Violet finished reading and frowned. "What is this obsession with poetry?"

"You loved poetry once. I remember that well. Maybe that's why he's been selecting poems for your messages."

True, she'd loved poetry . . . once upon a time, maybe. Back when she'd been romantic and silly. She'd lost all interest in it when reality had slapped her in the face. Ignoring Jonathan's astute comment, she scanned the letter again, looking for hints. "I don't see a clue like before. There must be a message in the meaning of the poem itself. Either that, or yours has the message and mine is just fluff." She looked over at him. "Do you recognize this poem?"

Jonathan took the letter from her and considered it. After a pause, he shook his head. "It sounds vaguely familiar, but I don't know who wrote it."

"Well, we can research it on the Internet," she told him, taking her letter back and folding it carefully. "What does yours say?"

He opened his envelope and a small chuckle escaped him.

"What?" She tried to peer over his shoulder without seeming too eager.

He offered her the letter. She took it and scanned the contents. It was two simple words: *Kallista Hotel.*

Violet gasped. "The Kallista?" That was the hotel she and Jonathan had stayed at together, back during that fateful summer in Santorini.

"I know. It immediately made me think of the Akrotiri dig. Your father has to be leading us there for a reason."

Her throat dry, Violet said nothing for a long moment. She didn't know what to think. She didn't want to go back to Santorini, that magical isle where she and Jonathan had fallen in love.

But it seemed like her father was determined to send them back. Was this just so he could throw the past in their faces and remind Jonathan of his connection to Violet? Surely there were easier ways; she knew Jonathan was generous when it came to her father's projects. All he had to do was ask and Jonathan would pull out the checkbook. So why this? Why send them there?

"Are you all right?" he asked her, his hand brushing down her arm in a way that made her shiver.

She shook her head as if to clear it and handed the letter back to him.

"You look pale," he said in a firm voice. He got to his feet and offered her his hand. "Come."

"I'm fine," she said irritably, pushing his hand away.

"You're not fine," he insisted, and offered her his hand again. "Let me take care of you for once, Violet. You're pale and you're shaking. I don't like to see that." His voice softened. "Let me take care of you."

Her skin prickled at the intensity in his voice, and she looked up at him. That focus was back in his eyes, that ardor, that burning need that was all-consuming. She was trembling, too, but not because of the letter. Because of Jonathan. Because she was still attracted to him and she didn't know what to do, and every location her father sent them to seemed designed to get them to rekindle that ill-fated romance from ten years ago.

But she could no more resist Jonathan Lyons now than she could ten years ago. Placing her quivering hand in his, she allowed him to haul her upright. If he held her against him for a bit longer than necessary, she didn't complain. When he looped an arm over her shoulders and pulled her under his arm, she didn't protest. She liked it. Heaven help her, she *liked* it.

"Come," he said gently. "Let's get you some coffee and breakfast, and we'll talk."

He led her across the green, grassy park. The sun was coming out and the fog had lifted, but the air was still brisk and she still shivered in Jonathan's jacket. He led her to the nearest coffeehouse and pulled out a chair for her at a table near the window. "Sit here and I'll get you something to eat and drink."

She should have protested, really. She should have been strong, needs-no-one Violet and ordered her own damn breakfast. Instead, she shivered at the table and clutched her envelope with the poem in it while Jonathan ordered her food and a hot drink.

Let me take care of you, he'd insisted. Violet wasn't good at letting others take control. It was hard to trust people enough to leave your own well-being in their hands, and Violet was used to just fending for herself. She'd done so as a child, especially when her mother was in one of her depressive spells, and she'd done so as an adult when she'd found herself abandoned and pregnant.

But when Jonathan returned with two hot cups of coffee and two delicious, fresh muffins, she was . . . grateful for him. She didn't even mind when he stroked his fingers over her cheek, brushing a lock of wet hair off her face.

"Your lips are blue," he told her in that fierce, disapproving voice. "Drink."

She nodded and raised the coffee to her lips. It was scalding hot and utterly delicious. After a few more sips, she gave him a hesitant smile. "Thank you."

He simply placed a muffin in front of her. "Eat, too. You're fragile."

Her? Fragile? That was flattering. Her mouth twisted in

a wry expression, and Violet broke off a corner of the muffin and popped it into her mouth. Lemon poppyseed. Her favorite. How did he remember all these things about her?

"Better now?"

She nodded, still chewing.

An expression of relief crossed his face and he relaxed in his chair, his posture easing. She hadn't realized how tense he was. "Are *you* okay?" she asked, putting a teasing note in her voice.

"I just don't like to see you upset."

Violet wanted to protest that she wasn't upset. Not really. She was just fine. But it'd be a lie. She *was* upset. "I just feel . . ."

"Manipulated?" he guessed.

She nodded and toyed with her muffin. "Messages for each of us to ensure we'd have to work together, and now sending us back to Santorini . . ." Her voice trailed off as memories swept over her. It wasn't a time she'd wanted to remember. Back then she'd been so happy . . . so stupid.

"I don't like to see you this miserable, Violet," Jonathan said. "Whether or not you believe it, your peace of mind is of the utmost importance to me."

She didn't answer. She simply sipped her coffee and thought.

"Do you want to go home, Violet?" Jonathan's voice was full of tension, his face unreadable. His hand clenched on the table, as if anticipating her response.

Did she? A few days ago, she would have said yes and had her bags packed before Jonathan could take his next breath. But that was before this morning, when he'd watched her with such stark, blatant need as she'd stripped off her stocking. And that was before they'd vowed friendship.

And that was before he'd drank himself into a stupor upon hearing that there had been a baby.

So now Violet didn't know what to think. All she knew was that she felt vulnerable and confused about Jonathan. Her world had been so much easier when she'd hated him.

But it was hard to hate a man who quoted love poetry when he was drunk.

Violet wrapped her hands around the warm cardboard of her cup. "Do you want me to stay, Jonathan?"

"I can honestly say I've wanted nothing more in my life."

A pleased warmth flushed her cheeks, and she nodded, then set down her coffee cup. "Then I'll stay."

His hand—clenched into a fist for so long—flexed, and then impulsively, he reached out and took one of her hands in his. "Thank you."

She could have sworn his thumb grazed over the back of her hand in a caress before he pulled away again.

Two hours later, they were back at the airport and in the tiny jet once more. Violet had changed into a pair of yoga pants and a long-sleeved tunic to be comfortable for the flight. Her hair was wavy from air-drying but she just tucked it behind her ears and ignored it. For some reason, she never felt ugly around Jonathan. It was impossible to, considering he looked at her as if she were a slice of his favorite cheesecake.

She wasn't surprised, either, when she picked a window seat and Jonathan selected the seat right next to hers. It didn't matter that the rest of the cabin was empty. Flight time felt like private time with Jonathan, and maybe she was a little crazy herself, but she was starting to crave those interludes alone with him.

She stared out the plane window with longing as they left the teeming streets of London behind. "Someday, I'd love to explore that city."

Jonathan froze next to her. "Do you want to turn around?"

"What?" She glanced over at him, but he was serious. Violet laughed and shook her head. "No, no. We need to head out to Santorini. I was just saying. I've never been to London."

"You should have said something," Jonathan told her. "I would have stayed for you."

Funny how the way he worded that made her entire body tingle. "This is your trip, Jonathan, not mine. I'm just your hired assistant, remember?"

"You are never *just* anything, Violet."

She shifted in her seat, feeling a little uncomfortable with her own reaction to his words. She shouldn't be thrilled at him saying that. She shouldn't. "So," she said lightly. "Looks like it's just you and me and the next six hours in the plane."

"Are you tired? Do you want to sleep?"

"A little tired," she admitted. Even though it was the middle of the day, she was suppressing yawns. Travel took a lot out of a person, and in addition to that, Violet felt as if she'd been on an emotional roller coaster for the last week.

"Use my arm as a pillow if you need to," he told her, pulling out his tablet computer.

He didn't need to tell her twice. For some reason, she craved being able to touch him. Maybe it was because she'd grown up so starved for love as a child, ignored by both parents, that she'd gone the opposite direction in her relationships.

Violet freely admitted she was a clinger. She liked to touch, she loved public displays of affection, and she adored any sort of physical contact when she could trust a person. Unfortunately her relationships had been few and far between. But now that Jonathan and she were friends again, he felt safe to cuddle with.

And she did love a good cuddle.

Violet wrapped her arms around his biceps and rested her chin against his shoulder, peering over as he began to pull up a search engine. "What are you looking at?"

"I thought I'd research your poem. See who the author was. Maybe there's a connection there we're supposed to pick up, like the Marlow Bridge."

"Mmm. Good idea."

He looked over at her, surprised. "Why, thank you, Violet."

Why was he so surprised and pleased by her compliment? She wasn't that mean, was she? Her fingers stroked his arm idly. "Jeez, I must be really rough to be around if you're thrilled about me saying 'Good idea.'"

"Not at all. I just . . . I thought you hated me." His expressive face was grave, his eyes soulfully dark.

"Oh, Jonathan," she said softly, and patted his arm. His rather nicely muscled arm. "I don't hate you. Not anymore."

"I didn't know about the baby." He stared ahead, as if unable to look at her. His voice was grave, wounded. "If I'd have known, nothing on earth would have stopped me from coming to your side. I swear."

But I left you a note, she wanted to protest, but kept those bitter words silent. Jonathan had been firmly in her father's clutches, and who knew better than she how much of a manipulator the old man had been? So she only squeezed his arm. "I believe you."

Strangely enough, she did. For the first time in what felt like forever, she was able to think of the lost baby and her abandonment without resentment, just a pang of sadness. The frustration and grief in Jonathan's face actually made her ache for the pain he was going through. At least she'd had ten years to adjust to it. It was fresh to him, and it seemed childish to throw this in his face now.

So she distracted him. Deliberately brushing her breast against his arm, she leaned over and gave him a curious look. "My poem?"

His eyes took on a glazed look, and then he seemed to give himself a mental shake. "Of course." His fingers danced over the tablet, and she watched him type a few of the phrases in. "Ah. Here we go. Lord Tennyson. The poem is called 'Idylls of the King; Song from the Marriage of

Geraint.'" He read on for a moment more and made a disgusted sound in his throat. "Apparently it's a poem about one of King Arthur's knights and his marriage was torn apart by lies. Well, damn. Your father *is* a bastard."

Violet couldn't help it; she giggled. He looked so very disgruntled.

At her laugh, Jonathan gave her a sour look, his entire body tense with anger. "Do you think that's the message your father is intending for us to take away from this?"

"I certainly hope not," Violet said, her mouth still twitching with amusement. "Do you see yourself as one of Arthur's knights?"

His shoulders relaxed a bit and she gave his arm a placating rub. "I suppose that's a stretch, yeah. What is the message here, then?"

"I don't know," Violet admitted. "Is it something to do with Lord Tennyson himself?"

He tapped on the tablet for a bit longer, reading, and eventually shook his head. "The man had a colorful life, but I don't see a connection to Santorini." He looked over at her. "I feel like my clue pertains to us. I'm just not sure how we tie in with the poem unless it's in an insulting way."

"Well, I wouldn't put it past my father to throw in a few barbs from beyond the grave," Violet said. "Don't worry about it too much, really. I'm sure something will be glaringly obvious to us once we get to Santorini. And you figured out the bridge, so I'm sure you'll puzzle out this next part."

He nodded absently and rubbed his chin, still staring down at the information on his tablet. A line of worry creased his brow.

For some reason, she didn't like seeing that worry there. "Since we're on the subject of poetry, do you know more?"

"More poetry?" he asked her, distracted. "What do you mean?"

"I don't recall you being a poetry buff when I knew you

before," she teased. "If I remember correctly, *I* was the one with the English minor."

His mouth crooked in a half-smile as he put the tablet away and leaned back in his chair, focusing his attention on Violet. "I had a change of heart about the English language after we parted. I ended up minoring in English Poetry, actually. Major in business. It's a weird combination."

"I'll say." She was fascinated, though. Business and . . . poetry? Had she influenced that? Did he take up his love of poetry because he'd wanted to be closer to her? Violet's heart squeezed. "Can you recite me something?"

"Poetry?"

"No, the starting lineup of the New York Yankees." She rolled her eyes. "Of course, poetry."

A smile flashed across his face. He rubbed his chin, thinking, and then turned to her, eyes gleaming. "How about some more Shelley?"

She shrugged. "That's fine. Hit me with it."

"You don't 'hit' people with poetry. You astound them with your eruditeness and your learning." He wagged his eyebrows at her.

Violet laughed and shook her head. "Just hit me with it already!"

He made a great show of clearing his throat, and Violet couldn't stop laughing. Then, grinning at her, he began to softly recite.

> *"The fountains mingle with the river,*
> *And the rivers with the ocean;*
> *The winds of heaven mix for ever*
> *With a sweet emotion;*
> *Nothing in the world is single;*
> *All things by a law divine*
> *In one spirit meet and mingle—*
> *Why not I with thine?*

See, the mountains kiss high heaven,
And the waves clasp one another;
No sister flower could be forgiven
If it disdained its brother;
And the sunlight clasps the earth,
And the moonbeams kiss the sea;—
What is all this sweet work worth,
If thou kiss not me?"

The breath caught in Violet's throat. He'd recited every line in an achingly tender voice, gazing directly at her. There was no mistaking the look in his eyes, the soft caress of his words. Her heart fluttered and she was filled with longing for him, for what they'd had once upon a time, back before everything changed and went to hell.

Her hand lifted to his cheek and she gently stroked the curve of his jaw with the backs of her fingers, admiring his beauty, his intensity, his love for her burning in his eyes.

And she wanted to experience that again. So badly. She was terrified of it, though. What if she fell for him again and he hurt her worse than before? She wouldn't be able to handle it.

And yet . . . she couldn't stop touching him. Her fingers brushed under his chin and she tilted his face toward hers, compelled.

The look in Jonathan's eyes was smoky with need. "What is all this sweet work worth?" he whispered, leaning in. "If thou kiss not me?"

Hell if she knew the answer to that. She kissed him.

NINE

～

If this was a dream, Jonathan didn't want to wake up.

Violet, his Violet, was cuddled up next to him on the plane, looking at him with soft eyes as he recited love poetry to her. Then, she'd touched his jaw and drawn him toward her. And incredibly, she'd kissed him.

It was no more than a quick brush of her lips over his, but it was enough. When she didn't pull away, he took the initiative. If she was waiting for him to kiss her back, he wouldn't let the opportunity escape. His lips parted against hers, his tongue stroking against the soft seam of her mouth. To his surprise, Violet's mouth opened against his, accepting his unspoken request.

With a groan, Jonathan turned and slid a hand to her nape, holding her against him as he deepened the kiss. His tongue slid against hers, and she was just as delicious, and soft, and wonderful as he remembered. And she kissed as fiercely now as she did then. Violet didn't sit back and appreciate a kiss; her tongue moved against his, her lips caressing his own, and she made fierce little noises of pleasure in the back of her throat with every stroke of his tongue, as if she were tasting a delicious dish. It made his cock excruciatingly hard, and his craving for her intensified.

He pulled away from her mouth and she made a protesting sound, her eyes closed. Unable to resist that tiny plea, Jonathan continued to kiss and nibble at her soft upper lip. *I love you*, he wanted to tell her. *I've never stopped loving you.*

But he knew that saying it again would scare her away. When she came to her senses, she'd likely regret this moment, see it as weakness. He needed to say something to keep her with him, to let her know that everything he did, every breath he took, was wholly hers.

Jonathan's teeth tugged on her lower lip, and he noticed how her head tilted along with his, following his movements, her eyes closed in sheer bliss. He loved that. He wanted to continue to watch her lose herself in ecstasy. Her hands clung to him as if she were starved for love, and it gave him hope. "Let me pleasure you, Violet," he whispered against her mouth.

Her eyes flew open. "W-what—"

He silenced her protest with another fervent kiss. "Let me do this, Violet. I won't ask for anything more. Let me make you feel good."

Another tiny whimper rose in her throat. Her eyelashes fluttered, but she didn't push him away. Instead, he felt her fingers dig into his hair at the nape of his neck.

She was holding *tighter* to him.

Triumphant, Jonathan pressed his mouth to her jaw and began to issue quick, desperate kisses to her soft skin. God, she was lovely. He craved her like oxygen. He'd longed for that blissful look that was currently on her face. It haunted his dreams, made it impossible for him to see another woman. Not when Violet was still consuming his mind.

He nibbled at her throat, licking and nipping the soft skin there, waiting for her to push him away, to protest that this wasn't what friends did. But she only moaned and clung to him, and he had to fight back his own groan of delight. She was enjoying his touch.

He vowed then and there that he'd make it so damn good for her that she'd come back for more. This time, it'd be all about her. Pleasuring her. Watching her face light up with ecstasy. Feeling her tremble in his arms. That would be satisfaction enough for him.

And he'd take nothing for himself. Because there was nothing on earth that could compare with the softest flutter of Violet's eyelashes in response to his touch. Nothing he could do that would bring him half as much pleasure as making her quiver.

He wanted to do more than just kiss her on her face and neck. An image of him burying his face between her legs surged into his mind and he had to bite back his response. If this was about Violet, she had to want it, too. He'd have to kiss her and caress her until she was begging for it.

And he remembered that his Violet loved to be touched more than anything.

Jonathan brushed a hand up and down her arm, enjoying the feel of her small frame under his. She was wearing a long-sleeved knit top that he wanted to rip off so he could feel the soft skin underneath, but he'd follow her lead. His hand smoothed over her shoulder and brushed over her nape, caressing.

She moaned in response, her head tilting back even as she pressed her body closer in his arms. "Jonathan," she breathed.

God, he loved the sound of his name on her lips. "I'm here," he murmured softly, gliding his hands over her clothed form, stroking down her back and then smoothing over her hip.

"Your hands feel unbelievable," she told him. "Why do you feel so incredible?"

"Because I know just how you like to be touched," he

told her, nipping at her ear. "Your body remembers how good I can be to you."

She shuddered against him. For a moment, he worried he'd pushed her too hard, but then her mouth pressed against his neck and she practically crawled into his lap. "Touch me."

"Take off your top," he told her. "Then I can touch you everywhere."

She hesitated for a moment, and his heart thudded a warning. Had he lost her? But she only opened her eyes and gave him a dazed look. "What . . . what about . . ." She licked her lips. "Will someone see?"

"Violet, love, we're at thirty thousand feet. There's no one on this jet but you and me and the pilot, and he's not coming out of the cockpit. We're completely alone." For the first time that evening, he was thankful they'd elected to fly without an attendant hovering. It truly was just him and Violet in the back of the small jet, and he intended to take full advantage of the situation.

She licked her lips again, sitting back in her chair, indecision on her lovely face. "If you're sure . . ."

"I won't do anything you don't want," he told her, brushing the back of his knuckles along the sweetly stubborn curve of her jaw. "Never."

"I want you to keep touching me," she admitted, reaching for him.

He dragged her into his lap this time, pushing the armrest between them up into the chair. She went into his arms eagerly, her hands on his shoulders and her thighs straddling his. His cock nestled between the part of her legs and he was unable to stop the groan from escaping his throat. He had to remain in control; this was about her, not him.

But she gave a little wiggle in his lap at his response, as if she enjoyed hearing it. Her hand slid down the front of his shirt, pressing against his muscles. "Will you take this off for me? I want to look at you."

She wanted to look at him? "If it'd give you pleasure," Jonathan said.

She nodded, the expression in her eyes eager, hungry.

He sat upright in the chair and Violet clung to him as he carefully maneuvered and pulled the T-shirt over his head without dumping her off of his lap. Then he sat back again, drawing her against him.

Her hands went to his chest, pressing against his muscles, and she gave a sigh of pleasure. "You sure did turn out pretty," she breathed, her fingers tracing along his pectorals. "Oh, man."

He let her explore him, remaining silent lest he interrupt her and distract her from her focus.

"And so warm, too," she murmured, her fingers trailing along his skin. She looked pale against his tan, a sharp contrast reminding him of the different paths their lives had taken. Violet should be as tanned as he was, Jonathan thought fiercely. She should be at his side on his adventures, not trapped in a classroom.

Grasping her hand in his, he brought the palm to his mouth and kissed the center. "I'd be even warmer if your bare skin was pressed to mine."

She shivered, her dark lashes fluttering again. He watched her bite her lip, deciding, and then to his intense joy, she reached for the hem of her body-masking tunic top that hid her lush curves. "I haven't been exercising as much as you in the last ten years."

"I don't care," he told her. He didn't give a fuck. If she was fat and lumpy—and she wasn't—she'd still be gorgeous to him because she was his Violet. "I want to see you. *All* of you. I want to press you against my skin."

Her eyes went wide at his words, and he mentally cursed himself for losing his cool. Maybe he'd been a bit too vehement in that statement.

But she leaned in and kissed him again, and then she

slowly tugged her top over her head, her messy hair fluttering against her jaw and curving there.

And then she was straddling him in nothing but a bra and her yoga pants.

Her bra was plain white. Boring, she probably thought. But he liked that boring bra. He fucking loved it, because it told him that she wasn't a woman with a closet full of lingerie designed to torment lovers. He wanted to be her only lover. He wanted to be the only one to touch her soft skin, to feel the press of her curves against him. So he tugged at one serviceable strap and then ran a finger along the seam of the bra cup. "Take this off."

She shivered again, and he watched her skin break out in goose bumps, her nipples erect. Her breath was coming in sharp, short little gasps. Slowly, her hands reached behind her back and he heard the pop of the clasp, watched the tight fabric over her full breasts loosen and then fall forward.

And then she shrugged it off her shoulders and cast it aside. Violet tossed her head back and sat on his lap, half naked and defiant, as if daring him to say something about the changes in her body.

Violet had never been lean. Even back when they were teenagers, her figure had tended to ripeness. That hadn't changed; her breasts were fuller than before, her stomach slightly more rounded, her hips a little plumper, her ass less of a tight apple and more of a juicy bouncing pair of curves that taunted him when she walked. But she was utterly and completely gorgeous. Her nipples were that dark pink he remembered, still upthrust and tight little circles that begged for his mouth and fingers. Her breasts were full and heavy, shifting with every rapid rise and fall of her chest, and her waist tapered in before spreading to her hips.

She was obscenely gorgeous.

"You are so lovely you steal my breath," Jonathan told her reverently.

He watched her tremble against him, her fingers digging

against his lower arms where she rested them. "That . . . that's not another poem, is it?"

"That's me," he said bluntly. "Speaking to you. You're gorgeous." His gaze devoured her, the heaving breasts, the taut nipples, the smooth skin. "May I touch you, Violet?"

Her fingers went to his neck, played with his hair. "Will you tell me more poetry?"

"Anything you want," he agreed. Anything so he could get his hands on her.

"I'd like that."

He racked his brain, trying to think of something that came to mind that would suit the moment. He normally had a sharp memory for these kinds of things, but with Violet straddling him, her breasts inches from his wanting hands, it was difficult to concentrate. He mentally went down his list of favorite poets anyhow. Not Frost, his personal favorite. He didn't tend to romantic moments. A few love poems came to mind, but he suspected that if he started vowing love to Violet—however poetically—she'd skitter away again. The first few lines of a filthy poem by John Wilmot he'd memorized in college sprung to mind, and he began to speak. "'Naked she lay, clasped in my longing arms,'" he began, his voice husky. The next line was "I filled with love" but he modified it. "'I filled with *lust*, and she all over charms.'"

Her eyes shone as he began to recite, fascination in her gaze.

Jonathan's hand traveled up her arm and to her shoulder in slow, deliberate motions as he recited the next stanza. "'Both equally inspired with eager fire, melting through kindness, flaming in desire. With arms, legs, lips close clinging to embrace, she clips me to her breast, and sucks me to her face.'"

Surprise flickered on Violet's face and she laughed, the sound sweet and pure. Her breasts jiggled with her laugh, and he was momentarily speechless at the gorgeous sight. "'Sucks me to her face'?" She echoed, giggling. "Is that supposed to be poetic?"

"It is," he said, a bit of a smile on his own face. He tried to tear his gaze away from those magnificent breasts and failed. "This is also the only poem I know of that uses the word 'cunt.'"

"Cunt? Really? How?"

"Patience, my lovely," he said with a playful wag of his eyebrows.

She snorted and tilted her head, regarding him with amusement. "I'll try to be patient."

"You're interrupting my seductive moment," he chastised her.

"Seductive? That was supposed to be seductive when you talk about sucking people to your face?"

"It gets better, I promise."

She nodded, biting her lip to contain more laughter. "I'll do my best not to laugh, then."

"Laugh all you want," he told her. "It makes your breasts bounce very enticingly." She sucked in a breath at his words, and he was pleased to see the soft desire return to her eyes. His hand went to her waist and brushed against the soft skin there, and he felt her tremble. "Shall I go on?"

"Please," she whispered, all laughter vanished, replaced by need.

His fingers caressed her shoulder and then moved to brush against the curve of her mouth. "'Her nimble tongue,'" he continued in a low voice, "'love's lesser lightning, played within my mouth, and to my thoughts conveyed swift orders that I should prepare to throw the all-dissolving thunderbolt below.'" Before she could laugh at the newest absurd euphemism, he went on. "'My fluttering soul, sprung with the pointed kiss, hangs hovering o'er her balmy brinks of bliss.'"

And he trailed his fingers down her neck to her breastbone, and waited.

A whimper escaped her throat. "If you don't touch me—"

He leaned in and kissed her mouth gently, feeling her breasts brush against his own bare chest. "'But whilst her busy hand would guide that part which should convey my soul up to her heart, in liquid raptures I dissolve all o'er . . .'" Jonathan trailed off as she burst into giggles. "I think I forgot what this poem was about," he said sheepishly. "All I remembered were the dirty words."

"Jonathan Lyons," she said, sliding her fingers over the lines of his shoulders playfully. "Have you been reciting me a poem about premature ejaculation?"

Hell, this was embarrassing. "I might have been."

She giggled again, and damn, he loved that sound. "By all means, please keep going."

Since he loved her laughter almost as much as he loved her whimpers of desire, he did. "'In liquid raptures I dissolve all o'er,'" he repeated. "'Melt into sperm, and spend at every pore. A touch from any part of her had done't: Her hand, her foot, her very look's a cunt.'"

"Mmm, there's the naughty little cunt," she said, sliding a finger over his nipple playfully. "It's almost . . . sweet, really, the way it's used in the poem."

He took her hand in his and pressed his mouth to her palm. "It's true, you know. Every look, every touch from you and I feel like losing control."

The amusement in her eyes quickly spun back to desire. "Still after all this time?"

"Worse after all this time," he told her. "Because now I know what it's like to wake up without you."

Her breath caught. "Jonathan—"

"Hush. Tonight is about me giving you pleasure. Let's not think about anything else." He gently kissed her palm again, and then placed it on his chest, over his heart. Then, he brushed a knuckle along her jaw and slid it down to between her breasts to distract her.

"All right," she said softly, her gaze rapt on him.

He forgot about everything but the need to pleasure her, and, his eyes locked on hers, he grazed his knuckle over the mound of her breast, circling one nipple slowly. "I remember these breasts," he told her in a low voice. "I remember the taste of the tips on my tongue, the weight of each breast in my hand. I remember how they bounced when I thrust into you. And I know how sensitive the undersides are," he said, tracing his knuckle down and curving it over the rounded slope.

She shivered in response, arching against his touch. Her eyes closed, and it was clear to him that Violet was determined to lose herself in the moment.

He loved that. He wanted that. He wanted to see her wrecked within herself, made wild by his touch.

And the best thing was, he knew her body intimately. He knew how to make her need turn into an inferno of desire.

And he knew that, for starters? Violet needed her breasts played with. She needed her nipples toyed with, her flesh kneaded and fingered, the peaks teased until she was breathless. He set to making her crazy, using both hands to palm and cup her breasts. "These look sweeter than I remember. Just as full and plump as before, but more soft and inviting. I can't wait to put my mouth on them."

She gave a little shiver in his lap that told him she liked his words.

"In fact, I think I will," he told her. He wanted to lean forward and suck on one of those juicy-looking nipples, but with the way she was sitting on his lap, it'd be an awkward position. So he hauled her forward, dragging her body toward him. When her belly was inches away from his mouth, he took one of her breasts in hand and made it point, the tip aiming for his mouth. He knew from the flutter of her lashes that she was excited by the anticipation, so he drew his motions out a little. Instead of taking her nipple fully into his mouth like he wanted to and sucking on its sweet, pebbled tip, he brought it to his lips and . . . waited.

She practically wriggled off of his lap, pressing her breast toward him. Inching closer.

Jonathan looked up at her face, at the need and tension on her lovely features, the anticipation etched there as she watched him breathlessly, waiting for his mouth on her skin. He tilted his head forward, that dark pink treat so close that he could smell the fresh scent of her skin, and gently rubbed the tip across his lower lip, not quite taking it into his mouth. It was deliciously hard.

Violet gasped, her eyes dark slits intent on his mouth as she watched him roll her nipple back and forth across his lips, never quite taking it between his teeth or touching it with his tongue. It was a tease. A tormenting, heavenly tease.

Her fingers tightened in his hair and she pressed hard against him, pushing her breast forward. "Oh, God, please, Jonathan."

Hearing her say his name did all kinds of things to his resolve. Without further ado, he flicked his tongue forward and lashed it against her nipple.

She moaned.

He loved the sound of that, so he tongued the nipple hard again, stroking it with the broad flat of his tongue, then circling it with the tip. Then, he gently took it between his teeth and flicked against it again.

Now she was whimpering, her breath coming in small pants, her hands plastered to the sides of his face as she held him to her. Her eyes were closed, and the look on her face was pure ecstasy.

He wanted more of it.

Jonathan nuzzled her breast, teasing and coaxing with teeth and lips and tongue, using every caress in his arsenal to drive her wild. His hand went behind her back to hold her steady and his other slid to the waist of her yoga pants. The stretchy material was bunched at her waist, and he pushed at it, wanting to shove his fingers into her waiting warmth so close nearby. He imagined the hot feel of her pussy lips over his fingers, slick with need, and nearly lost his mind. His cock was so hard it felt close to bursting, but he'd control it. Violet's pleasure was more important than his own.

She made a soft mewing sound as he lightly nipped, surprised by the bite of his teeth. He soothed it away with soft licks and kisses, murmuring her name over and over again. His other hand pushed at the yoga pants, wanting them to give and slide down her hips. When they didn't, he gave up on that and just pushed his hand down into the material and pressed against her skin, seeking the warm cradle of her sex.

She panted as he brushed his fingers over the crinkle of curls shielding her pussy. Jonathan groaned against her breast, nearly overcome, but when she directed his mouth to her other breast, he attacked it with relish, biting and licking and teasing it until she was whimpering and wild in his arms all over again. His hand, paused just above her pussy, then slid downward, and he cupped her mound. *This is mine,* he wanted to tell her. *This is mine and no one else's.*

But he bit those words back and tongued her nipple, sending her into new sighs of pleasure. Ever so slowly, he pressed his middle finger forward . . . and nearly lost control when it slid easily between her soaking wet folds. Holy Christ, she was turned on. He mentally cursed and had to take a moment to compose himself, pressing his forehead against her pillowy breasts and trying to retain control.

Violet shifted on his lap, his hand. "Is . . . everything all right?" Her fingers dragged through his hair.

"I just need a moment. You're too much. It's making me lose control, and I don't want to. I want this to be about you."

"Take as long as you want," she said softly. "I'm right here." And she stroked his hair again, the move almost loving. When she touched him like that, he almost believed she loved him again. Almost.

The realization that this was probably no more than a quick release for her dashed his erection faster than anything. He continued to press his face against her breasts, heartache nearly destroying him. He was touching Violet's skin, breathing Violet's scent, his fingers buried in Violet's pussy.

And yet, it still wasn't enough. He wanted her heart.

But when she rubbed against his hand, sliding his fingers up and down the folds of her sex, he knew she needed this. Hadn't he said this would be about her, not him? It should be, and so he'd pleasure her even if it broke his own heart to do so.

So he kissed the sides of those soft breasts and looked up at her, easing a finger forward until it dragged against the hood of her clit.

She nearly jumped off of his lap, crying out, "Oh!"

Now, that? That was beautiful. He rubbed over it again, even as she squirmed against his hand, half trying to pull away and half trying to brush against his fingers harder. When she arched her back again, his mouth latched on to one of her nipples and he sucked hard even as he rubbed her clit, enjoying the tiny wail that escaped her throat. His sensitive, delicious, lovely Violet. He could never get enough of her, never have enough even if he lived to be a hundred years old.

And he wanted more. Jonathan released her nipple with an audible pop, pleased to see the tip wet and gleaming from his mouth, and a dusky red from his sucking. "I want you to lay back on these chairs for me," he murmured, still gliding his finger back and forth across her sensitive clit.

"W-where?" Violet panted, glancing around the small cabin.

"Here." Jonathan reluctantly pulled his fingers from her sweet, wet warmth and dragged her off of his lap and onto the seat next to him. She sat there, blinking and dazed, still drugged by passion.

"Do . . . do you want me to lie down?"

"Nope." He grabbed the waistband of her pants. "But

these have to go, because I'm burying my face between your legs."

She gave a shuddering gasp and fell back against the leather seats, her heavy breasts bouncing with the movement, and for a moment, Jonathan wanted to go back to them, to suck and tease and lick them until she was crying out all over again. But the scent of her arousal was in his nostrils, and he wanted more of her. Fighting his own need again, he tapped her hip. "Lift, please."

She did, and he dragged the pants off her hips in one smooth move, until the fabric bunched at her thighs. Her hips were exposed, the sweet, rounded curves of them just as generous and beautiful as he remembered, the thatch of hair between her legs wet with need above her creamy thighs. His mouth watered at the sight.

One more tug, and the pants were at her knees. She wiggled a bit and kicked them off, then pressed back against the seat, watching him with heavy-lidded eyes. "What do you want me to do now?"

"I want you to scream my name," he told her in a low voice, pushing forward. She was seated in the leather airline chairs, the armrest pushed up so they made a little couch, and it didn't leave much room for him. That was fine. All he needed was a place to kneel. He pushed her legs apart and slid to the floor, kneeling there.

And then her thighs were spread before him, and the lusciousness of her was inches away, and he couldn't resist. Like a starving man, he dropped his mouth to her and began to feed.

Her gasp of delight was almost as delicious as the taste of her on his tongue. Hot, musky, and just a bit sweet, he couldn't help his own groan as he lapped at her warmth. She'd always had the prettiest pussy he'd ever seen. Soft, beautiful folds that surrounded her clit and her core like it was a flower. He pushed his tongue deeper between those folds and savored each long, delicious lick.

There were few things on earth better than Violet DeWitt's pussy on his face, and he intended to savor every moment of this. Each flick of his tongue brought more of her slickness to the fore, and he lapped it up as if she were his favorite treat. Each brush of his lips against her skin told him something: where she was the most sensitive, what nips made her shiver in response, what brought more of that sweet honey to the forefront for his tongue. He studied her like he'd studied poetry, analyzing each sound, each phrase, and then memorizing it for later.

But for now, he wanted to worship at her clit, that tiny center of desire. He tilted his face and angled his mouth, heading for it like a beacon, and began to kiss and lick it with small, methodical strokes. He knew from the past that she liked a slow and steady build. Violet never got off fast, but when she did get off, it was magnificent. He wanted to see that again, and so he took his fingers and parted the lips of her sex, spreading her before him like a feast, and focused his attentions on the clit that poked out, begging for attention.

"Jonathan," she sobbed, and when he looked up from her lap and saw her eyes, he saw need written there. Sharp, clawing need. He could relate. His own erection had returned, full force, and was pressing hard against the edge of the seat as he leaned over and lavished his tongue on her flesh.

"I'm so close," she begged. "Please, please push me over."

"I will," he promised, and returned his mouth to her flesh, teasing the little stiff nub of her clit with his tongue. Her hips bucked against his mouth and his steady, slow licking motions, and he couldn't resist sliding his fingers between the seam of her sex and searching for her core.

He paired two of his fingers together and teased at her entrance, circling it the way his tongue circled her clit.

She nearly came off of the chair in ecstasy. "Oh, God. Oh, yes!"

"Be still," he growled at her, though his own hips were thrusting unmercifully, uselessly, against the edge of the chair that he was pressed against.

She nodded, clutching at the chair she rested on. She was a gorgeous sight, all flushed cheeks and pale skin, her breasts heaving with every gasped breath, her hair a messy nimbus about her face. Her legs were sprawled wide with his face between them, and he wanted to memorize the sight of her like this, so full of need and so utterly beautiful that it made his heart ache.

"Please," she said again, urgency in her tone.

He set upon her once more, back to the slow, steady licking of her surely aching little clit. He pressed his fingers into the well of her sex, having to stifle his own groan at the way her cunt clenched and pulled at him, as if she were trying to suck him in deeper.

Violet's moans of pleasure grew louder, and so he began to pump his fingers slowly in and out of her, curling them ever so slightly and dragging them against the front wall of her core as he pulled them out, looking for the spot that would guarantee a deliciously brutal orgasm. The rhythm of his tongue against her clit continued, his pace picking up just a bit and matching her quick, panting breaths as if they were the metronome he had to follow. Gasp, lick, gasp, lick. Her juices covered his mouth, her scent was in his nostrils and coating his fingers, and he was in heaven. He never wanted to leave this spot, ever. If he died at this moment, he'd die a happy man.

But his Violet needed to come.

He crooked his fingers inside her and rubbed hard, and was rewarded with her choked cry of surprise. Ah yes, that was a new trick he'd picked up in the intervening years. He'd never done that to her before, and he was guessing that her other lovers had never bothered to try and find it. For a moment, he was filled with a vicious jealousy that gave way to a possessive sort of pleasure at the way she arched and sobbed when he brushed his curled finger against it again.

She was his. This was her, and she was all his. No man had touched her like him, and he was going to fucking give her the best orgasm she'd ever had.

So, fingers rubbing against her inner wall, he bent over her clit with a new fervor, increasing the strokes of his tongue to a new rapidity.

She made a wordless sound, noisy and completely unmindful of the fact that her cries were echoing in the cabin even as he sprawled between her legs, eating her out at thirty thousand feet in the air. Her hips moved, jerking, as if trying to follow his fingers, and he knew he couldn't let up now. To do so would mean she'd have to chase her orgasm all over again, and the way she was clenching around him, the lips of her pussy swollen with need, she was close. So close. So he continued, mentally chanting his own poem.

Come for me, Violet. Come on my face, on my lips, and let me taste your sweetness.

A few more rubs and arches of her back, and he felt her entire body shiver, and then she gave a little cry of release. Her legs jerked on his shoulders, and he felt her pussy clench hard at his fingers, felt her clit quiver under his tongue.

Perfection. He groaned his own pleasure at her response and kept licking and stroking, dragging out the orgasm to enhance her pleasure for as long as possible. She writhed against him, his name dragged out of her lips like a benediction. "Jonathan. Jonathan. Jonathan."

"This pleasure's all for you, Violet," he rasped against her soft, dewy skin. "I'd give this to you every day if you'd let me. There's nothing better than making you wet with need, and watching you squeeze around my hand."

She moaned, her hips riding his fingers as she lost herself in the orgasm, and he felt stark pride at how disheveled, pleased, and thoroughly fucked she looked.

He'd done that to her.

He pulled away from that sweet cradle of her hips, bitterly reluctant but knowing he couldn't stay there all night. At least, not yet. Maybe in a week or two she'd let him feast between her legs for hours on end. For now, he'd be content with whatever scraps of attention she gave him.

But most of all, he had to act as if this were no big deal. As if they were just friends. Friends with benefits.

His lip curled at the thought.

He'd give his "friend" so many benefits her head would spin. He'd give her so many goddamn benefits that her legs wouldn't be able to hold her upright.

And then he'd see if she just wanted to be friends with him.

So Jonathan got to his feet and licked the taste of the woman he loved off of his lips. "I'll get a towel for you."

Under the pretense of retrieving a towel, he left to go jerk his cock in the airplane's tiny bathroom so she wouldn't see his need and feel obligated to reciprocate.

He hated that fucking word, *obligated*.

―――――――――

Violet stared at Jonathan's bronzed shoulders as he stalked toward the airplane bathroom at the back of the jet. She was dazed, and breathless, and just all over . . . wow.

Okay, so he'd learned a few things since they'd last had sex together. The sex had always been great with Jonathan. But that right there? That right there had just blown her ever-loving mind. She'd never come so hard. Hell, she was wondering if she could ever walk again. She felt deliciously, thoroughly used.

And she felt really, really good.

And yet . . . as she watched him disappear into the bathroom, the old doubts resurfaced. Oral sex on an old flame and demanding nothing in return? That wasn't how friends acted. This? This was a one-way trip back to heartbreak.

Some of the things Jonathan had said to her in the heat of passion weren't the words of a man just having a casual diddle with his "good buddy." And now that her mind was clearing, she remembered each groan he struggled to hide, the way his lips clung to hers as if he wanted to memorize every caress.

Even though Jonathan was giving lip service to being her friend, he was still the same intense, possessive Jonathan Lyons who had broken her heart the last time.

Violet sat up and straightened her hair, tried to get her racing heart back under control.

No matter how good he was at sex now, fooling around with him could only lead to more hurt. She needed to tell him that they couldn't do this again. Not if they wanted to maintain their fragile, newly rebuilt friendship.

But as she pulled her shirt over her breasts, she felt suddenly so very tired of the walls she kept erected to keep herself safe. Couldn't she just relax for one day and not worry about emotions? Couldn't she just enjoy?

Violet pulled her pants on and lay back in the seat, thinking.

She'd tell him in the morning, when both of them had clear minds and a few hours of distance. Tonight, she'd allow herself to wallow in pleasure for a bit.

TEN

~⌐

When the plane landed at Santorini's airport, Violet was roused from her nap by Jonathan's gentle caress. "Come on, sleepy," he murmured as he woke her. "Let's get you to the hotel."

She might have protested or said something about working on the envelope hunt, but her brain was mush after the intense orgasm she'd had earlier. She'd fallen asleep before he'd even emerged from the bathroom. Now, it was late at night and Santorini was lit up and beautiful, but her eyelids were so heavy they wouldn't stay up.

She vaguely remembered a taxi ride to the hotel and checking in to the hotel while leaning against Jonathan's arm, and then sleep. Blissful, delicious sleep.

When Violet awoke the next morning, she was in a room by herself. That was . . . a little disappointing. *No, it isn't*, she chided herself. *He's giving you space like you're always demanding.* Still, she glanced around the room, frowning. Where was Jonathan if not with her?

Her gaze fell to a note on the bedside table, scrawled in his familiar bold handwriting.

I'm in room 211 if you need me. Call me when you get up and we'll have breakfast & plan our next move.—J

She studied the note, looking for hidden meanings, some signal about what they'd done on the plane. Any regret? Any declarations of love? Did "plan our next move" refer to something relationship-wise or was she reading too much into it? Violet didn't know. It seemed . . . awfully casual.

She showered and dressed, opting for jeans and a blousy, off-the-shoulder top with a tank underneath. The time for her schoolteacher armor was past, she supposed. Tucking her hair behind her ears in a nervous habit, Violet dialed Jonathan's room.

"This is Jonathan," he answered.

"Hey, it's me."

A pause. "Good. You up for breakfast?"

For some reason, his nonchalant tone bothered her. This was Jonathan, Mr. Born-and-Bred-Intensity. Wasn't he supposed to be reciting poetry to her beauty and vowing that he loved her above all others? That was his normal MO. To have him so casual after the mind-blowing incident on the plane rattled her. She cleared her throat, settling her thoughts. "Breakfast is fine."

"Downstairs, then? I can be there in ten."

"See you then," she said, and hung up, vaguely disgruntled and not sure why. She got up, slicked on a bit more lip gloss, and added a touch of mascara so her eyes would seem bolder, and headed down to the hotel lobby.

The Kallista Hotel hadn't changed much in the last ten years, and as she walked through the lobby, the Greek columns and tiled floor reminded her of times past. She crossed her arms, feeling vulnerable, and waited for Jonathan in the lobby.

He arrived a few minutes later in his usual casual blazer, T-shirt, and jeans. He was unshaven and his hair was a bit tousled, as if he hadn't bothered to fix it since it was just Violet he was meeting. She wasn't sure if that irritated her or if she wanted to run her fingers through his hair and smooth it into place.

"Shall we eat?" Jonathan asked, gesturing at the doorway to the hotel restaurant.

She nodded and let him open the door for her, lost in thought.

They got a table and sat down, ordering a pair of coffees. Jonathan glanced at the menu and set it down, then pulled a small tablet out of an interior pocket of his jacket. "I had scans made of our newest letters while we were flying," he told her, tapping the screen. "Now that we're here at the hotel, maybe we can figure out our next move."

"Sure," she said lamely, and fought a swell of irritation. Was he just going to ignore what happened between them last night? She couldn't. Every time she looked at him, her gaze went to his mouth, and she remembered how he'd teased her clit with his tongue for what felt like hours. When he reached for his silverware, she gaped at his hands, remembering how those fingers had found just the right spot inside her to drive her mad with need.

"Do you have any ideas?" Jonathan asked, spreading his napkin on his lap.

Oh, she had ideas, all right. Violet watched his strong, blunt hands move to the table surface again. Those were distracting her. He said something else that she didn't catch. "Hmm?"

"Violet? Any ideas on where we go next? I'll follow your lead."

She blinked. "Follow my lead?"

He tilted his head, eyes narrowing at her. "You seem distracted this morning."

Why wouldn't she be distracted? Irritation flared and she

grabbed her own napkin-rolled silverware and tore the bundle apart. "Of course I'm distracted."

"Thinking about the clue?"

Fuck the clue. "No," she bit out. "About what happened on the plane last night."

His gaze was steady, his face unreadable. "What about it?"

Her jaw dropped a little. "Well, it shouldn't have happened, for starters."

He shrugged.

A shrug? That was all she got? Violet fought back her temper as she patted her napkin in her lap. The waitress came by and brought coffee, and they were momentarily distracted with ordering breakfast. "Just toast," Violet said, hating the snappish tone in her voice. God, she sounded like a bitch. When the waitress left, Violet wrapped her hands around her coffee cup—so she'd resist lobbing it at Jonathan's oh-so-casual head—and frowned at him. "I feel like we need to talk about what happened."

Again, he shrugged. "I'm listening."

She ground her teeth at his casualness. "I just . . . I feel like friends with benefits is not the direction we want to head."

"All right." He picked up his cup and took a sip, then set it down and picked up his tablet again, studying the screen.

That was it? Violet clenched her fists. What about protests? Utterances of undying love for her? Didn't he say he'd always loved her and wouldn't stop? Hadn't he vowed it just yesterday when he was between her damn legs? And now he just didn't give a shit?

What the ever-loving fuck?

A horrible thought occurred to Violet. What if . . . what if he was disappointed in her? What if that was why he was so cool now? She tugged at the low neckline of her loose top, suddenly feeling self-conscious and dowdy. She wasn't as thin and athletic as she'd been ten years ago. A few extra pounds—okay, twenty—had settled on her already hour-glass figure and made her a little curvier than most. He'd picked up some damn impressive tricks in the last ten years and made her come like wild. But what if he had built her up in his imagination and now he found her performance lacking?

For some reason, that was like a stab in the heart.

It was like . . . when she knew Jonathan was still in love with her, she could hold him at arm's length, until she was ready to let go of the past and accept him again. If she held on to her bitterness and anger for another year or two, she knew he wouldn't give up on her. She'd been comfortable to hold him away. It was safe, and Violet liked safe.

But this new, casual Jonathan, who didn't give a shit if they had sex or not?

This man was a stranger, and she didn't know what to do. And she wasn't sure she liked it. "All right?" she echoed. "That's all you have to say?"

He looked up at her again. "What do you want me to say? I told you that you could call the shots. I said it was about you. If you don't want to do it again, that's fine."

That was fine? He'd given her the best orgasm of her life and taken nothing for himself and that was *fine*?

"Okay then," she said, feeling a bit lost. "Let's go back to just friends."

"Just friends," he agreed.

Why did she feel like she was the one losing this battle?

"So . . ." Violet said after taking a steadying sip of her coffee. "We're here at the hotel. We have a poem that talks about nothing in particular. What do we do?"

Jonathan shrugged again—a gesture she was beginning to hate. "I'm sure something will come to us. Maybe we need to explore the city. The poem mentioned wheels. Maybe we need to look for wheels of some kind."

It was as good a lead as any. "Just looking for wheels

seems rather vague to me. And if we don't find the wheel my father referred to?"

"Then we wait here for a while and see what hits us. Something will pop up."

He seemed so very casual about the entire thing. "So we just lounge around on a Greek island and enjoy the sun and sand? Is that what you're saying?"

He grinned, a flicker of the old Jonathan rising to the surface. "Is that such a bad thing?"

It wasn't, not really. Santorini was lovely from what she remembered, and the weather seemed to be nice today. "Do you think we should check out the ruins?"

"We're not part of any sort of archaeological dig, so I don't know if they'd just let us out there unless we pulled strings. We can, but if it wasn't one of your father's digs, it would seem strange for him to send us out there."

That was true. She knew that he'd been heavily involved in the Akrotiri ruins for about five years, and then had abruptly changed his mind, heading for Spain instead. Why Spain, she hadn't known and hadn't cared. "So . . . we're basically stranded at the moment."

"I guess we are. Want to go sightseeing?"

She blinked at his suggestion. "Shouldn't we work on this?"

"We should. And we will. But for now, why don't we just enjoy the day? Take some time off? You seem tired."

If she was tired, it was because she was still a puddle of jelly after last night's interlude. It was an interlude which had rattled her to her core and hadn't seemed to affect him at all. Sheesh. "I'm not tired."

"Good. Then shall we go exploring?"

"Can't I eat breakfast first?"

"I never said we'd skip out on the eating," Jonathan said in a low murmur.

And that made her blush, thinking again of the plane ride over. Damn it, she was pretty sure he'd said that just to bug her. And that made her all confused again.

Which Jonathan was he? Jonathan of all shrugs and not caring if they ever touched each other again? Or suggestive, madly in love with her after ten years Jonathan?

She was so confused.

They spent the day in the warm sun. Santorini was just as idyllic as she remembered it. The island itself was formed from the remnants of a volcano, the city hugging the edges of the caldera. It had been one of the oldest civilizations in existence thirty-six hundred years ago when the volcano had erupted and destroyed Akrotiri. In the present day, Fira town was its own little white cluster of buildings crawling over the rocky soil, surrounded by the impossibly beautiful ocean and jagged cliffs. It was utterly lovely, and the sky overhead was a sea of endless blue.

She'd loved this place when she'd snuck away here with Jonathan so many years ago. They'd left the Akrotiri dig behind for a weekend of passionate lovemaking in the Kallista Hotel back when they were teenagers, and walking the streets ten years later, she couldn't stop thinking about that weekend.

Back then, Jonathan had held her hand as they'd explored the narrow streets.

Today, he walked at her side. As a *friend*. The thought left a sour note in her mind.

Fira's shops lined the streets, colorful fabrics and beach souvenirs catching the eye. Delicious smells lingered in the marketplace, and she couldn't resist stopping for a bite of baklava, or a delicious gyro. She bought a colorful linen wrap intended for the beach, and took her time browsing as they shopped. It was pleasant . . . and infuriating at the same time.

They went sightseeing and talked about nothing in particular. They read the poem repeatedly, scanned the streets for wheels or things that might have matched up with their clues, and came away empty-handed. By the end of the evening, Violet's feet ached from walking, her nose was sunburned, and she was a good, achy tired again. They'd eaten all day as they'd walked, so there was no need for dinner. Still, when it came time to part, Violet hesitated. Did Jonathan want to spend time with her? Maybe come up to her room? Have a little more "friends with benefits" time?

Not that she wanted to, she assured herself. But if he wanted to, then at least she'd know he was still interested.

But Jonathan seemingly didn't care. He gave her a quick smile, told her he'd call her in the morning when he woke up, and headed down the hall to his own room.

And for some reason, that bugged Violet. It seemed like the more mixed-up she became emotionally, the more he retreated.

She hated that. She wanted him to be just as torn and confused as she was. She wanted him to think about their interlude on the plane when he laid down to sleep that night, because lord knew she was.

She dreamed about him, too. Dark, delicious dreams of his mouth and his hands, and him murmuring filthy poetry in her ear as he made love to her.

It was depressing to wake up and find she was in bed alone.

The next day went much like the first. They headed to the beaches, and when Violet protested that they probably wouldn't find any hints toward her father's poem, Jonathan suggested that they simply enjoy themselves. It would come to them at some point. They just had to be patient and wait, and until they came across it, they could enjoy the island paradise that Santorini had to offer. She just needed to think of it as a working vacation, Jonathan teased.

And Violet thought she was good at being patient, but she wasn't. She really wasn't. Because when they walked the beach and strolled in the surf, she wanted Jonathan to hold her hand like the other couples they saw. She wanted to run her hands over those flexing muscles and know that he belonged to her.

She was falling for him all over again, and that was dangerous. The harder she fought to pull away from him, the closer she was dragged.

It seemed to be the opposite for him. Jonathan was cheerful and friendly, but there was a definite distance between them. It was like he didn't care if he ever kissed or touched her again.

She should have been happy with that. Just like she should have been happy to have a few days of paradise on the beaches of Santorini, enjoying the sun and relaxing in a beautiful Mediterranean island.

But she wasn't. She was more tense than ever, and it had nothing to do with her father's silly scavenger hunt and everything to do with the gorgeous, sexy man at her side who was determined to just be her friend.

Why on earth had she ever said she wanted to just be friends? Worse than that, why was he okay with it?

Violet felt like she was in a hellish sort of limbo. A friendly, no-strings-attached, no-hearts-on-the-line sort of limbo. It was a limbo she would have been perfectly happy with two weeks ago, before Jonathan was back in her life.

But now that he was, it seemed her heart wanted all or nothing. And she was utterly terrified of that, just like she was terrified that he was no longer attracted to her.

What if she fell for him again—a very real possibility—and he was no longer interested? She'd be left behind, hung out to dry once more.

And it scared the hell out of her.

But as day three merged into day four in the island paradise, business and pleasure continued to mix together. When Jonathan suggested that they check out the local scuba diving in case of any submerged wheels, Violet knew it was a long shot, but she went along with it, and they spent a day diving in the blue Mediterranean waters. Following that train of thought, they visited every tour of the ruins on the island, and Violet hated that she enjoyed it so very much. Each day was pleasant, and utterly, completely frustrating. She couldn't keep living in this wonderful, terrible limbo. She just couldn't.

Something had to be done.

It was clear that Jonathan wasn't pursuing her anymore. If she wanted him, she'd have to pursue him and make it obvious that she desired him. She'd have to put her heart out on the line and offer it up to him, not knowing if he was even attracted to her anymore. Maybe he was content with their now-friendship.

Violet would have to be the one taking all the risks. And it frightened her, but it didn't make her as miserable as the thought of more torturous days of a remote Jonathan who was cordial and polite and treated her about as intimately as he did the staff at the hotel.

She thought she'd wanted to be his friend.

She didn't. Not in the slightest.

So . . . Violet began to plan. If she was going to break through this friend-zone they found themselves in, she needed to go all out.

The next day, when Violet suggested they spend another afternoon at the beach, Jonathan was surprised. She'd been antsy with every day spent on the island. It was obvious to him from her frustrated body language, and from the way she kept frowning at him like he was doing something wrong.

But what exactly he was doing wrong, Jonathan didn't know. He was giving her space, just like she wanted. He didn't touch her anymore, even though it was fucking killing him. Every evening, he slept like shit because his bed was empty, and he spent hours in the shower each night, jerking off and trying to relieve his body from the endless, aching lust he had for her.

If Violet wanted nothing more than to be friends, he wouldn't push her. He'd take whatever she would give him and be happy with that.

She was clearly upset that they were stuck on the clue, though. Each day, she seemed more and more distressed that they were getting nowhere. He wasn't unhappy at all, though; he loved that he got to spend these extra days with her. They'd both memorized the poem and looked for wheels all over the city. They'd asked about Dr. DeWitt at every location they could think of, and there was nothing to follow up on. Every day, Jonathan lived in fear that Violet would turn to him and say "I'm done. There's nothing to be found." And then he'd have no choice but to send her home and out of his life.

He was a shitty person because he was glad they weren't able to find anything. Because every day they were stalled meant another day he could drink in her presence, watch her dainty motions as she ate, watch the way she turned her pretty face up to the sun to catch a bit more sunlight. The way she smiled. The smell of her hair. The way she put her fingers to her full lips to bite her nails.

So her suggestion to go to the beach had taken him by surprise. Not that he was complaining. Another day of leisure with Violet at his side? He'd take it.

As soon as they got to the beach and she stripped off her cover-up, though, his mouth went dry.

Instead of the sensible black one-piece Violet had been wearing for the past few visits to the beach, she'd purchased a bikini. Not just any bikini, but a tiny, bright blue one that barely covered her curvy ass with a triangle of fabric, and a top that seemed to push her magnificent breasts together into two plump mounds that bounced with every step.

He'd had to adjust himself several times at the sight of it.

Not that she'd notice—Violet had barely glanced at him, her gaze on the water. "Weather's lovely today."

They were going to talk about the weather, were they? When her jiggling breasts were just begging to be freed from those creative straps holding them together?

She squinted up at the sun and put down her towel. "I think I need some suntan lotion or I'm going to burn. Would you do me the honors?" She held out a small white tube to him and presented him her back.

He took it from her, wondering if this was some kind of torture. At the base of her spine, he could see two dimples that framed her tattoo: *Carpe Diem*. Staring at that tattoo was going to get him into trouble. His gaze moved up, to her shoulders. Probably a bad call. Jonathan stared at Violet's nape for a long moment, tempted by the tiny bow of her swimsuit tied there. It was just begging to be pulled apart, and then her breasts would tumble free from their confinement . . .

And then he'd have everyone at the beach staring at his woman. Well, more than they were already staring. He was already casting scowls in the direction of a few men.

With an angry squirt of suntan lotion, Jonathan pressed his hand to Violet's shoulder.

She shivered, squirming. "That's cold!"

God, his dick was so fucking hard at the moment. He was going to embarrass himself if anyone saw the hard-on he was sporting in his own swim trunks. But Violet needed to be protected from the sun's rays, so he continued to stroke the lotion into her skin—a rather delicious kind of torture, especially with the soft little sounds of pleasure she was making at his touch.

"Mmm, thank you," she said when he was done.

He didn't say anything in response, just stormed right into the water so he could hide his erection. When it was waist high, he dropped in to his neck and stared out at the blue sea, trying to compose himself.

To his annoyance, Violet swam out to him, ignoring the fact that he was trying to flee. "Have you had any luck with the poem?"

"None," he bit out. He wasn't thinking about it. Hell, he wasn't even trying. If it took a month for them to figure out Dr. DeWitt's cryptic message, he'd be ecstatic. That was time he'd get to spend with Violet. Looking at her, absorbing her presence, listening to her soft voice. "I haven't worked on it today."

"That's all right," she told him. "I'm kind of at a dead end, too." She stood up in the water and let it sluice down her skimpy top, her breasts magnificent and gleaming.

He couldn't stop staring at them. At her. Was she torturing him on purpose? She was the one who said she wanted to be friends. He was letting her lead.

So why did it feel like she was determined to rub it in his face that he couldn't have her? Jonathan dunked his head to cool it.

They swam for a few hours. Eventually, they returned to their separate hotel rooms, Violet claiming she wanted a nap.

Jonathan took a cold shower, and when that didn't ease his need, he jacked off.

She called him a few hours later. "What time are we meeting for dinner?"

"I'm ready whenever you are," he told her.

"Great. Downstairs in a half hour?"

That was fine with him, and he dressed casually and headed down to the lobby.

Once he got there, though, his jaw clenched at the sight of her. Violet was . . . stunning. She was wearing jeans, but they were skin tight, and her feet were encased in strappy sandals. In addition, she was wearing a white tank top with a loose, low-swooping neckline that showed off her breasts magnificently. Her lips were a plump pink and her skin was sun-kissed.

She was gorgeous.

She was torturing him.

Violet gave him a brilliant smile as he walked toward her. "There you are. I'm positively starving." Her hands went to her stomach, and of course his gaze was drawn to the cleavage practically spilling out of her top. "I need something in my mouth right now."

Definitely torture.

When they sat down to dinner, instead of their regular table, Violet insisted on a booth. And when he sat down at the booth, she slid in next to him. "I figure I can peek over your shoulder while you do some more research online about wheels in Santorini. I'm sure we'll eventually hit on the connection."

He stared down at her, trying to keep his face impassive. Violet was short, her head only coming up to his shoulder when she stood. He liked that she was tiny, but tonight he both loved and hated it, because whenever he looked over at her, he had a bird's-eye view of what might be the best cleavage in all of the Mediterranean.

And he had to act like he wasn't affected, because they were supposed to be *friends*.

Jonathan pulled out his tablet and tried to focus his gaze on it and only it. Looking over at Violet would just mean more staring at her magnificent torso. And he couldn't stare if he was her friend, because nothing about that pair of breasts screamed *friend* to him. They screamed for attention, for his mouth, for touching, for hours of attention to be lavished upon them.

When the waitress put a glass of water down in front of him, he grabbed it and sucked it down, trying to ignore the fact that his arm brushed Violet's breast. Goddamn it.

"Can you pull up the poem?" Violet asked him, her voice low. She leaned in close to read over his shoulder, and her breasts brushed against his arm again.

"Of course," he said, glad for the table surface that would hide his erection. He mentally willed it to go away even as he pulled up the all-too-familiar file and held the tablet out to her.

She didn't take it, just leaned against his arm and read, her lips moving in a way that made him think of sex. Then again, everything she did made him think of sex.

After a moment, she shook her head. "I've still got nothing. You?"

How on earth could she possibly expect him to be able to concentrate when her thigh pressed against his in the booth and every movement made her magnificent breasts rub up against him? "Nothing."

She leaned a bit closer and pointed at the first paragraph of the poem that had them stumped. "'Turn, Fortune, turn thy wheel and lower the proud.' It mentions fortune and wheels several times in there. You don't think we need to look for a local fortune-teller, do you?"

"We can do whatever you like," Jonathan said briskly, offering her the tablet again.

She ignored it and nudged his arm. "We're supposed to solve this together."

"I'm afraid I'm no help on this. I shall be the pockets, you can be the brain."

Violet gazed at him with a frown on her pretty face, but she let it go.

They ate their dinner in silence, Violet picking at her food. He scarfed his own down as quickly as possible so he could get back to his room and jerk off. Sad how he was now needing to seek release for his body on a regular basis. Just being around Violet cranked his libido to the extreme.

Violet ordered a dessert. He declined, and since he didn't want to seem rude and abandon her, got a coffee for himself. The dessert was a confection of whipped cream over cake, topped with a cherry, and it made him think of her breasts again, how they were soft, pillowy mounds tipped by cherry-red nipples, and . . .

And hell. He needed that cold shower as soon as possible.

She took a small spoonful of the dessert and lifted it to her lips. When she gave a small moan of pleasure, his entire body went rigid in response.

"Oh, my God, this is so good. Do you want a taste, Jonathan?"

He looked over at her—damn it, he needed to quit looking over, because now he had an eyeful of her deep cleavage, so creamy and looking far more delicious than any dessert. And even though he should have told her no, when she lifted the spoon toward him, he opened his mouth for it.

She fed him the bite, watching him expectantly. He tasted nothing, his mind full of Violet's skin, Violet's taste. "Good," he said gruffly, and nearly groaned aloud when she licked her own lips again. He wanted to thank every deity in the world when she didn't offer him another bite, and grimly drank his coffee, staring ahead at nothing.

It was the longest dinner in the world. By the time the check arrived and he paid, he'd ignored Violet as she moaned and chatted her way through her dessert, licking her fingers and lips with gusto. He paid, and he got the hell out of there.

As soon as he was back in his room, Jonathan practically ran for the damn shower. He turned it on—straight-up cold—and began to undress, ripping his clothing off. He'd jerk off a few times and then maybe he'd be able to concentrate on something other than Violet. He hoped. Christ, he was reaching for his cock more often than a schoolboy lately.

A knock sounded at his door. Cursing, Jonathan zipped his pants again. When his cock continued to jut out, a blatant sign of what he was about to do, he reached into his pants and adjusted himself, flattening the length and tucking the head of his cock against his belt. It was painful, but fuck it. A little pain might distract him. With that, Jonathan headed for the door, shirtless.

A quick look through the peephole showed that it was

Violet. Concerned, he unlatched the door and opened it. "Is everything all right?"

Her gaze went to his naked chest, and then she looked up at him. He could have sworn her eyelashes fluttered a bit. "I do have a bit of a problem. Can we talk?"

"Of course." He opened the door wider and gestured for her to enter. If Violet had a problem, it was his problem as well. His heart panged. He hoped she wasn't asking to leave; he wasn't ready to let her go yet. Even if her being here tortured him, it was the sweetest, most delicious torture he'd ever experienced, and he wasn't about to give it up. He turned to face her, hating the slight frown marring her forehead. "What can I help you with?"

"I, well, it's hard for me to say." She twisted her hands and bit her lip, then began to pace in his room.

Damn it, she was going to ask to leave, wasn't she? Fury and possessiveness swept through him, and he clenched his fists as he slammed the door to his room. "If you're asking to go home, my answer is no. Not until we find whatever it is your father left us."

She looked surprised at his short temper. "What the hell crawled up your ass?"

You, he wanted to snarl. *You, because you don't want to be here with me and I've done everything in my power to try to make you mine again, and it still isn't enough.* "Nothing."

"It doesn't sound like nothing to me," she said, and put her hands on her hips. The movement only emphasized her curves, and he almost wished she'd put her arms down again. Almost. "Do you want to sit down so we can talk?"

"I don't know. Is this going to take long?"

Her nostrils flared, and for a moment, she looked as if she wanted to punch him. "Why are you being such a dick to me? What did I do?"

He *was* being a dick, and that was unfair to her. "It's not you. It's me," he said gruffly, and turned to the bathroom.

A moment later, he had the shower off and emerged to see her sitting on the edge of the bed, her hands twisted in that nervous way again. "I'm sorry. Now, tell me what's wrong and maybe I can help."

"Well," she began, and tucked a lock of hair behind one ear nervously. "I . . . See, there's this thing."

He crossed his arms over his chest, waiting.

She put her hands back in her lap, and then tucked her hair behind her other ear, a sure sign of nerves if there was one. "Let's say I had a craving for baklava."

Now it was his turn to frown. He gestured at the phone. "Are you hungry? Did you want me to order you something—"

Her glare intensified, became withering. "Let me finish."

Jonathan lifted his hands in a silent apology, indicating she should continue. He watched her body language, noticing the tension there. Even distressed, she was beautiful to look at. He'd never tire of gazing at her exquisite form.

She shifted on the edge of the bed and placed her hands next to her thighs. "All right. Let's say that the last time I had baklava, it gave me vicious food poisoning. I swore off baklava for the rest of my life. Then, let's say someone shows up with a tray of it and it looks delicious, and I remember how much I like it. The question is, do I take a chance, knowing I could possibly get burned once more? Or do I keep my promise and stay away knowing that it's safer?"

He wasn't listening to a word she said. She'd started leaning forward as she spoke, and the neckline of her loose top kept sliding down, and all he could see were the tops of Violet's breasts. That shirt was a fucking cruel tease. Why she'd worn it—

"Jonathan?"

"Hmm?" He forced himself to look away from those magnificent breasts, to refocus on her intent face.

"Did you hear what I was saying?"

Something about baklava. And food poisoning. And . . .

Christ, were her nipples erect under that blouse? Jesus God in Heaven, he needed that cold shower. "You want me to order you something from room service?"

"No!" she cried out, angry. Her hands clenched at her sides and she sat upright, all stiffness. "You're not listening to me at all, are you?"

"I'm a bit distracted." *By your breasts and your nearness.*

Violet jerked to her feet in a fluid motion that made her breasts bounce. Not that he noticed. Much. "Damn it, Jonathan," she cried. "What does a girl have to do to get you to notice her? If you're not attracted to me anymore, just freaking say so! Don't dance around it like an idiot."

ELEVEN

Jonathan stared at Violet as she straightened her clothing.

She tilted her head back in a haughty stare.

"Not . . . attracted to you?" he asked slowly. Was she insane? He'd been fighting his attraction tooth and nail to ensure he didn't overstep the "friends" boundary.

Her eyes glittered with unshed tears. "I'm practically throwing myself at you here."

She was? Was that what this was about? The bikini and the dinner where she practically rubbed up against him? Jonathan was in shock.

"But if you're not interested, just tell me. I know I've changed in the last few years, and I'm terrified I'm just going to get hurt again, but it seems like I'm the only one—"

Jonathan rushed forward and cupped her face between his hands. He kissed her before she could change her mind, silencing any protest she might make. "Never think that," he murmured between kisses. "Never think for a moment that I don't love and adore you."

"I'm afraid," Violet whispered, even as she clutched at his shoulders. "I'm so afraid of getting hurt again. Last time . . . it nearly broke me."

Pain shot through him at the fear in her eyes, the heartfelt emotion there. He'd done this to her. Tenderly, he brushed a thumb across one of her lovely cheeks and leaned in to kiss her again. Softly. Reverently. Then, he said, "I won't ever hurt you again. This I promise."

She gazed up at him, clearly uncertain. Then, she nodded slowly and leaned into his touch. "It's so hard for me to trust, but . . . I trust you."

He felt as if he'd been given a gift. Jonathan kissed her again, poetry springing to his mind as he gazed upon her upturned face.

> *"I loved you; even now I may confess*
> *Some embers of my love their fire retain;*
> *But do not let it cause you more distress,*
> *I do not want to sadden you again.*
> *Hopeless and tongue-tied, yet I loved you dearly*
> *With pangs the jealous and the timid know;*
> *So tenderly I loved you, so sincerely,*
> *I pray God grant another love you so."*

"That was lovely," she said in a soft, aching voice. "Who was that?"

"Pushkin," he murmured, leaning in and kissing her eyebrow reverently. He wanted to cover her entire face with kisses, and began to do so, touching his lips to her forehead, her cheek, her nose, in gentle touches. "I thought of you every time I heard that poem. Except, I fear, the last part."

"The last part?" she murmured, leaning in to each kiss that he pressed to her face.

"I don't want another to love you," he confessed, lightly placing his fingers under her chin so he could turn her heart-shaped face up to his. "Because I wanted you for myself.

I've never stopped loving you. Never stopped wanting you. Every second of every day, my heart has always been yours."

Violet's beautiful eyes gazed up at him, shimmering with emotion. She didn't respond, but her hand curled behind his neck and she pulled him down for a kiss. As his lips met hers, she murmured against his mouth, "Make love to me."

"Everything I do for you is out of love," he told her between quick, fervent kisses. "It is all making love, because I do it out of love for you. But touching you? That is worship."

"Then worship me," she murmured, her other hand sliding to the front of his chest and pressing over his heart. "Show me your love."

He groaned, a surge of need flaring hot and hard through him. A mental image of tossing Violet on the bed and ripping her clothing off, savagely pounding into her as she screamed her pleasure and dragged her nails over his back, filled his mind. He shuddered. There'd be time enough for that later. For now, he wanted to seduce her. To make love to her so slowly and sweetly that she couldn't help but fall in love with him again.

He'd confessed his love. Over and over again, he'd confessed it. She'd never responded in kind. He knew that. He knew her heart was guarded, and it was up to him to break those barriers once more.

"Are you on the pill?" he asked her, making sure she knew exactly what he was asking for.

A wry smile curved her lovely mouth. "Always."

He nodded. "I'm clean."

Hesitation stiffened her body. "I am too, but I still want you to use a condom. Just, you know, in case." She bit her lip.

In case the pill failed? She didn't want to be left alone and pregnant again? For a moment, he felt like the world's biggest asshole. He'd left the woman he loved pregnant and abandoned all those years ago. "Condoms," he agreed thickly. He went to his bathroom and dug through the toiletries packed by one of his assistants. He always kept condoms on hand, and found a strip of them after a moment's searching. Taking one in hand, he returned from the bathroom, placed it on a nightstand, and saw her face lined with worry again.

He hated that she was so anxious about what should be a beautiful act of love. It had been love between them once. Jonathan resolved that it would be again. He'd make her lose that worry. He wanted her to drown in his touch, not stress about whether she would get pregnant again.

This would be all about her, once more.

Striding across the room to her, Jonathan took Violet in his arms and kissed her again. The kiss started out soft and sweet, a gentle press of lips. When her mouth parted under his and her body relaxed, his kisses became more focused, more intense. His tongue feathered over her soft lips in a tease, and when she gave a soft little gasp of pleasure, he nearly groaned in response. God, he loved this woman. "Let me make love to you, Violet. Let me worship you. Let me give you nothing but pleasure. Let me show you how much I adore you."

She nodded, and he felt her head move against his, ever so slightly, felt the tension in her fingers as she curled them against his chest. She was clinging to him, but not quite lost in the moment yet. He had to break through that fear of hers, that wariness that kept her from losing herself to him. What would it take? He remembered her response to him on the plane. That had been sweetly beautiful. Had she been off her guard and that was how he'd been able to break down her defenses?

Was it time for him to take her off her guard again? Did Violet have to be pushed out from behind her walls in order for her to enjoy herself with him once more?

If that was what it took, he'd do it. He'd give anything to see her screaming her pleasure again. His mind filled with glorious images of her on the plane, her hands pressed to his head as her hips quaked against his face, and his mouth was filled with the delicious taste of her.

He groaned in pain and need. God, he needed that again.

"What is it?" she whispered, her fingers tightening on his jacket.

"Do you trust me?" he asked, his voice a little harsher than he'd intended.

She blinked up at him, surprised. "I . . . Why?"

"Just answer me, Violet. Do you trust me?"

Violet stared up at him for so long that he thought she would answer in the negative. Her gaze searched his face, and then after what felt like forever, she nodded slowly. "I trust you," she whispered.

"Good." That surge of possessiveness slammed through him again. His fingers worked through her hair, then cupped her sweet face. "Good."

She tilted her face toward him, eyes closed, implicitly trusting him.

And that gave him an idea.

"I want to tie you up, Violet."

Her eyes widened. "W-what?"

But as soon as he said it aloud, he knew it was a perfect idea. "You trust me, right? Let me tie you up." It would push her trust past just verbal assurance and into a physical realm. She would truly have to trust him to let him tie her up and do what he wanted to her. It would require more than just lip service. He wanted to be absolutely sure that she trusted him. That she wasn't just saying it.

Her eyelashes fluttered, and he watched indecision cross her face. Then, after a long moment of doubt, she slowly nodded. "I . . . All right." She glanced at the bed, then at him. "How do you want to do this?"

"Get on the bed," he told her. "Remove your clothes for me."

She trembled visibly, but nodded. He loved her willingness.

He wanted to shower her with kisses all over again, but that would have to wait.

As she moved toward the bed, he turned to his dresser and pulled out two silk neckties. He carried them with him at all times, in case of impromptu meetings or important business visitors, and now they were perfect for what he wanted. He tied the smaller ends together to create one long, soft rope, and then turned back toward Violet and the bed.

She sat on the edge of the bed and had removed her silky, flowing top and cast it on the floor while he'd been preoccupied with his neckties. She'd pulled off her leggings, too, and now wore nothing but a black pair of high-cut panties and a black lacy bra that seemed designed more for enticement than functionality. Had she dressed with the intention of seducing him, then? The thought sent a thrill through his body, that the woman he'd lusted after and dreamed of for so long was in his bed, and had come after him.

He was determined not to disappoint her.

Approaching the bed, he extended the ties in his hand out to her. "Are you sure you wish to do this, Violet? I won't hold it against you if you change your mind."

She looked down at the ties, licked her lips, then gazed up at him. "I want this."

He brushed his fingers over the curve of her cheek. "If you get frightened, what's your safe word?"

Violet thought for a moment. "Stop?"

He chuckled, still tracing her face with his fingertips, fascinated by the way she leaned into his touch. "It's supposed to be something you wouldn't call out in the heat of passion."

"Well, I should hope I wouldn't be screaming out 'stop,'" she told him, sounding a bit peeved.

"Pick something unusual, that I wouldn't expect you to call out."

A wicked gleam shone in her eyes. "Daddy?"

"You're really trying to kill my erection, aren't you?" But he laughed.

She grinned, and that weird tension between them dissipated. "Who was the poet from earlier?"

"Pushkin?"

To his surprise, she gave a prim shake of her head. "Sounds awfully close to 'push it in.' Maybe I should pick a different safe word. Let's go with Ozymandias."

He grinned. Count on his Violet to give a safe word—something he didn't intend on her needing to use—such thorough consideration. "All right then, Ozymandias it is. Now, give me your hands."

She held them out, wrists up and together in the air, the look on her face full of trust and nervousness.

He felt like he was being given a gift. Jonathan took her wrists in his hands and gently placed a kiss on each one. "Before we begin, I want to say thank you, Violet."

She looked surprised. "Thank you?"

"For trusting me." The ache in his throat left it knotted. Did she not realize how much her trust in him moved him?

She gave him a tremulous smile. "I do trust you. I'm just scared to."

He'd make sure he never betrayed that trust again. Carefully, he wrapped her wrists in the silk of the tie in a figure eight motion and then wove the fabric through the middle again. "Too tight?"

She tested her hands. "No, it's fine."

"Good. I want to tie these to the headboard now." He moved to the side and fluffed the pillows on his bed into a big stack, then gestured that she should lay back on them. "Here."

Her eyes widened but she nodded. Glancing behind her, she scooted back on the bed with little wiggles of her body that made him hot with need. When she finally backed up against the pillows, she lay down and experimentally raised her hands above her head.

"Perfect." Jonathan grasped the tie dangling between her wrists and examined the headboard. It was thick, heavy wood with a cutout Greek key design that was ideal for him to secure his knots. He slid one end of the tie through and knotted it. "Still good?"

She nodded. "Do you do this a lot? I feel like I should ask that."

"Never," he told her. "Never had the urge before now."

She thought for a moment. "I'm guessing this is a bad time to ask, but . . . did you have anyone seriously after we, you know . . ."

"No," he told her honestly. "For me, there has never been anyone but you."

"I don't know if that makes me feel better or terrifies me." Her hands twisted against the ties, testing them.

"Why should it terrify you?" He trailed his fingers down one extended arm. Her skin was so soft.

"Because I feel like I can't live up to any image in your head you have of me from back then. I'm not the same person."

"I know." This Violet was more guarded, and when she let him in under her walls, intensely more vulnerable. "I don't mind the changes. In fact, I love them."

"My ass isn't as small as it was—"

"Your ass is beautiful." His hand moved down her side, skimmed her hip.

She snorted.

"It's true. It's big and juicy and I'd love to take a bite out of it."

She gave a nervous giggle at that.

"What?" he asked, chuckling a bit himself. "I can't want to sink my teeth into that creamy skin of yours?"

"You make me sound like dinner."

"No, you're dessert. Sweet, delicious, and I can't wait to taste you on my lips."

Her breath caught in her throat and he watched her lashes flutter again.

"Shall I get undressed?" he asked her, skimming his hand down one lovely thigh.

She nodded, silent.

His hands went to his belt and he began to slowly unbuckle it. Jonathan was pleased that her gaze went to his waist and she watched him, eyes hot, as he slid his belt out of the loops and dropped it to the ground, then unbuttoned his pants and dropped them. His cock was hard and aching through his boxers. It would have to wait for relief. He intended on making Violet come until she was limp with pleasure. And then maybe once more after that.

With that thought in mind, Jonathan dropped his boxers and stepped out of his clothing.

Her eyes widened and she licked her lips at the sight of him, which just made him harder. "I forgot how good you look naked. That's so unfair."

"How is that unfair?" He took his cock in hand and slowly stroked it, tip to balls, just to watch her reaction. Sure enough, her gaze followed his hand, riveted. He liked that.

"Because you shouldn't look that delicious. Here I was trying to get over you, and you look better than ever. I mean, you've got a six-pack practically up to your throat."

As he stroked his hand down his cock again, her gaze followed and she licked her lips once more, then made a soft whimper in her throat.

"Are you just going to sit there and tease me?" she asked.

"Nothing wrong with a bit of teasing," Jonathan told her, and gave his cock another fierce stroke with his hand, enjoying the way her eyes gleamed in response. "Whets the appetite."

"But I already had a healthy appetite," she told him.

"Mmm. Healthy, but not ravenous."

"And are *you* ravenous?"

"For you, I am."

She gave a little shiver. "Then show me."

How could he resist that suggestion?

Jonathan took a few steps toward the bed and crawled in next to her, his gaze locked on her face. He watched her nervous eyes flicker over his body as he draped his bigger form over hers, and then he was on all fours over her helpless form. Her body was trapped below his. Jonathan grinned down at her, feeling wickedly in control. He liked that Violet was his to do with as he liked, and he intended to exercise that control. "Still trust me?"

"Of course." She sounded more confident than she looked.

"Good." He leaned in and gave her a light, nipping kiss.

She lifted her mouth, her tongue slicking against his, and he lost himself in the taste of her. Violet was delicious. Everything about her—the soft feel of her lips, the tease of her tongue against his, her hot, wet mouth—everything was perfection. Jonathan groaned against her, then took control of the kiss, slicking his tongue against hers and intensifying the kiss until it felt as if they were devouring each other. Violet gave little whimpers underneath him, whimpers of pleasure and need, and they made his cock ache. He longed to press it against her, but with her tied up and laid flat, maneuvering was limited. Still, this gave him the opportunity to crawl all over her and do as he pleased, and he certainly would.

Reluctantly, he ended the kiss, then couldn't resist biting down on her lower lip and sucking on it even as he pulled back.

She gasped, her eyes sleepy with desire as she gazed up at him. "Oh, man, you're a good kisser. I'd forgotten how good up until a few weeks ago."

"And then I was so good that you kneed me in the balls?" He kissed along her jaw, reminding her of their first meeting.

She gave a girlish giggle that delighted him. "It's your own fault. You don't just maul a woman you haven't seen in ten years."

"Not even if she's the most beautiful creature I've ever seen and I've fantasized about her for a decade?"

Violet moaned as he bit down on her earlobe. "Not even then."

"Now that's unfair," he told her, licking down her throat. Her breasts brushed up against his chest, and he could feel how hard her nipples were even through the fabric of her bra. That would be coming off very soon. He wanted to feel her bare skin against his chest.

"Jonathan?" she asked, breathless.

He continued to kiss down her throat. "Hmm?"

"You haven't asked me if I had anyone else in the last ten years." Tension vibrated through her body.

He hadn't, because the thought drove him insane. "Do you have anyone else you're seeing?"

"No! Of course not!"

"Then no one else matters, because from this moment on, you're fully mine. Body and soul." He pressed his mouth to her throat and sucked. He wanted to mark her, brand her as his, though he knew that was crazy. His intense love for Violet drove him to madness though. She'd been his first and only love, and having her back in his arms was a dream made reality.

"Oh, Jonathan," she sighed, arching her throat so he could continue to kiss and suck on it. "Sometimes you know just the right thing to say to make a girl's knees weak."

"I'm not saying it just for a reaction, Violet. It's how I feel. It's how I've always felt. You are, and have always been, mine. You have always owned all of my heart. I've never stopped loving you."

She bit her lip and then gave him a teasing smile. "You've never stopped talking, either. I thought we were going to make love?" She gave a little shake of the bonds over her head.

Was he making her uncomfortable with his vows of love? He'd silence them, then. Anything for her. He just wanted her to know how he felt. "I didn't realize you were so eager," he murmured, lifting his head and dragging one hand over her breast and cupping it. Her nipple was pointed through the lacy fabric of her bra.

"Of course I'm eager," she said, her words sweetly sarcastic. "I've been throwing myself at you all day."

"Is that what the bikini was for? It covered less than this." His finger slid under the edge of one of her bra cups, teasing the skin underneath. "I liked it."

"That was the point," she said, her voice a little more breathless at his touch.

"To entice me? Minx." He kissed the delicate skin at her collarbone. "I am flattered. And, I'll have to make sure you're amply compensated for your efforts."

His hand slid under her back, and she arched, allowing him easier access to the clasp behind her. She was breathing rapidly, excitement coloring her skin a pretty, flushed pink. He undid her bra with one hand and began to push it out of the way.

"You did that rather easily," she murmured. "Lots of practice?"

"If you're fishing for answers, the one you seek is 'professionals.' No relationships. Just lots and lots of working girls."

"I . . ." She shook her head. "I can't decide if I'm appalled or amused. I thought you were a playboy."

"Only for show." He'd taken the odd girl with him to high-profile events when a date was required, but usually a friend of a colleague, and never the same girl twice.

"I'm just surprised. Professionals? Really?"

"They're easier than a relationship," he explained, sliding her bra up around her collarbones so he could admire her newly-exposed breasts. God, they were glorious. All soft and cream and pink. "They require nothing more than a condom and money. If I had an itch that needed scratching, I'd call up a service that had clean, vetted girls and get it taken care of."

"You make sex sound like a business transaction."

"That's all it was," he said bluntly. "There was no emotion involved."

"And . . . with me?" There was a soft catch in her voice.

He leaned down and licked the slope of one breast, nearly groaning at the delicious taste of her skin. "With you, I'm making love. There is no comparison."

"Is it . . . weird that I'm glad? That there's no one else?"

Only if it was weird that he was glad of it, too, if only so he could be free for her here, now. "I never pursued anyone else. It wasn't fair to them if my heart was still yours."

"God," she murmured, and her body clenched underneath his. "Are you trying to seduce me with words alone?"

"No, I plan on using my tongue quite a bit." And to prove it, he took one lovely nipple into his mouth.

She moaned, arching against him, her arms pulling against the bonds over her head. The little tip was tight with need, and he swirled his tongue over it, teasing her. He knew the touches she liked the best—rough, quick licks on the underside of her nipple—but he wanted to draw out the pleasure. He wanted her entire body to quiver and ache.

His mouth worked on the one nipple while he shifted his weight, easing his body over hers. He wanted to press the entire length of his skin against hers, to rub his cock against her sex and feel her rock against it. All in time, he told himself. He needed to pace himself. The most important thing was blowing Violet's mind. That was his goal.

He wanted to palm her other breast and work it even as his mouth worked the first, but he needed the hand to prop himself up on the bed. For a moment, he cursed his "great" idea of tying her hands up. He wanted nothing more than for Violet to touch him, to show that she wanted him as much as he wanted her. Christ, he was dying for her touch on his skin.

As she wiggled underneath him and moaned, again he regretted his idea. He wanted Violet wild and writhing in his arms, fully participating. She was helpless while tied down to the bed—

Then an idea hit.

He pulled his mouth from her nipple, pleased with her murmur of protest. "Tell me what you want me to do to you, Violet."

Her gaze was unfocused, passion-glazed. "W-what . . . ?"

He leaned down and kissed her breast. "Do you like my mouth here?"

"Yes," she breathed.

"Then tell me where you want it next."

She stared at him for a long moment, as if incredulous that he was going to make her take the driver's seat. Then, she flung her head back and groaned. "Can't you just . . . wing it? You're doing great so far."

"I want you to lead me," he told her. "This is about your pleasure. You tell me where you want it, and I'll put my mouth there."

She sucked in a breath at that, but was silent.

Was Violet . . . shy about asking for what she wanted in bed? He tried to remember, but his memories were of equal partners, of greedy hands and passionate kisses stolen after long days at the dig. But now, Violet had gone silent.

He rested his chin on her soft, lovely skin and waited.

She shifted. "You . . . you're really going to make me say it?"

"Why wouldn't I?"

"Because I'm not as thin or as pretty as I was when I was younger. I'm not . . . exciting." She bit her lip. "I grew up and got boring and dowdy."

Was she insane?

"And I was fine with that until I saw you and you turned all breathtakingly gorgeous, and now I feel like . . . well." She sighed. "I feel like I'm not holding up my end."

"You're mad," he said, leaning down and licking one pert

nipple. "I see no flaws when I look at you. Nothing but lush skin and delicious curves just begging to be tasted."

"That's kind of you," she said with a small, nervous smile.

"I'm not being kind, Violet." He tongued her nipple again. "Being kind would have nothing to do with taking you into my bed. I desire you. I want you more fiercely now than I did in the past. My cock aches to be buried deep inside you once again. And I want you. The you with the short hair and the mistrust in your eyes, because that's the woman I loved once and still love. The things I loved about you—your sharp wit, your sharper tongue, your smile—none of those have changed. You're still the same woman I fell in love with ten years ago, and the same woman I fell in love with all over again yesterday and the day before."

She seemed to tremble underneath him. "Why is it that the poetry sounds sweet, but your words sound even sweeter?"

"Because you know they come from my soul," he told her, and kissed between her breasts. "And you know I want to pleasure you more than anything else in the world. You know that, right?"

He felt her tremble again, and when she was silent, he looked up.

She gave a jerky nod.

"Then . . . tell me what you want."

TWELVE

Oh, sure. He made it sound so easy. *Tell me what you want me to do to you, Violet.* Great words in theory, but now that she was in bed with Jonathan, naked, and he was all glorious and tanned and she was not? It wasn't quite so easy to spit out things like *I want your face between my thighs* or *I want your cock deep inside me.*

All Violet could see were her pasty-pale thighs against his sun-browned skin, her soft curves against his hard muscles. One of them had been working out in the last ten years and it wasn't her.

She had no idea why she was so fidgety. He'd seduced her on the plane and she'd been a little anxious, but not wildly nervous like this. He'd gone down on her and had made her feel beautiful. So why was she trembling like a schoolgirl at the thought of demanding that he do the same now?

Because the stakes were different.

Because now her heart was fully committed, and she didn't want him to be disappointed in her. Because for the last week, she'd been wondering if he'd been repulsed by touching her, and it had made her question her own desirability.

Violet didn't think she was disgusting, of course. She was just shorter and a little curvier than most. The problem was that she wasn't the same long-haired wild child she'd been when he'd known her.

She didn't want him to be disappointed, because she wasn't disappointed in him at all. If anything, she loved the changes in his body.

So she licked her lips and tried to push her nervousness away. He was gazing up at her with those intense eyes, that full-on stare that told her she was the center of his universe, and nothing else mattered. It was hard to speak up under that intense scrutiny. To say lewd, dirty things about what she wanted.

"Tell me," Jonathan murmured, and leaned down to tongue her nipple again.

She gasped, arching her back so she could thrust her breast against his mouth. "But you're doing so well on your own."

"I want more, though. I want to make you wrung out and limp from pleasure."

"You're already on your way there," she protested.

That heat was back in his eyes. "Tell me what you want from me."

"I . . . I want more kisses." God, she was such a coward.

One eyebrow raised, and just that small gesture made her wetter. "Anywhere in particular?"

She sucked in a breath. "My mouth?"

He crawled over her again, and Violet strained at the ties on her hands. His big body covering hers was sinfully delicious. She liked that he was almost a foot taller than her, liked that when he prowled on top of her, he could cover her entirely. It made her feel dainty and delicate in a way most men didn't.

Jonathan braced his hands at her sides and gave her a

slow, sultry smile before he leaned in and lightly brushed his lips against hers. As he did, his cock brushed against her sex, and she realized he'd dropped his knees so his erection would rub against her sensitive flesh with every touch of his mouth against hers.

Violet moaned.

When her mouth fell open, Jonathan's tongue slicked inside and he began to slowly, sensuously kiss her. Soft, licking kisses that seemed to take all the time in the world to explore her mouth, to savor her taste. She was entranced by those kisses, drugged by their sweetness. And with every flick of his tongue, he'd give a little thrust of his hips, grinding his cock against her folds. Folds that were already slick with need and aching for a touch.

Her breath came in a ragged gasp that he swallowed with his mouth. She'd asked for kisses, and he was going to give them to her. Over and over, he made love to her mouth, slicking and tonguing until she was lost in the feel of his mouth, his lips against hers, the taste of him on her tongue, the feel of his cock pressed against her pussy in a silent but firm suggestion.

It was so good. So, so damn good. Violet's legs fell open farther, until she was spread wide on the bed underneath him, and when his cock dragged between her folds, she felt all of him.

And it was incredible.

She moaned again, lost in the sensation.

His tongue danced over her lips. "What do you want now, Violet?"

Oh. She was being asked to think? She couldn't think of anything but his mouth on hers, his cock gliding through her folds and brushing against her clit with every little movement of his hips.

"Violet?"

"Hmmm?" Her lips clung to his, not wanting him to pull away. God, he had great lips.

"Tell me what you want or I'm going to stop."

She whimpered. "You're cruel."

"No," he said softly, and kissed her parted mouth again. "I just want you to be a full participant in this, love. I don't want you to feel like you don't have a say in things just because your hands are tied. You might be the one in the ropes, but you're still the one in charge."

She shivered at that. Slowly, she dragged one leg up and wrapped it around his hips, pushing with her foot to press his cock harder against her pussy. "I want more of that."

This time, Jonathan groaned. His mouth dragged across her jaw. "You want my cock inside you?"

Oh, hell yes, she did. But not yet. "Soon," she promised. "But I want you to keep teasing me."

"Is that so." He licked at the side of her neck. "I think I can manage that."

She lifted her other leg, both now hitched around his hips. "Show me." God, she felt so wicked, demanding this of him.

"Look at me," he told her, and his face lifted from her neck. "Look at me when I touch you."

She hadn't realized that her eyes were closed. She'd just been lost in the way he was making her feel. It seemed insanely difficult to drag her eyelids open, but she did, and saw the strain on his gorgeous, intense face, the dark pupils, the thick eyelashes, the strong features.

He rubbed his nose against hers in a surprisingly tender gesture, and as he did, he swiveled his hips. The motion ground his cock against her pussy, dragging over her sensitive clit with exquisite sensation. And as he did, he continued to watch her.

That was . . . so erotic. Violet sucked in a breath, her gaze locked to his. To his dark blue eyes with their amber flecks. To the gaze that seemed to be demanding more and more of her. And all the while, he continued to slowly grind against her clit, until she could feel her juices dragging over his skin and wetting them both.

She moaned.

"Like that, Violet?"

She nodded, unable to look away, unable to speak. She was wrapped up in Jonathan's intensity.

He pushed against her, the surge focused on rubbing the head of his cock against her clit. He spread her lips with his erection and dragged back and forth through her juices, his face hovering inches away from hers.

"You're mine," he told her in a soft voice, even as his cock slid against her clit again. "My Violet. My love. You know that, right?"

She trembled underneath him again. "I—I—"

"Shhh," he said, and leaned in to kiss her. "You don't have to say anything. Just know it."

Her body flexed underneath his as he rocked against her again. This was a sensual feast, but it was also torture. Her body demanded more than just rubbing. Her nipples ached, begging for more attention.

She strained at the bonds on her wrists again.

"Are your arms all right, sweetheart?"

"They want to be around you," she said breathlessly.

"Not this time," he told her. "This time, I'm pleasuring you."

But he'd done that last time, too. When would it be her turn to pleasure him? Violet opened her mouth to object, and he nipped at her lower lip again.

"Tell me what you want."

She arched so her breasts pushed up, begging for attention. "Penetration," she breathed.

He groaned, the first sign of loss of control he'd shown thus far. Violet was fascinated, and excitement flashed through her. She wanted more of that. She wanted him to lose control, too. While his control was exciting, the thought of him losing his mind while touching her was even more gratifying.

So she decided to talk dirty to him, getting bold now with that groan echoing in her mind. "Is that all right?" she asked him, and she nipped at his lip. "Or did you want to keep dragging this out? Because I've been aching to have you deep inside me for days now."

His eyes closed, his dark lashes fanning as his jaw clenched. It looked as if he were struggling to keep control.

She nipped at his lip again, even as he rocked his cock against her pussy once more, a bit rougher this time. "Don't get me wrong," she murmured. "I love the feel of that big, thick cock against my pussy, but I love the thought of it deep inside me even more. Love the thought of you filling me up and making me ache because you're so big that you're stretching me around you."

He groaned again. "Violet—"

"It's true, you know. You're big. You're always a tight fit. I remember that." She wriggled her hips against his, gasping when it did wicked things to her clit. "I loved how tight you were inside me, how you filled me up. It always makes me so hot to think about. And you know I've been thinking about it since you touched me on the plane."

"Have you?" he rasped, his voice ragged. His mouth dragged over hers, his tongue slicking against her own for a fierce, quick kiss.

"Mmmhmm," she said when he pulled away. "I've dreamed about it. About you grabbing me and tossing me down on your bed and drilling into me—"

He groaned and pressed his face to her neck. "Fuck, Violet, hush or I'm going to lose control." His hips thrust against hers roughly, and she felt him draw back. She lifted her hips, tilting them, and the head of his cock pressed against her core, taunting her.

She bucked against him. "Condoms," she breathed. "Need condoms."

"Condoms," he agreed thickly, but he didn't get up from her. He held his body clenched against her own, making her crazy. Then, his mouth sought hers and he gave her another slow, lingering kiss.

He wasn't moving fast enough, though. She was aching with desire and need, and she felt so empty that she might scream from the delicious ache of it. "Don't you want to sink deep inside me, Jonathan? Bury yourself balls deep and make me scream with pleasure?"

Jonathan groaned again and pulled away from her clinging legs. He tore off the bed, heading for the condom he'd left on a nearby dresser.

She watched, eyes greedy, as he opened it and rolled it down his thick length. The head of his cock was a deep, delicious reddish-purple, and she imagined he ached to be inside her as much as she ached to have him there.

Condom on, he approached the bed, the hooded look in his eyes making her quiver with need. She wanted him to climb on top of her and start thrusting away. To take her savagely and fill her up. God, she wanted that so bad.

But he was determined to drive her crazy with lust, it seemed. He sat on the edge of the bed, next to where she lay panting and sprawled, and just gazed down at her.

"You're beautiful, Violet. Have I told you that?" His fingers caressed the line of her jaw.

"You've mentioned it once or twice," she said, trying to keep her voice playful. When his fingers got near her mouth, she tried to nip them.

"I could stare at you all night," he said, his gaze going down to her aching breasts. His hand cupped one, his thumb teasing the nipple as she moaned and strained against the neckties holding her wrists, preventing her from reaching out and grabbing that big, delicious, condom-sheathed erection that was so close but so far away.

"I hope you're not going to," she told him breathlessly. "I don't think my pussy could stand it."

"We can't have that, can we?" He leaned in and gave her another intense, deep kiss, distracting her. She was so engrossed by the feel of his mouth on her own that she didn't notice his hand until it cupped her mound and he began to drag his fingers back and forth through her wet folds.

Violet whimpered and panted against his mouth. Her hips arched off the bed, bucking against his hand. "Oh, God, Jonathan, please."

"Please what, love?" he whispered against her mouth. "Tell me what you want."

She wanted relief from that maddening, erotic torment of his fingers. She wanted more of it. Hell, she didn't know what she wanted. She wanted the orgasm that was so close to rising to the surface. So she simply rolled her hips against his hand and when he brushed his fingers against her clit again, she gasped. "Right there!"

"Right here, sweetheart?" He dragged a finger through her slickness, down to her core.

"No, no," she moaned. Cruel tease.

"Here?" he murmured, and circled her clit with two of his fingers.

She gasped. "Yes! Oh, God, yes. Right there."

"Tell me it's what you want."

Violet moaned. He was torturing her. "I want it, Jonathan," she said, practically sobbing the words. "Please, please, play with my clit."

"I love hearing you say that," he told her, then shifted on the bed. He leaned over and tongued one of her nipples even as he continued to rub against her clit. Violet moaned, the dual sensations bringing the budding orgasm closer to the front. She forgot all about wanting penetration and wanting to drive him crazy. She was the one losing her mind, now.

His fingers found a slow, steady pace against her clit, and it was as maddening as it was delicious. "Faster," she moaned, even as he gently bit down on her nipple. "Oh, God! And keep doing that!"

"I will." His voice was thick. "Sweet, beautiful Violet." She felt his hand shift, and his thumb pressed against her clit, then he began to rub slowly back and forth, even as she felt his forefingers push into her core.

Violet moaned, tightening her muscles against him. "Yes," she cried out again. "I'm so close!" The sensations were overwhelming her, and her entire body felt like it was being pulled tight, like a bow, as he continued to stroke and pet her clit with his thumb, his other fingers pushed deep inside her, his mouth tormenting her nipple.

A moment later, she felt it peak inside her, and she gasped, the orgasm ripping through her body with a ferocity that surprised her. She quivered, limbs locked in place as he continued to rub and stroke her through waves of the orgasm, until she was left trembling and panting with need. Then, limp, she relaxed against the pillows, breathing hard. "Oh," she whispered. "Lord have mercy." That had been intense.

He lifted his head and she looked down just to see him slowly tongue her nipple. That sent a quivering aftershock through her, and she felt her pussy clench around his fingers, still buried deep inside her. Slowly, he dragged his thumb over her clit again, and she felt another aftershock ripple through her. A moan built in her throat.

"I want you to come again for me," he told her in that low, intense voice. His fingers pulled back and thrust deep, and she arched as he pushed in, her muscles quivering in response. "I need to see that again. You were so fucking lovely it nearly stopped my heart."

"Jonathan, please," she murmured. "I want you inside me. Don't you ache?"

"I do, but I'm enjoying watching you too much," he told her.

Time for more dirty talk. She was breathless and wriggling against his touch as he continued to glide his thumb over her oversensitive clit. God, she wanted him to pull away—and to keep going. Little orgasmic quivers kept rocking through her, reminding her that she could have another one at any moment. "But you promised me penetration if I asked for it," she told him softly. "And I asked for it. I practically begged you for it."

His fingers thrust deep inside her again, eliciting another moan. "I am penetrating you."

"No, I want all of you," she told him. "I want that big thick cock deep inside me, filling me up until I can't stand it. Your fingers feel good, but your cock feels better, and it's been too long since I've had it inside me."

His dark eyes were practically black with need. "Don't you want me to bury my face between your legs and make you come again, Violet? I love licking you. Love the taste of you on my mouth."

Violet quivered. He knew just what to say to make her weak, didn't he? That mental image haunted her, and she thought of the screaming orgasm he'd given her on the plane. But the ache deep inside her wouldn't go away, and she wanted to see him come this time. She'd come twice under his hands; she wanted to see that same release on her lover's face. She wanted to see Jonathan let go.

"Please, Jonathan," she begged. "I need you deep inside me."

"Come again for me," he demanded.

She tightened her interior muscles, trying to clench his dragging fingers inside her. "Not until you're in me and we can come together."

He hesitated, then groaned and pressed his face against her stomach. "Damn, I love you, woman."

She hoped that meant she was going to get her way. "Hurry," she encouraged him. "I'm aching so badly for you."

Jonathan turned and climbed onto the bed fully again, then leaned down and kissed her, and she eagerly wrapped her legs around his hips. He groaned against her mouth, and she felt his hand move between them, guiding his cock to that perfect spot between her legs. When he placed the head of it at her core, he hesitated.

She bucked against him, trying to encourage him forward. "Yes!" But he only rubbed it against her, that wicked beast. She groaned as he thrust against her entrance, but no further. "Do it!"

"I love you, Violet," he said hoarsely. Then, he pushed deep and sank to the hilt.

She gasped. Not only because of his heartfelt words, but because of the sensation of him, the memory of him filling her like this so many years ago. Sex with Jonathan had always been good, even when they were two fumbling teenagers. Sex with Jonathan as an adult was reaching new levels of amazing. She tightened her inner muscles around him, reveling in the feel of his cock deep inside her. God, he felt so good. So perfect for her.

He groaned, his eyes closing, and she watched his face, hungry to see his desire. To see him lose control. She wanted to feel him stroke deep inside her, but more than that, she wanted to see him as he lost control, to see his face tighten with his own orgasm, to watch the release move across his handsome features.

She was hungry for it. And so Violet flexed her hips, encouraging him to start moving. "You feel incredible, Jonathan. You're so deep inside me, aren't you?"

"Violet," he murmured thickly. "My Violet."

"All yours," she agreed, and gasped when he rocked his hips, thrusting into her. Oh, that was sinfully magnificent.

"All mine," he said in a low voice, and pushed into her again, his movements steady. "You are, aren't you?"

She didn't answer. She didn't have to. It was in the way she greedily raised her hips for his next drive, the way her arms twisted in the bonds, dying to touch him. She wanted all of him. And so she dug her heels into his ass and lifted her hips with each powerful thrust he gave her.

If Jonathan had thought to make her wild with slow, measured thrusts, he'd clearly underestimated himself. She felt his body tremor against her own, and she watched his face go tight, as if struggling to hold on. One hand clasped her hip and he held her firmly, even as he hammered deep again.

"Yes," she told him, lifting her hips and squeezing her internal muscles with every thrust. "Yes, Jonathan. Give it to me."

His control was ebbing. His next few thrusts lost their measured cadence, and then Jonathan lifted one of her legs from his hip and dragged her ankle to his shoulder. He pressed a kiss there and pushed into her again, and it made his penetration even deeper, even more wonderful than before. Violet gave a soft cry and bit her lip. Oh, God, that was wonderful.

And all the while, he started to thrust harder and harder. She heard the slap of his balls against her ass, felt his skin smack against her own with the power of his drives. It was wonderful. More than that, the look on his face had gone rigid, inches away from losing control. He was thrusting into her so hard that her breasts were bouncing with every movement, and the bed in the hotel room was squeaking loudly.

She didn't care. She loved it.

She was so fixed on Jonathan's pleasure and the look on his face that she was surprised when she felt the onset of an orgasm begin to bloom deep in her own belly again. "Oh," she cried out, shocked. Normally she needed for her clit to be manipulated in order for her to come, but Jonathan's wild driving into her was doing it for her. "Oh, Jonathan," she gasped, urgency building inside her. Her toes curled, and her ankle dug into his shoulder. "Oh, keep going!"

"Come for me," he growled, voice harsh with need. The bed squeaked louder, and Jonathan slammed into her harder and harder. His hand had left her hip and he was using both to support his body as he drove into her. Her breasts were bouncing wildly, and she was loving it, her moans escalating with each thrust. Violet was pretty sure they were being noisy as hell.

She was also pretty sure she didn't care. She closed her eyes and bit her lip again, focused on that elusive orgasm, on the feel of Jonathan pounding into her. "Oh, God, please keep going. Just like that. Oh, God, yes. Yes!" It built and built, and then she was trying to lift her hips to meet his hammering thrusts as he moved impossibly fast within her. She couldn't keep up with his rhythm, their bodies out of sync. It didn't matter. She didn't care. All that mattered was closing in on that orgasm—

And suddenly it was there. Violet gave a little scream as her body shuddered, her pussy clenching tight around the thick length of Jonathan's cock, and she came and came and came. Sparks exploded behind her eyes and her entire body quaked, and oh, God, it was so good.

Her name dragged out of his throat between thrusts. "Violet."

She opened her eyes, even as her body quivered with the orgasm, and wished she could touch his face. "Come for me, Jonathan," she whispered. "Oh, God, come with me."

Even as she came down, he tilted his head back and groaned, the cords in his neck straining as he came on his own. She watched in wonder as his body tensed, his face flushing, and she thought she'd never seen anything more beautiful than Jonathan Lyons, face tight in the rictus of orgasm. His thrusts became erratic and slowed, his panting equally so, and then he dragged his cock in and out of her in one last, almost exhausted thrust, and his sleepy eyes opened to stare at her in wonder.

"Violet," he murmured thickly.

"I'm here," she said in a soft voice. "I'm here."

Breathing hard, he rolled off of her and headed to a nearby garbage can, peeling off the condom. She watched his buttocks flex as he walked, admiring them and the tan lines separating his waist from his ass. He turned back to the bed and moved to the headboard, his fingers undoing the knots that held her wrists in place. "You okay?"

"I can honestly say I completely forgot what my safe word was supposed to be," she said breathlessly.

He tensed. "Did I hurt you?"

She snorted and sat up as the bonds on her wrists released and she rubbed them. They didn't hurt except for where she'd been straining against them. "Don't be ridiculous, Jonathan. If I was screaming, it was because I was out of my mind with pleasure."

He relaxed and got back into the bed. Before she could head to the bathroom to clean up, he put his hands around her waist and dragged her body against him. "Don't leave me yet."

Those words were like knives in her heart. *Don't leave me yet.* Poor Jonathan. She snuggled close to him and enjoyed that she got to touch him now, finally. She rolled onto her side, facing him, and began to slide her fingers up and down his flat stomach.

"Mmm," he said softly when she dragged her fingers through the thin line of hair below his belly button. "Next time, no hands tied. I like your touch too much."

Would there be a next time, Violet wondered? Then she decided, yes, there would be. She wasn't an idiot; if Jonathan gave her mind-blowing, weak-in-the-knees sex, she'd gladly take it every chance she could get before they had to part.

Then she frowned. They did have to part. It wasn't a good idea to fall in love with Jonathan again. She might always be fond of him. She might love the sex he gave her. But she didn't know that she was ready to go all-in once again. Her heart still carried the bruises from last time.

Troubled, Violet rolled onto her back and stared up at the ceiling.

"You all right?" Jonathan's hand brushed her arm.

"Just thinking." Her thoughts sucked, too. They were full of her returning to her quiet teaching job back in Detroit, and Jonathan going back to his whirlwind lifestyle of fascinating projects and exploring famous and dangerous places and running his car company. Even though they'd fit together as college students, she'd switched directions once she'd returned home. They didn't fit as adults. Jonathan was a billionaire with a hectic lifestyle. Violet was, well . . . boring. She was just a schoolteacher.

He'd get tired of her in another week or two.

Which was why it was so important that she keep her heart locked down, no matter what. They could have sex, they could laugh and play together both in and out of bed, and she could kiss him, but she had to keep her heart her own.

Because if it broke again, she'd never be able to recover.

Violet sighed and stared at the ceiling without seeing it. She did notice, however, that they'd knocked the picture on the wall askew. It hung over their heads, a few feet above the headboard, and was tilted distinctly to one side. That was rather funny. "I think we were a little overly vigorous," Violet said with a smile and pointed at the picture.

And just then, she noticed the picture itself. With a gasp, she sat up and whirled around to stare at the picture. It was a giclee, a mass-produced print of a pastoral scene that was probably sold in multiple hotel catalogs full of ugly but unobtrusive furnishings. She hadn't paid a bit of attention to it before, and she probably wouldn't have noticed it now except for one thing: the pastoral scene of a river that flowed toward a mill and a gigantic waterwheel.

A wheel.

"Do you see what I see?" she asked, pointing at the picture.

Jonathan sat up. After a moment, he laughed and quoted the first line of the poem again. "'Turn, Fortune, turn thy wheel.'"

"You think that's our wheel?" Violet asked eagerly. She hobbled forward on her knees on the bed and pulled the picture off the wall, looking at the back of it. Nothing.

"Well, my note did say Kallista Hotel," Jonathan agreed. He ran a hand over the cardboard backing of the cheap picture. "So it has to be something with this hotel."

Violet stared at it, thinking. "This isn't an original. I wonder if the other rooms have a similar painting in them?"

Jonathan gave her a musing look. "You want me to rent out the entire hotel?"

"Can you do that?"

He gave her that slow, lazy smile that made her heart turn over. "A billionaire can do whatever he wants, love."

THIRTEEN

⟨⟩

The next morning, Jonathan had rented out every room on their floor—the second floor. They'd gone through every room and only found two with the same painting as the one she'd been staring at in bed, and neither had a message written on them.

They'd returned back to Jonathan's room, no closer than when they'd started.

Puzzled and frustrated, Violet returned to the poem, studying it over and over again. "That has to be the wheel. It has to."

She leaned over the tablet, staring at the scanned message and wishing inspiration would strike.

As she did, Jonathan leaned over and murmured in her ear, "Shall I rent out another floor?"

"That's just a waste of money if we're on the wrong track," Violet said, though she shivered at the feel of his breath caressing her ear.

"You know I don't care about the money," he said, and leaned in and kissed the side of her neck.

Violet gasped and arched, giving him more access to her throat. After last night's marathon loving, they'd slept for a few hours, and she'd woken up to Jonathan's hungry kisses in the middle of the night. They'd made love twice more, each time more fierce than the last, and when dawn had hit, Violet had fallen into an exhausted, dazed slumber.

Even now she was curled up in the blankets, naked, and seated at the table in their room despite the late afternoon hour. After finding no luck with the second floor, they'd returned to their room and made love again.

And again.

Jonathan had just showered and he smelled fresh and clean, and she wanted to lick the droplets of water off of his bronzed skin. God, the man was delicious.

"Some of us are trying to work here," she teased him as he continued to nibble at her neck. She squirmed away from him with a grin and pointed at the tablet. "Look what you made me do." Her fingers had hit the screen when he'd kissed her and she'd accidentally zoomed in, the handwriting on the note enlarging to an extreme degree.

"It's fine," Jonathan said, his mouth moving to her ear and his nibbling continuing onto her earlobe. "Just ignore it. We'll work on it later."

"You're incorrigible," she told him with a grin.

"Mmm, big teacher word there." He gently bit her earlobe and slid a hand into the blanket, cupping one of her breasts. "That turns me on."

"Everything turns you on," she teased.

"Everything about you," he agreed, and she forgot all about working for the next few hours.

———

When Violet begged for mercy, Jonathan got dressed and headed downstairs to get them something to drink. They'd cleaned out the minibar of bottled water during their steamy night, and they were both thirsty. As she waited for Jonathan,

Violet took a quick shower and pulled on one of Jonathan's shirts, since her clothes were still in her room. He wouldn't mind her borrowing it; heck, he'd probably like the way the slogan on the front of the T-shirt stretched tight across her breasts.

While she waited for him, Violet grabbed the tablet and returned to the bed, determined to puzzle out the poem. The tablet was still open to the screen she'd left it at, and the giant font glared at her as soon as she tapped the screen. She flicked her fingers over the surface, trying to reduce the font down, and as she did, she noticed something curious: the "i" in the second line seemed to be darker than the rest of the lettering. It was impossible to tell when she was viewing it from afar, but close up, it was clearly darker.

Curious, Violet scanned through the rest of the poem. A few more letters were also darker. She got a pen and a piece of scratch paper from the bedside table and began to mark them down.

Turn, Fortune, turn thy wheel, and lower the proud;
Turn thy wild wheel thro' sunshine, storm, and cloud;
Thy wheel and thee we neither love nor hate.

Turn, Fortune, turn thy wheel with smile or frown;
With that wild wheel we go not up or down;
Our hoard is little, but our hearts are great.

Smile and we smile, the lords of many lands;
Frown and we smile, the lords of our own hands;
For man is man and master of his fate.

Turn, turn thy wheel above the staring crowd;
Thy wheel and thou are shadows in the cloud;
Thy wheel and thee we neither love nor hate.

She stared at her notes, thinking. IVIIIII meant nothing to her. There were no darker symbols in the last paragraph, so she wondered if the spacing had anything to do with it. On a hunch, she separated out the letters by paragraph. IV III III.

Roman numerals.

433.

The Kallista Hotel had four floors.

She gasped. That was it. It had been in front of their faces all this time. They just hadn't paid attention to the lettering because they'd been so focused on the poem.

The door opened and Jonathan came into the room with a plastic grocery bag filled with bottles of water and a small bag of what smelled like fresh baklava. "I thought you might be hungry—"

She launched herself from the bed with a squeal and leapt for his arms. "I figured it out!"

Jonathan dropped the bags and held on to her as she flung herself against him. "You got it?"

"I got it! Room 433!" She grinned up at him, her arms going around his neck. "Ten bucks says that the room has one of these ugly wheel paintings."

"How did you solve it?" His hands went to her backside, and he groaned. "And why aren't you wearing panties?"

She was dressed in nothing but one of his T-shirts. "I'm wearing this because I haven't left your room in the past twenty-four hours," she teased. She grabbed his hand and dragged him to the bed. "Look, I'll show you."

He sat down on the bed and she crawled in next to him, pulling over the tablet and her notes, showing him her discovery.

"That's incredible," Jonathan murmured, and then turned to look at her, a smile on his face. "*You're* incredible."

Violet beamed at him, ecstatic. She'd figured this one out on her own. And with him smiling at her, she did feel pretty incredible. At that moment, Violet felt like she could take over the world.

And when his gaze went from smiling at her to down at her mouth, Violet realized he was aroused. Grabbing her bare ass had distracted him, it seemed. And she was feeling rather sexy and empowered herself. She wanted him, and she wanted to be the one in control.

So, with a wicked expression on her face, Violet leaned in for a kiss. As his mouth met hers, she placed her hand between his legs and stroked the bulge in his pants.

Jonathan groaned, his hand tightening over hers. "What about the room?"

"It can wait," she said, stroking his cock through his jeans. "It's my turn to be in charge." With a smile, she moved her hand to his chest and gave him a subtle nudge, indicating he should lie back.

Jonathan fell backward onto the bed, his eyes hot as he watched her.

With sure hands, she grabbed the buckle of his belt and undid it, stroking her hand over his cock every so often to keep him excited. Next were the buttons on his fly, and then she was shoving his jeans down his hips. He lifted them to help her, and she grabbed his boxers next, pulling them down and exposing what she wanted—his cock.

He was erect and ready for her, thick and hard already. Violet gave a little shiver of pleasure at the sight of that and leaned over him. "I've been wanting to do this to you for days."

"Have you?" he whispered, his voice ragged.

"Oh, yes." Her hand slid around the base of him, encircling him with her fingers. She loved the thickness of him, loved the smooth flesh of his cock, the soft skin peppered with raised veins that felt fascinating under her fingers. "That's why it was such torture for me to have my hands bound last night. I wanted to grab this and take it into my mouth."

He groaned.

"But there's nothing stopping me now, is there?" Her

voice was breathy with desire. She leaned down and licked the head of him, loving the way his body clenched and tensed as she did. "And it's just as tasty as I thought."

Jonathan said nothing, but his hand went to her hair and wrapped in the strands there, as if needing an anchor.

She liked that. Violet licked him again, and again, using her tongue to bathe the head of his cock in firm, teasing strokes. She circled the divot in the center with her tongue, lapping up the pre-cum that beaded there. "You're delicious, you know that?"

"Not as delicious as you," he murmured. "I love the taste of you on my tongue."

"Yes, but now it's my turn," she purred. "So don't distract me." And when he started to speak again, she took the head of him fully into her mouth and sucked.

His head fell back on the blankets and he groaned.

Violet made a soft sound of pleasure low in her throat, and with one hand on his shaft, the other moved to his sac and began to massage it as she continued to suck on the head of his cock, rubbing it with the tip of her tongue. She pumped him with one hand, leaning over him, and then began to take him deeper, working him into her mouth with slow, easy motions. She loved teasing him with her lips and tongue, his cock filling up her mouth and making her stretch to take him in.

"Violet," he groaned as she squeezed her hand around the base and continued to suck him deep. "I'm not going to last."

She released him with an audible pop. "Poor baby," she murmured, not sorry in the slightest, and leaned down to give him another wicked lick. "Is big bad Violet going to make you lose control?"

His fingers dug into her scalp. "She is. She's a wicked woman."

"Mmm, I like that," she said in a low voice, and then bent over his cock again to take him into her mouth once more.

This time, when she took him deep, she felt his hand press against the back of her head, a silent suggestion for more. She was happy to oblige, pumping him with her mouth over and over again.

Then, she felt him tense underneath her. "Violet, I'm going to come—"

She made a little hum in her throat, to let him know that was all right, and sucked him deeper.

With a curse, she felt him buck, and his cock hit the back of her throat. Then, she felt his hot seed spurt, pouring down the back of her throat, and he gave a pained, ecstatic groan. "Oh, God, *Violet.*"

She pulled off of him slowly, swallowing his spend, and then gave the head of his cock a parting kiss. That, she decided, was entirely too fun. "You certainly didn't last long for a man who can torture me for hours on end."

He groaned and threw an arm over his forehead, still panting. "I can't help it. You have an incredible mouth."

"Flattery," she teased, then slid off the bed.

"Where are you going?"

"I'm going to brush my teeth, and then we're going to go check out room 433," she called to him, feeling rather satisfied with herself.

He groaned again and didn't move from the bed. "Give a guy a minute to recover?"

"A minute," she teased again. "But only that long."

———

Violet returned to her own hotel room to get dressed.

She'd snuck out of Jonathan's room wearing not much more than a towel and dashed to her own room, which was just a few doors down. Thank goodness they had the whole floor to themselves. Then, after she'd dressed and fuxed her hair, Violet stared at her reflection in the mirror, blushing. Her neck was covered with bright red hickies that her short hair didn't quite sweep over. That was going to be rather obvious to the world, wasn't it? But . . . she kinda didn't mind it. Slipping on a pair of shoes, Violet headed back out of her room and Jonathan was waiting for her in the hallway.

Downstairs, the girl at the front desk had bad news for them. "I'm afraid room 433 is occupied."

"It's important that I have that room," Jonathan explained, pulling out his money clip and dragging crisp hundred-dollar bills from the stack. "What will it take?"

"I'm sorry, sir," the girl at the desk said apologetically. "I can contact the people currently in the room and see if they're willing to switch, but I can't force them to."

Violet put her hand over Jonathan's money, lowering his hand before he could start flinging money at the girl. She smiled at the front desk attendant and then snagged Jonathan's arm, dragging him away. When they were out of earshot, Violet suggested, "Why don't we go up and ask if we can talk to them for a minute?" They didn't need the whole room, just the painting.

Theoretically. They could still be wrong about it.

Jonathan looked over at Violet and then nodded, putting his money away. He pulled her under his arm, casually dragging her against his side. "Let's see what we can do, then."

A few minutes later, they'd headed up to the fourth floor and found the room they were looking for. A "Do Not Disturb" tag was hanging from the door.

"Oh, no," Violet said. "Maybe we should come back later."

Jonathan ignored it and knocked on the door.

She winced, anticipating an angry man showing up to berate them. A minute passed, and then she heard someone shuffling to the door. It opened a crack a moment later, the chain still on the door, and an old man peered out at them. He stared at Violet and Jonathan. "We have enough towels."

"I'm not here with towels, sir," Jonathan said, smiling.

"We were wondering if we could see the painting in your room," Violet interjected. The man was looking at them rather suspiciously, and the last thing she wanted was for him to call the front desk and get them kicked out of the hotel. It didn't matter how many rooms Jonathan was renting; if he harassed the other guests, he could still get booted.

The man shook his head, and started to close the door.

Jonathan stuck his foot in the crack. "I will pay you ten thousand dollars to give us that painting on the wall."

The man's eyes widened.

"It's true," Violet chimed in. "He's loaded. I promise. Show him, Jonathan."

On cue, Jonathan took out his money clip and waved it at the man.

He stared at it for a moment longer, and then held out his hand. Jonathan removed his foot from the door and handed the man the wad of money. The door shut and Violet felt a twinge of worry. What if he didn't open it again?

But a moment later, he did, and Violet and Jonathan smiled nervously at the old man, who was dressed in nothing but an undershirt and a pair of old boxers. On the bed, his elderly wife sat, wearing a floral bathrobe, the remote in her hand.

He gestured that Violet and Jonathan could enter.

"We just want the painting," Violet said quickly. This was so awkward.

"Take it," the man said. "It's an ugly thing."

"Thank you," Jonathan said, and strode for the bed. Violet bit her cheek to keep her face impassive as Jonathan pulled the painting off of the wall, nodded at the old couple, and then headed out the door. She trailed behind him, holding in her excitement. Jonathan was unreadable, his face stone, as they walked to the elevator.

When the elevator doors shut, he turned and grinned at her. "That went well."

She snorted, twisting her hands together as she stared at the painting in his hands. "If you call handing over all your money 'well,' then yes, I guess it did."

"That's pocket change."

For him, maybe. For the rest of the world, it was a life-changing amount. She shook her head and focused on the picture. "Is there anything on the back of the painting?"

"Not that I see. We'll pull it apart once we get back to my room. Our room," he corrected. "I want you moving into it tonight."

That was high-handed of him. "You haven't asked me," she said in a light voice.

"That's because you're mine, and I plan on licking you for hours to ensure that you know it," he said, that intense look on his face again.

All right, that convinced her. "Well, then." Violet fanned her flushed cheeks with her hand.

The elevator dinged and they returned to their floor. She wanted to run for the room, her anticipation sky-high, but she forced herself to walk slowly and steadily next to Jonathan, who didn't seem to be in the same anxious hurry that she was.

But then, a few moments later, they were in his room. Jonathan set the painting down on the bed and it was almost identical to the painting in their room. This one was a different angle of the pastoral scene, and the water-wheel dominated most of the picture.

"This has to be it," Violet said excitedly.

Jonathan turned it over and ran a hand along the cheap cardboard backing. "Let's see if we can't pull this off."

Violet watched anxiously as he pried up the tabs on the back and slowly removed the backing. There, on the underside, taped to the mat, were two envelopes with a single word written on the cover of each. The handwriting was familiar. *Violet. Jonathan.* One for each of them.

"That's it," Violet breathed. She reached for the envelope with her name, tracing her fingers over her father's handwriting. On the back, she could feel her father's wax seal. He'd gone to so much trouble for all of this. She didn't understand.

In her experience, her father was a man who was interested in little beyond his own personal wants. To arrange all of this for her to discover—with Jonathan at her side—after his death? It made her wonder if there would only be the stele and journals at the end of this scavenger hunt, or if there would be something more meaningful.

Jonathan picked up the envelope with his name. "Do you want to open yours first?"

She ran a finger along the edges of the thick envelope, curiously hesitant. "Ten bucks says it's another poem," she told him, trying to keep the teasing note in her voice and failing. For some reason, she was oddly emotional. What if this was the last envelope? It would be the last tie to her father. A man she'd never been close to, yet who, after his death, had wanted to involve her in this enough that he'd dragged Jonathan into it.

She didn't know how she felt about any of this. Steeling herself, she broke the wax seal on the envelope and pulled out the paper inside and began to read.

> *"I went to the Garden of Love,*
> *And saw what I never had seen:*
> *A Chapel was built in the midst,*
> *Where I used to play on the green.*
>
> *And the gates of this Chapel were shut,*
> *And Thou shalt not writ over the door;*
> *So I turn'd to the Garden of Love,*
> *That so many sweet flowers bore.*
>
> *And I saw it was filled with graves,*
> *And tomb-stones where flowers should be:*
> *And Priests in black gowns, were walking their*
> *   rounds,*
> *And binding with briars, my joys & desires."*

Violet blinked as she finished reading it. "Wow. That's . . . grim." She looked at Jonathan. "What do you think?"

His mouth tightened. "Seems to me that it's about the loss of love."

Of course it was. Was this another slap from her father beyond the grave? Violet examined the writing but didn't see anything bolded or out of the ordinary. She shook her head and folded the note, returning it to its envelope. "I'm not sure what I make of that."

"Perhaps it makes more sense with mine," Jonathan suggested, and ripped open one end of his envelope, removing his own slip of paper. He scanned it quickly, then made a sound in his throat.

"What?" Violet asked, scarcely breathing. "What does it say?"

Wordless, he held the paper out to her.

She plucked it from his hand and read it. *There is a latch under my gravestone that opens a secret compartment. You'll find the answers you seek there.*

Violet felt cold. Goose bumps rose on her arms. He was sending them back to his grave? His grave was in Detroit. At home. He'd sent them to England and New Mexico, and now Greece . . . all so she could go back home? "I don't understand."

"Violet," Jonathan said softly. He reached out and stroked her arm. "Are you all right?"

"I don't know," she answered. It was an honest response, too. She didn't know how she felt. Part of her was furiously angry, and part of her was disappointed. "He sent us all over the place just to have us turn around and go right back to Detroit? What was the point? Why not just send us there in the first place?"

"Maybe there was a message, a meaning of some kind, in each of the locations and the poems."

Her lip curled with anger. "Each poem basically sounded like it was berating me for being a bad daughter who ignored her dear old dad. If that's his message and I'm supposed to be shamed by it, he failed."

"It's all right," he soothed her, pulling her against him in a one-armed hug. "We'll figure it out once we go to his grave. The note says that all our answers are there."

She pulled away from Jonathan, shaking her head. "I don't want to go."

"What?"

"This is nothing but manipulation. All of this." She gestured at the letters "It's just another one of his stupid games. What are we going to find at the end of this? A copy of his favorite lecture? His favorite book?"

"I'm hoping to find my stele," Jonathan said quietly. "His notes would be a bonus, of course, but I want to take the stele back to the excavation in Cadiz."

She shook her head. After all this emotional turmoil between herself and Jonathan, after being dragged from country to country, only to find out that her father just wanted her to visit his grave? She felt manipulated by him once again. "I don't want to go."

Jonathan's voice was low, calm. "I'll be with you, Violet. It's fine. He can't hurt you any longer. We're together again. It's like the last ten years didn't happen."

It was like he'd slapped her across the face.

The last ten years didn't happen? Like hell they didn't. Violet's body went cold. Her heart felt like ice. "But the last ten years *did* happen. We can't change that."

"It's just a bad memory now."

She flinched. It wasn't just a bad memory for her. Fuck that. She'd been abandoned and devastated, and had lost everything. He'd mooned over her while living the high life. She'd rebuilt herself over again.

He might have spent the last ten years longing for her in-between archaeological expeditions and trips all over the world, but she'd been through hell. She'd been through hell . . . and come out the other side a stronger, more independent person. She knew the difference between love, lust, and need.

And she wasn't about to forget the last ten years simply because she was lusting after Jonathan right now.

Ten years ago, Violet DeWitt had needed Jonathan Lyons and he'd abandoned her. The twenty-nine-year-old Violet DeWitt didn't need anyone.

And even after ten years, Jonathan Lyons still didn't understand her.

Calmly, Violet refolded the letter and placed it in its envelope, and held it out to Jonathan to take. "Just because you don't want to think about the last ten years doesn't mean that they didn't happen. They aren't a mistake you can erase. You can't pretend they don't exist. It happened, and we need to learn from it."

Even as she said the words, she felt a twinge of remorse. Ten years ago, being in Jonathan's bed had gotten her pregnant and abandoned. Now it seemed she was making the same mistakes all over again.

"Violet, that's not what I meant—" He reached for her.

She drew away, getting to her feet. "I need to think, Jonathan."

He got to his feet as well, following her as she headed for the door. "Where are you going?"

"Back to my room."

"So you can think? Think about what?"

She looked at him calmly. "Maybe I'm going to think about the last ten years. Because they sure as hell happened for me."

"Violet, you know I didn't mean it like that—"

"Actually, Jonathan, I don't know that." Her voice was ice. "I do know I made a mistake ten years ago when I fell into your bed, got into trouble, and expected you to come rescue me. That rescue never came and I had to learn the hard way that you can't depend on anyone but yourself. And here I am, ten years later, back in the same position I found myself in before. And I'm not very proud of that."

Jonathan's face had gone stark. "Violet," he breathed. "I love you. That hasn't changed—"

Softly, she patted him on the chest. "You might not have changed, Jonathan, but I have. And now I need time to think."

She turned to the door and opened it, only to find Jonathan's hand on her arm. "Violet. Please don't go." There was a wealth of pain in his voice. "What I said, I'm sorry. I didn't mean—"

"I know," she said. "I know you didn't mean it harshly. But it still stands—you don't mind forgetting the last ten years, and I do. I can't go back to that girl I was. And I need you to want the woman I am."

"I do—"

She gave him a soft, sweet smile. "And I need to see if I still want the same things I did ten years ago." She pulled her hand from his chest. "I need to think, Jonathan. Just let me be for a bit, all right?"

And Violet turned and left, not entirely sure if she was pleased or relieved—or disappointed—that he didn't follow her out.

———

It's like the last ten years didn't happen.

It's just a bad memory now.

Those two lines played in Violet's mind over and over again, like a bad recording stuck on a loop. She lay flat on her back on her bed all afternoon, unmoving and staring at the ceiling as she thought.

She thought about Jonathan—the Jonathan of the past, and the Jonathan of the present. She thought about her father and his manipulative games. She thought about the baby she'd lost ten years ago. She thought about her job back in Detroit, her students, her friends, and her colleagues there.

Jonathan wanted to pretend like the past just didn't happen, and she couldn't do that. And it hurt to think that he'd even suggest such a thing. Mistakes had happened, and she'd learned from them, grown from them. Grew smarter, stronger, tougher. She'd hurt, she'd cried, and she'd learned.

She couldn't go back to the girl she was ten years ago, and she didn't want to.

And for Jonathan to ask her to do that wounded her soul.

He didn't know her at all if he said that to her. Then again, he hadn't gone through the pain of loss that she had. She'd grieved both a relationship and a baby. His words made her wonder if he'd ever really felt as if he'd lost her, or if he'd temporarily written her off.

And now that they'd spent a few weeks together, he expected her to just jump back into bed with him and into his life as if no time had passed?

To be fair, she was the idiot crawling all over his bed, so she wasn't blameless. Even though she loved being with Jonathan again, sexually, she still didn't know how she felt about that gap in their relationship. She didn't know if she could ever get past that. The sex was great, but what was sex without love? Jonathan said he loved her, but . . . she didn't know.

She just didn't know anything anymore.

FOURTEEN

After agonizing for hours, Violet made up her mind.

She quietly packed her bags and dressed for a flight home. She called in a ticket at the airport, arranged for a taxi, and when she could put it off no longer, she headed down the hall for Jonathan's room.

Her heart ached and felt like a stone in her breast. Just this morning, she'd been happy, so incredibly, stupidly happy. But that happiness was exceedingly fragile; it had only taken one offhand comment from Jonathan for her to realize just how much they didn't know about each other.

And she was too responsible now to plunge headlong into another bad relationship that would only leave her aching and empty again. Better to cut her losses now, while she still could. If she got in any deeper, she might not be able to stand it.

Tucking her hair behind her ears, Violet clutched her purse close and knocked at Jonathan's hotel room door. She heard him bound across the room and the door swung open. Jonathan stood there, his shirt rumpled, his hair a mess, and his face looking tired and aged, despite the fact she'd seen him only a few hours ago.

"Violet," he murmured, and held the door open wider. "Come in."

"Actually," she said softly, "I can't." Her heart ached and tears threatened. "I came to tell you good-bye."

"No," he breathed. His eyes narrowed, grew hard. "Violet, no. Don't do this to me." He reached for her as if he wanted to hold her, and then drew back, as if sensing she would pull away. "Violet, please. Let's talk about this—"

"There's nothing to talk about, Jonathan. I just . . . Coming here was a mistake. I allowed myself to be sucked in, and I think it's time I went home and went back to my normal life before I get pulled in too deep. It was great seeing you, but I can't do this."

"We don't have to go to your father's grave," he said quickly. The look in his eyes was tense. "We can forget he ever started this scavenger hunt bullshit. Just stay with me. *Please.*"

She shook her head, backing away a step or two. "Don't make this more difficult than it already is—"

"Make this more difficult?" He barked a laugh and it was hard, ugly. "It doesn't seem like it's difficult for you to leave me at all. This is the second time things have gotten intense and you've turned and ran."

"That's not fair." She clutched her purse against her side like it was a lifeline.

"I don't give a shit about fair, Violet. I love you." His voice was ragged, and the pain on his face was terrible to see. "I've always loved you. It's never changed."

"But *I've* changed, Jonathan. I think that's where we keep having a difference of opinion. I have changed and I don't know that you have." Her smile was apologetic, sad.

"You're not even giving me a chance. Goddamn it, Violet, at least give me a chance!"

She knew she wasn't. But she also knew she didn't have to give him a chance. It was obvious to her how these things would turn out. "Let's say I did. Let's say I jumped right back into your bed and we continued on our merry way. What then?"

His brows furrowed. "What do you mean?"

"I mean, what happens next for us?"

He looked exasperated by her question. "Whatever you want. I don't care, Violet, as long as we're together. That's all that matters to me."

"Yes, but you have a life, and friends. So do I. You have archaeological expeditions you're supporting and a car company to run. I have school to teach. You're based out of New York, aren't you? I'm in Detroit. These things don't mesh really well. When would we see each other?"

He opened his mouth, and then snapped it shut again, eyes narrowing as if sensing a trap.

She raised a hand into the air, a mute apology. "I know. There's no right answer. You can't just give up your business and your pursuits to come hang out with me while I teach, and I can't just abandon school and my students just so I can be your girlfriend."

"Violet—"

She shook her head. "Don't you see? We've moved on. Moved past."

"I don't see that at all," he said, his voice rising. "I see you trying to shut me out again—"

"That's not true—"

"You won't even let me finish a sentence," he snapped. "Is it because you won't like what I'm trying to say? Because it's easier to just decide that you already have your mind made up about me, and you'll just go on with your life without me?"

Her mouth clamped shut and she glared at him, irritation rising to the forefront. She'd been hurting when she'd approached his door, and now he was trying to turn this around on her? When he didn't say anything else—heaven forbid she interrupt him—she gave a small sigh. "I'm not here to argue with you—"

"No, you're just here to leave me." He raked a hand through his hair and looked so tormented that she felt a twinge of doubt. "Violet, please. Whatever you want, I'll make it happen. I just don't want to lose you again."

Her mouth forced itself into a wobbling smile. "What's that old saying about loving something and setting it free?"

"Don't," he said harshly, and he averted his face, as if in pain.

"I'm sorry, Jonathan. I just . . . I just can't. I can't rely on anyone else for my happiness. It has to come from within me."

"You make me happy, Violet."

His eyes were curiously shiny, and that made her heart ache even more. It made what she had to say doubly difficult. "Yes, but I'm not sure if I feel the same."

He closed his eyes. "Let me try to make you happy. Please, Violet. Just give me a chance."

She shook her head. "Good-bye, Jonathan. Don't come after me, okay? Set me free."

Before he could say anything else, she leaned forward, gave him a quick peck on the cheek, and then turned and raced for the elevator. If she looked back, she'd regret it. If she saw the pain in his eyes, it would just compound the pain she was feeling right now. But she knew that this was pain she could get over. She'd gotten over it once. She could do so again.

As she hit the button for the elevator, she distantly heard the sound of a lamp smashing into a wall.

———

Violet was gone again. His Violet had abandoned him once more. She said it was to spare them both, but he knew the truth. Violet was scared, and so she was running again.

Don't come after me, okay? Set me free.

God. He clenched his fists, his shoulders heaving as he looked for something else to throw. The TV was close by, and he grabbed the flatscreen and slammed it into the wall, viciously enjoying the shower of broken pieces that rained down onto the carpets.

Fuck *everything*.

His heart had just been pulled out of his chest and stomped on by a petite, gorgeous woman who he loved with all of his soul. Someone who he didn't make happy. That gnawed at him worse than anything. *He couldn't make her happy*. Even if she stayed with him, she'd still be miserable.

He couldn't win her love back. There was no love for her to give him.

Violet didn't even want to try. He thought she was letting down her walls, letting him back into her heart. Instead, she'd closed right back up again and shut him out as if she felt nothing for him. As if *he* was nothing.

And he was helpless to do anything about it. She didn't want him to come after her.

She didn't want him at all.

With an angry snarl of rage, he ran his hands over the dresser, smashing everything on it to the ground.

————

Without Violet's beautiful, smiling face at his side, Dr. DeWitt's postmortem scavenger hunt held no meaning for Jonathan. He left sunny Santorini and headed for his newest pet project, the dig in Cadiz, but even the glowingly enthusiastic reports from the archaeology team couldn't rouse him out of the dark cloud of apathy hanging over his head.

After two days in Spain, he headed back to New York to bury himself in work. While Lyons Motors had a fleet of extremely capable chairmen and his private company ran itself without much intervention from the owner, from time to time, he'd stick his hands in and toy with a new project. This time, he suggested that research and development come up with a new model of car to break into a different market. It was a distraction ploy, but not a great one. He called meetings and met with engineers and designers and listened to enthusiastic suggestions, hoping to feel that same spark inside himself.

It was useless. No matter what he did, he couldn't get Violet's dead eyes and her too-calm expression out of his mind. The way she'd so efficiently cut him out of her life again.

Last time, she'd begged him to come home with her. This time, it was obvious she was booting him before she had the chance to get hurt again. In the ten years since they'd been parted, Violet had learned to push everyone away. She'd been perfectly happy with him that morning, but as soon as her father's letters had been found, she'd shut him down and forced him out of her life.

And the sad thing was, he understood why she'd pushed him away. He knew she had been hurt terribly, both by her father and by him. He knew she was terrified of being hurt again. But how could he prove that he wouldn't hurt her when she didn't even want to try and let him into her life?

He couldn't sleep at night because he ached to have her beside him. He couldn't concentrate during the days because he kept wondering what Violet was doing. Was she as miserable as he was? Or was she already back into her old routine, her heart carefully armored? Or was she crying and miserable because she wanted to love him and she was terrified to? What if the condoms and her birth control had both failed and she was somehow pregnant again? And he'd abandoned her once more?

He picked up the phone and put it down a dozen times every day. If he called her, he'd be harassing her because she'd said specifically that she didn't want him to contact her. She had his information; she knew where to get him. He told himself that, and that if there was a problem, or if she wanted him, she'd call.

But Violet never called, and Jonathan was forced to admit to himself that maybe his love was one-sided after all. Maybe he loved Violet more than she'd ever loved him.

Maybe one person's love just wasn't enough for a relationship.

"You look like shit, man," Reese called as Jonathan sat in his familiar spot at the poker table.

"Business meeting ran late," he said tonelessly, picking up his empty glass and raising it with the other five men as they called their meeting of the Brotherhood to order. *"Fratres in prosperitatum,"* he announced with the others. They'd been waiting on him to start their weekly meeting.

"This meeting of the Brotherhood is called into session," Logan said. "Now, ante up, boys." He began to deal cards around the table as the men settled in for a long night of cards, cigars, and business talk.

Jonathan put down his empty glass and pushed it to the side of the table. Normally he'd enjoy a bit of Scotch with his cards, but he'd lost all taste for alcohol ever since he'd seen that awful look in Violet's eyes when he'd drunk himself into a stupor. Not that it mattered if he drank anymore, if Violet was cutting him out of her life. He considered the glass, and then shook his head. To Jonathan, it still mattered.

"Seriously, you look like shit," Reese told him, chewing on the end of an expensive cigar as he picked up his cards. "Everything okay?"

"Fine," Jonathan said, his tone clipped. Hopefully that would end the conversation.

"You should be in a good mood," Hunter said, his voice gravelly and rough. The scarred billionaire sat directly across from Jonathan, and for once, his fiancée wasn't perched in his lap. "No girls tonight."

Jonathan snorted to hide the twinge of envy he felt. It seemed like all his friends had paired off in the last year. Their weekly meetings were frequently interrupted by Reese's new wife, Hunter's fiancée, and Logan's bride-to-be. Even Griffin, the starchiest asshole of their bunch, had recently gotten engaged and tended to let his frizzy-headed girlfriend lead him around by the balls. Quite happily, if the content look on Griffin's face was any indicator. The last bachelor of their group was Cade.

He frowned. And himself. He was still a bachelor, even though in his heart, he'd always been claimed by Violet.

Hand after hand of poker blurred together with familiar discussions. Jonathan was mostly silent, though he mentioned the new line of roadsters he was developing when it came time for him to share his latest business dealings with the group. Mostly, though, he was just distracted.

He couldn't get his mind off of Violet. Was she regretting her hasty retreat? Or did she just not even care? If he knew Violet—and he thought he did—she was pushing any sort of emotion so far down inside that she wouldn't feel anything. She'd just go about her day, armored and icy, until something set her off. And then she'd explode in a fury of tears and misery.

And that made his heart clench even more. He wasn't even pissed at Violet for pushing him away; he just dreaded when her control finally slipped and she broke down, because he wanted to be the one to comfort her. She needed a shoulder to cry on, even if it was his.

Sometime close to midnight, Jonathan threw his last chips into the pile. "All in." He knew it was a bad hand— he'd been betting recklessly all night and had lost a small fortune on the table. Not that he cared. He just wanted to be done. He wanted to go home and lick his wounds and mull over the loss of Violet for a bit longer.

Frankly, he was shit company tonight.

He was glad when Cade won the hand. "I'm out," Jonathan said with a fake grimace. "Just as well. Time for me to call it a night anyhow." He stood from the table, said his good-byes to his friends, and headed up the stairs and out of the club, heading to his reserved parking spot.

"Wait up," a voice called behind him as he pulled his keys out.

Jonathan turned, frowning at Cade Archer, who'd followed him out. The blond man had his hands shoved in his light-colored jacket and was squinting down the street, looking for his driver who was likely hovering nearby with Cade's ride. Archer headed over to Jonathan and paused nearby.

"What is it?" Jonathan asked, his voice terse.

"Just wondering how things went with Violet," Cade inquired. "You two have a lot of history."

"Fuck off."

"That well, huh?" Cade's grin remained. "I'm sorry to hear that. I know you care for her very much."

Jonathan clenched his teeth, his hand tight around his keys. Part of him wanted to punch Cade in the mouth—Cade, who was the definition of kindness—and part of him wanted to spill his guts.

"Can I ask what happened?" Cade said after Jonathan hesitated.

"She closed me out again."

"Again?"

He gritted his teeth. "I thought you knew this story already?"

"Humor me."

"Ten years ago, Violet asked me to run away with her. I declined and she left without me. It seems she begged me to come after her and I never got the message. She was pregnant and miscarried my baby." It felt like a raw wound just admitting it aloud. God, he was a shitty man. He didn't deserve a woman like Violet. He had to force the next words out of his throat. "This time, we fucked and she got scared and left me again. Told me not to follow her."

"Mmm," was all Cade said.

That wasn't what Jonathan wanted to hear. "What the hell does that mean?"

"So she asked you to follow her before and you didn't?"

"I didn't know she was pregnant. Her father told me she'd gone home and married someone else. I thought . . . I thought she was gone."

"So you didn't fight for her. Did you even call her to see if she was okay? To close the door? So you could both move on?"

He ground his teeth again, his jaw clenched. "No. I was pissed." And hurt. And nineteen, fresh off of losing his first and only love.

"Mmm."

"Goddamn it, *what*?"

"She got scared and left you this time, and you're here?"

He scowled at Cade. "She told me not to follow her."

Cade looked nonplussed at Jonathan's increasingly violent mood. He scuffed one of his expensive leather shoes on the sidewalk and glanced back at the club, which was still throbbing with bass despite the late hour. "When I talked with Violet, I got the impression that she didn't have a very happy childhood. She seems to resent her father quite a bit. That so?"

Jonathan nodded brusquely, not sure where this was going.

"So did it ever occur to you that Violet expects everyone she cares for to disappoint her? Maybe it's easier for her to retreat than to extend herself and try to make things work."

Jonathan just stared at him.

"And so I wonder . . . I mean, of course she's going to push you away. You've hurt her in the past and she's afraid of being hurt again. I guess I'm wondering why you're not fighting for her."

His mouth went dry.

Of course.

He was so fucking stupid. So lost in his own misery that it didn't even occur to him to go after her. It all seemed so incredibly obvious now. Violet was pushing him away because she was scared of being hurt. He didn't go after her last time and he'd lost her for ten years. This time, there was nothing holding them back but fear.

And Jonathan needed to show Violet he wasn't afraid.

He grabbed Cade by the collar. "You are a genius, you know that?"

Cade grinned. "Glad I could be of help."

FIFTEEN

Violet sipped her cup of coffee and stared at the new sign in front of Neptune Middle School as the workers adjusted it. There was some sort of sick irony in knowing that she'd have to walk in to work every day at Jonathan Lyons Middle School. Fate was a cruel, cruel bitch that way.

"Hey, long time, no see," someone said behind her, and Violet turned away from the sign and saw her friend Kirsten. "Glad to have you back," Kirsten said with a grin, an identical cup of drive-thru coffee in her hand. "How was the vacation?"

"It was interesting," Violet said, keeping her voice light. She sipped her coffee so she wouldn't have to say more than that. Kirsten fell into step next to her, and the two teachers headed into the school.

"Well, you didn't miss too much here," Kirsten said, tucking her brown hair into a clip with her other hand in a way that bespoke years of practice. "More meetings, more detentions, though we did get some additional funding for the band program thanks to your mysterious benefactor."

She sounded thrilled; Kirsten was the band teacher, and for her, everything circled back to woodwinds and brasses. "You got a nice tan, at least. Where did you guys go?"

"Greece," Violet murmured, and at Kirsten's groan of excitement, she added, "purely for research, though."

"Man. Greece! You tell that billionaire if he needs a band teacher, I'm first in line."

A stab of jealousy shot through Violet. Kirsten would be Jonathan's type, wouldn't she? She was bubbly and pretty and easygoing, like Violet used to be. Like Violet no longer was. If she was a good friend, she'd fix them up and kill two birds with one stone. Make Kirsten happy, and get Jonathan out of her hair for good.

But she didn't say anything. The thought bothered the hell out of her.

It's just because you're still too attached, Violet told herself. *Give yourself a few months to get over him and you'll be fine.*

She'd been repeating that as a mantra for the last week or so. It didn't stop her from crying in weak moments, or waking up at night and wishing he was there next to her. It didn't stop her from being in a foul mood, and she'd avoided returning to school until she could put it off no longer.

She just needed time, Violet told herself. Time healed all wounds. Theoretically. This one hadn't even had time to scab over yet.

So Violet listened to Kirsten chatter on about the newest piece that her students were learning, and how her only tuba player was eternally flat on every note, poor kid, and eventually Violet made it to her classroom, where her students weren't thrilled to have her back. The substitute had been letting them watch movies while she was gone, and Violet didn't see the harm in continuing that for a few days more. She put on a historical documentary about mummies and left them alone, staring out the window. Something about being home felt a bit . . . off. Violet couldn't describe it. It just felt wrong.

It wasn't until she was in the teachers' lounge bathroom during lunch hour that she got her first inkling as to what was bothering her. She was seated in one of the stalls, her head cradled in her hands. She wasn't using the bathroom, just hiding from the world. If she was in the bathroom, she wouldn't have to answer questions about Jonathan, or the trip she'd been on, and everyone at the school was curious. They meant no harm, but no one could tell from Violet's stiffly-smiling face that she didn't want to talk about it.

Someone in the next stall tapped on the adjoining wall. "You don't have a tampon, do you?"

"Of course," Violet murmured, reaching for her purse hanging on the hook. She pulled out a tampon and passed it under the stall.

"Thanks," the woman on the other side said. "Kinda snuck up on me this month."

"I've had that happen," Violet said sympathetically, and froze. Her blood felt like ice. That was what she was missing.

Her period.

Violet's heart pounded in her veins, so loud that she couldn't even hear herself think. Emotion crashed through her. No period. Oh, God. With numb fingers, she searched through her purse, pulling out her birth control compact. She popped it open and examined it. Not a day missed. And she and Jonathan had used protection, every time.

But . . . she didn't have her period.

It's just stress, Violet told herself. *Just stress. You're stressed with the whole Jonathan thing and that's why you can't sleep at night. It's throwing you off. You're not pregnant. You're not.*

But after work, she still went to the pharmacy and bought a pregnancy test. In a daze, she drove back to her condo and let herself in. The pregnancy test was in her purse, waiting.

All she had to do was pop it out of the package, pee on the stick, and she'd get results. Then she'd know if she was in the same situation that she had been ten years ago, or if she was just freaking out over nothing.

Instead of heading to the bathroom to end the torture of not knowing, though, Violet sat down on the couch and stared ahead, thinking.

She wasn't beside herself with terror this time. Maybe it was because she was no longer a college student; now, she had stability and years of living under her belt. Whatever happened, she could handle it now.

If she was pregnant . . .

She'd have to tell Jonathan. Strange how her heart leapt at the thought. They'd have a reason to be together other than pure animal lust. It would go against everything she'd been cautioning herself to avoid, but with a child, they'd have a reason to stay in each other's lives.

Her heart thrummed with excitement at the thought.

Maybe, just maybe, they could take it slow and raise the baby together, and learn each other. They could start fresh.

They could start over.

She shouldn't want to do that. It should be the last thing she wanted. But the thought of Jonathan at her side as they went to baby appointments, Jonathan touching her belly, Jonathan rocking their child back to sleep at night and then crawling back into bed with her . . .

God, she wanted that. She wanted that so badly it surprised even her. She'd broken off with Jonathan so she wouldn't get her heart hurt, but it seemed like her heart had already decided what it wanted, and it wanted Jonathan.

But she'd pushed him away.

Twisting her hands in her lap, Violet wondered what he'd think if she went to him and said she was pregnant. Would he be happy?

Or would he think she was messing with him? Her heart

dropped at the thought. He was a rich, handsome man. He could have any woman he wanted. He'd wanted Violet but she'd pushed him away twice now. He'd probably given up on her at this point.

Thanks to her own actions, she was back in the same spot she'd been ten years ago—alone, troubled, and possibly pregnant. And this time, she couldn't blame anything on her father, because she'd been the one to do all the pushing away.

She couldn't blame anyone but herself.

Violet pressed her fingertips to her mouth, feeling ill. Why had she freaked out so much when he'd said that the last ten years didn't matter?

She hadn't even wanted to listen to his explanations. She'd heard Jonathan's careless words, judged him lacking in her mind, and gone straight home. Any relationship hope? She'd cut and severed it in one fell swoop. She just decided that he was the same jerk she'd always thought he was and shut him down before he could explain. That was what she'd always done—run off and stuck her head in the sand when things got rough. And she'd done it again.

Oh, God, she was *really* going to be sick.

Her doorbell rang.

One hand pressed to her mouth, Violet stood up and automatically headed for the door. Of all the times for one of her neighbors to ask to borrow something, now was not the time. That pregnancy test was burning in the back of her mind like a brand, and she couldn't stop thinking about Jonathan, and—

She opened the door and stared dumbly at the man on her doorstep.

Jonathan looked like hell. He hadn't shaved in a few days, and there were dark circles under his eyes. His dark hair was a tousled mess, and his jacket and the shirt underneath both looked as if they'd been slept in. While his normal look was casual, she was surprised to see him so rumpled.

Heck, she was surprised to see him at all.

"Jonathan," she said, since she couldn't think of anything else to say. "W-what are you doing here?"

The look on his face was grim, stubborn. "I'm here to fight for you."

Her eyes widened. "You what?"

"I'm here to fight for you," he repeated, placing a hand on the door in case she was going to try and slam it in his face. He stepped forward, devouring her with his eyes. "I didn't fight for you last time. I just assumed you were out of reach and I let you go out of my life. I'm not making the same mistake again."

Blank with shock, she stepped aside and let him enter. "Come in."

He entered, and she watched him, still hardly able to believe he was here after all. His big shoulders seemed to eat up her tiny apartment. She wondered what he thought of her place. It was small and cluttered with books and miscellaneous objects that appealed to her. On one wall hung a map of the Roman Empire. On another, she had a row of delicate antique ginger jars. There weren't many personal pictures; she owned no pets, she had no ex-boyfriends who had left their stamp. She wasn't even a great housekeeper. How embarrassing. Swiping a messy throw off one of her chairs, Violet folded it nervously. "What are you doing here in Detroit again? I thought you were based out of New York."

"I am. I was." He scanned her apartment, then turned to look back at her. "I might be staying here for a while, though. Maybe for good."

Her heart pounded as if she'd run a mile. "Oh? Why is that?"

"Because you're here, Violet. If you're here, this is where I want to be." He moved toward her, stalking like some big, delicious predator, and took the trembling hand she had pressed to her lips and kissed her fingertips. "I know you said you didn't want me to follow you. You said this wouldn't work. That we were two different people. The thing is . . . I know we're different." His smile was soft, almost apologetic, even as his eyes devoured her face. "You're not the same girl you were ten years ago, and I'm not the same idiot boy. I like to think I've learned from my mistakes. So this time, I'm not letting you go."

"Y-you're not?"

"I'm not. We're doing this your way. However you want. If you want to ignore me for the next ten years, fuck me for one night, and then turn me out again, that's how we'll do this. Whenever, however you need me, I'll be here."

She flinched at his words. God, he made her sound so cold. She pulled her hand from his, hurting. "Jonathan, that's not fair—"

"I don't give a shit if it's fair or not. I'm tired of trying to do the right thing if that means I don't have you." He moved forward and put his hands on her shoulders, ever so gently. "You don't understand, Violet. I'm not saying this to hurt you. I'm telling you that I'm here for you, forever. Always. I know you're scared of being hurt and disappointed. I know you're afraid I'll hurt you again and leave you abandoned. I know the only man in your life was your father, and he neglected you. I know your mother was lost in her own problems, and you've never had anyone to depend on. I'm here to tell you that I will be that person, Violet. I'm here. I'll always be here for you. You can depend on me." His thumbs brushed her shoulders and he gave her a tender look that made her ache inside. "Always."

Violet's lips trembled. A wealth of emotion threatened to erupt inside her. He wasn't vowing intense, passionate love like he normally did.

He was promising to be by her side. Always.

And that was exactly what she needed to hear. What she needed so desperately and yet was terrified to ask for. "Jonathan—"

"Don't turn me away, Violet. Please. Whatever capacity

you want me in your life, I'll be here. Even if it's not as your lover. Even if you just want a friend, I'll be here."

Now the tears spilled down her cheeks. He was being so selfless. She didn't deserve him, didn't deserve his love. She was a wounded creature who had been deprived of love and affection so many times that she didn't even know how to ask for it anymore. She didn't know how to say *yes, that's great, thank you.*

But the understanding look in Jonathan's eyes told her that he knew that, too.

"I'm scared," she told him softly, her voice wobbling. "Every time I love, I get hurt."

"Sometimes love is about hurting, Violet." He brushed the backs of his fingers over her cheeks, dashing away her tears. "But the pleasure in love is greater than the pain. So much greater. You just have to be willing to take that leap."

"And what if, in ten years, we can't make it work? What happens if we part then?"

"Then I've had ten years of your love. Ten years of glorious, wonderful memories, and I'll regret not an iota of it. Every moment, every year, every hour matters. I've finally figured that out, now." His mouth twisted in a wry smile. "Remember when I told you that the last ten years didn't count? I was wrong. Because if we didn't have the last ten years, I wouldn't know what it was like to lose you. Without that, I might never have come here tonight, despite knowing that you didn't want me here. I might never have tried again. I would have just gone on. Those ten years let me learn from my mistakes."

Weeping openly now, Violet fell into his arms and snuggled against his chest. "I love you," she blubbered, all snot and tears and braying sobs. "I love you and I'm so, so scared." Her fingers curled into his jacket. "Just don't leave me again."

"You can't get rid of me, love. I promise. No matter what, I'm yours." He wrapped her in his arms and held her tightly while she cried out her emotions onto his jacket.

They remained like that for a long, long time, Violet struggling to compose herself, Jonathan's hands moving over her shoulders, her arms, her hair. She wasn't sure if it was because he was trying to soothe her, or if he just couldn't get enough of touching her. Either way, she loved it. She loved his touch, and she never wanted to be without it again.

With one last sniff, Violet pulled away from him and took a step back, gazing up at his face. His unshaven, hollow-eyed, beautiful, wonderful face. "I do love you. I just . . . didn't realize it until I pushed you out again."

"I love you too, Violet. I loved the girl I met ten years ago, but I love the woman she is now even more." His hand caressed her neck, drawing her closer, and when he brushed his lips against her mouth in the tenderest of kisses, she felt hope once more.

The world was suddenly full of hope.

"I'm so glad you're here," she whispered.

"I'm glad that you're glad," he murmured. "I figured you'd either listen to me or there would be a restraining order involved. I'm actually a little surprised it's not the latter."

She gave a watery chuckle. "I wanted you here. It just took me losing you again to realize what I had."

"You never lost me," he said, brushing her hair behind her ears in a tender gesture that took her breath away. "Never think that."

Her fingers curled in his clothes. "I was so worried that I'd pushed you away again and that you'd give up on me for good. That I wouldn't be able to fix the mistake." She hesitated, and then added, "I . . . missed my period."

She felt Jonathan's body tense against her own. "I thought you were on the pill?"

"I am. I never skip a dose."

"And we used condoms."

"I know. I still bought a pregnancy test." She bit her lip. "I know the odds are pretty much impossible, but . . ."

"There's always that slim hope."

It *was* hope, Violet realized. She'd wanted a child to anchor Jonathan to her, to force him to come back into her life. But now that he was here, she still wanted a baby. She'd always wanted a family. More than independence, more than travel, more than a career, she'd wanted an honest-to-goodness family. That core unit of people that would love her unconditionally. That core unit of people she felt like she'd never had.

Until now. So she looked up at Jonathan and gave him a wobbling smile. "Shall we go pee on a stick together?"

"Well, I don't know what mine will do, but if you want me to, I'm game."

Violet beamed at him through her tears.

———

Ten minutes later, Violet sat on the bathroom counter, waiting for the results. She'd done the deed and then let Jonathan in so they could wait on the results together.

It wasn't surprising to Violet that the test showed negative almost immediately. It had been too much to hope, really. "No baby," she said softly, and dumped the stick in the trash. She must have been crazy to be disappointed, but she was. "It's for the best."

"Is it strange if I'm disappointed?" Jonathan asked, pulling her off the counter and into his arms.

"Not strange," Violet said. She was oddly disappointed, too. The old, familiar worry returned. If there was no baby, then they didn't really have to stay together, did they? He was free to go at any time.

"Get that thought out of your head," Jonathan said softly, pressing a kiss to her forehead. "I can tell from the look on your face that you're expecting me to run."

She really was transparent, wasn't she? "I didn't say that."

"No, but you were thinking it." His mouth twitched in a smile. "Just because there's not a baby now doesn't mean there can't be one in a year or two."

Her skin prickled at his words; not fear, but anticipation

and excitement. Just the thought of being two years down the road with Jonathan filled her with an intense sense of pleasure. "So what happens now?"

"We leave the bathroom?"

Violet rolled her eyes but pulled out of his arms and walked down the hall. She was heading for the living room of her condo when Jonathan tugged her hand, heading toward her bedroom instead.

Well, she didn't have a problem with that. She let him pull her toward her bedroom, wincing when she spotted her unmade bed and the dirty clothes on the floor. "I'm not a great housekeeper."

"I'll get you one," he told her, moving to sit on the side of her bed and pulling her down next to him.

"I don't want you buying me a housekeeper," she told him. "I'm a teacher."

"Then you shall remain an impoverished teacher and I will take the housekeeper," he told her, dragging her smaller form against his so he could nibble on her ear.

"Do you have a house here in Detroit?" It was difficult to concentrate with his tongue flicking against her ear. "I thought you lived in New York."

"I fly in to Detroit a lot for business and live mostly in New York. I usually stay in a hotel when I'm in Detroit, but if you're here, this is where I want to be, too."

"But what about my teaching?"

"I wouldn't ask you to give up your job for me." He brushed her hair aside and kissed her neck, her cheek, everywhere he could kiss her. "I have a few private planes. I'll just fly back and forth a lot more, provided you'll fly with me occasionally. We'll make it work."

"I guess we will, won't we?" There was that hope, beating a frantic pattern in her breast again.

"I do have meetings every Thursday night that I can't miss, but if you don't mind losing me one night a week, the rest of them are yours."

"You'd relocate for me?" It sounded like he was going out of his way to convenience her. Her with the paltry job. He was a billionaire with an enormous company to run, and he was worried about inconveniencing *her*?

"Violet, you don't seem to get it. I'd do *anything* for you."

She turned to him and flung her arms around his neck. "I love you, Jonathan."

He fell backward on her bed, his arms going around her waist as she fell onto his chest. His eyes were mysteriously shiny again. "You know I'm never going to get tired of hearing you say that?"

"I'm scared of being in love," she admitted to him. "I'm afraid of putting myself out there and getting hurt."

"The last thing I want is to hurt you," he told her in a husky voice, gazing up at her with love.

"I'm starting to figure that out." Her fingers brushed through his hair and she leaned down to kiss him, then pulled back again. "But it's going to take me a while to get comfortable with things. I imagine I'm going to be difficult from time to time—"

"I like difficult."

"And I'll probably close you out when I get hurt or upset."

"I'll just have to push my way back in again."

"And I'm a terrible slob."

"It's a good thing I'm getting that housekeeper."

She laughed, feeling light and airy and wonderful. "I guess it is."

"Just as long as you never leave me again," Jonathan said, his fingers tightening on her waist. "I can put up with any difficult moments, any messy floors, anything you throw at me."

"I won't leave again. I promise," she said, and traced a finger through the stubble on his jaw. "I do love you."

"I love you more than anything in the world."

She smiled and snuggled against his chest, pressing her cheek against his heart. She loved hearing that. She had a feeling she was going to constantly need to hear it just to believe it, but Jonathan was good about telling her.

His hand slid down her body, caressing her hip. "Can I say how glad I am you didn't slam the door shut in my face?"

Her lips twitched with amusement. She felt so light, so wonderful, so utterly carefree at the moment. She loved him. She loved him, and he was all hers. For as many times as she wanted, for as long as she wanted. Violet felt a surge of possessive pleasure mixed with desire. Her hand moved down his front in a caress, gliding from his chest to his crotch. She felt him harden immediately under her hand. "You do seem glad. Nice and . . . glad."

Jonathan groaned, his hands tightening against her. "You're distracting me, aren't you?"

"Is that bad?"

"Hell no. Distract me all you want."

She couldn't stop smiling; her hand caressed his cock through the fabric of his jeans thoughtfully. "Tell me a poem?"

"A poem?" he echoed, clearly distracted.

"Yes. Tell me something romantic." She stroked her hand up and down his cock.

He was quiet for a long moment; as he thought, her fingers dragged over the outline of his cock, and she circled the head through the fabric, causing him to twitch underneath her. "Do you . . . like Rossetti?"

"I'm sure I will."

"All right, then." He sucked in a breath when she dragged her nails over the denim, and then began. "'I loved you first: but afterward your love, outsoaring mine, sang such a loftier song . . .' something something."

She giggled. "Something something?"

"I . . . can't seem to think of the rest of it at the moment. I'm rather distracted." His hand slid over her back, tugged at her bra clasp through the fabric of her top. "I think I'd remember more if we were naked."

"Is that so?"

"It can't hurt."

"I'm willing to give it a try," she teased, sitting up. She smiled down at him and pulled her blouse over her head, tossing it onto the floor. A moment later, her bra followed and she sat in front of him proudly, naked from the waist up.

Jonathan groaned and dragged her body back down against his, seeking her mouth in a kiss. "God, you're beautiful. I am the luckiest man alive."

She smiled down at him. She was the one feeling lucky. This wonderful, smart, gorgeous man loved her. Loved her ridiculously. Loved her even when she was being impractical and frightened. So she kissed him fiercely, trying to show him all the love that she was brimming with at the moment. Her tongue brushed against his lips, and then she pulled back. "How's that memory coming?"

He reached up and brushed his fingers over the tip of her breast. "Give me a minute. I'm sure it'll all come back to me."

"Oh, take your time," she murmured, arching into his touch. His other hand teased her nipple as well, and she tilted her head back, sighing with pleasure. "I'm in no rush."

"So you wouldn't mind if I did this to you all day?"

Goose bumps prickled her skin at the thought of just lying back and languidly letting Jonathan tease her with small touches all day long. "I can't say I'd mind, no."

"Mmm. I think parts of me would go crazy before too long, though." He sat up and dragged her against him. His face pressed against her cleavage and then he was nuzzling her breasts, kissing the soft skin. The unshaven whiskers on his face tickled and dragged at her flesh, sending a bevy of sensations through her. He tuned in to her shivers, biting and licking gently at her. "I love your breasts." He cupped one and lifted it to his mouth, dragging her nipple across his full lips.

"Are they your favorite part?"

"No, your brain is," he said, and she melted all over again. "But they're one of the tastiest parts."

She giggled at that. "It's good to know that I'm tasty, at least."

"The tastiest," he agreed.

"This is all to distract me from the fact that you don't know any other poetry, isn't it?"

He laughed, his breath fanning against her skin. "Not at all. This is so I can suck on these beauties for a while." His thumb teased one nipple before he popped it back into his mouth and began to flick it with his tongue.

Violet moaned, heat pooling between her legs, her pulse pounding a sensual beat in her body. He always made her feel so good, so sexy. It didn't matter that her breasts weren't as perky as they were ten years ago, and her hips wider. He made her feel like the most beautiful woman on earth. And maybe in his eyes, she was.

"I'm remembering another line now," he murmured even as his tongue circled the tip of her breast. "This is definitely helping."

"Mmm, keep going then. I'm glad I could be of help." Her fingers dragged through his hair lazily, brushing along his jaw, the stubble, any tactile experience she could derive from him. She could touch him all day and never get bored.

" 'Rich love knows nought of thine that is not mine. Both have the strength and both the length thereof, both of us, of the love which makes us one.' "

"That's beautiful," she told him softly, and for a moment, crushed him to her chest as if she could somehow drag him against her and give him some of the love that was pouring out of her heart. She was terrified, but she was on cloud nine nevertheless. For some reason, now that she'd accepted Jonathan's love, she knew he'd never hurt her again. It went against everything he was.

"It's true," he told her, and looked up into her eyes with

his own intense, solemn gaze. "'The love which makes us one.' When I'm with you, I feel whole again."

"Me, too." Violet tilted his face so she could kiss him, and he rolled them backward onto the bed. She lay on top of him for a moment, the kissing continuing, and then he rolled them both once more until Violet was under him, and he was on top of her.

"I want to see you naked, love. I want to put my mouth on all of you." His kisses moved from her mouth, to her jaw, then down to her breasts. All the while, his hand tugged and pulled at her skirt.

She wriggled under him, drowning in his touch. She wanted his mouth all over her, and just the thought of his lips delving into her pussy sent her moaning. She guided his hand to the zipper at her hip, and he began to slowly pull it down. It stopped halfway, stuck, and he swore an oath and ripped it the rest of the way down.

She didn't even care. "I want your mouth on me, Jonathan. Now. Please."

He bit the tip of her nipple in response, and she nearly came off the bed at the sweet shock of pleasure mixed with the hint of pain. "Patience. I'm still unwrapping my present."

"Unwrap faster," she told him, raising her hips wantonly. "I need you."

"We have all the time in the world, love." His tongue licked slowly at her nipple, soothing away the small bite he'd given it.

"But I ache for you," she told him in a low, pleading voice. "I've been dreaming about you, you know. Every night."

He groaned and buried his face against her gently rounded stomach, giving her skirt another tug. "Have you?"

"I have."

"I was a little afraid I was the only one still madly obsessed once you left me. I kept thinking that you just wouldn't care."

"That's not true," she said in a soft voice, sucking in when his tongue dipped against her belly button. She'd had no idea she was ticklish there, but his tongue was making her want to squirm and writhe with every licking caress. "I dreamed of you every night."

"Dirty dreams?"

"Very dirty," she told him. "Erotic, sweaty, blissful dreams."

"Mmm, tell me more."

She didn't remember much of them. All she knew was that she had his face in her mind, his body pressed against hers, and when she woke up, her panties were wet and she was aching with unfulfilled need. "They're never as good as the real you, but I woke up every day and ached for you."

His fingers slid under her skirt, still hitched around her hips, and cupped her mound through the silk of her panties. "Did you ache here?"

She moaned. "Yes."

One finger pushed against her slit, dragging against it through the now-wet fabric. "Is all this wetness for me?"

Violet spread her legs wider, encouraging him. "Oh, Jonathan, that feels so good."

"How good?" He continued to rub, pushing down against her flesh like she was a sculpture he was molding under his fingers.

"D-decadent," she panted, making a mewing sound every time his fingertips dragged over her clit.

"Mmm, I like that word. I do think *decadent* makes me think of sweet, delicious things. And are you sweet and delicious, Violet?"

"Why not taste me and find out?" she asked breathlessly, raising a knee until she was sprawled wide open against him, her open legs beckoning.

"Oh, I will. I'm just saving my dessert for a little while longer." His hand lifted from between her legs and he raised it to his mouth, licking his fingers. She watched as his eyes closed in delight. "God, you taste good."

"Still savoring?" Her hips rolled uselessly against the sheets at the hot look in his eyes. "Or is that just an excuse because you can't get my skirt off?"

He threw back his head and laughed. "I admit nothing."

Violet grinned and slid her hand to her skirt, working it down her hips with a bit of creative wiggling. Why, oh why, had she chosen to wear such a tight, inflexible fabric this morning? Sure it looked good on, but it was hell to take off. When she had the skirt down to her knees, though, he grabbed the material and hauled it off her legs, flinging it to the ground. She was left in nothing but her silky pink panties, the crotch damp from excitement, and he gazed down at her, studying her. Automatically she parted her knees and presented herself to him, waiting for more.

To her surprise, he put his palm on her stomach, just below her belly button, and gave her a thoughtful look. "Have you . . . thought about the future much?"

She sucked in a breath, suddenly flattened. "You mean, a baby?"

He nodded, his hand caressing her skin.

Oh, wow. Blinking back sudden tears, Violet forced a small shrug to her shoulders. "Earlier I did, of course. Now . . . I don't know."

"I think I'd like to see you carrying my child," he said in a soft voice, and leaned down to kiss her stomach again. "Maybe not right away. We still need time for us. But maybe in a few years."

Violet nodded, overcome. "I'd love that," she said, aching. It wouldn't replace the baby she'd lost—that unnamed child would always hold a special place in her heart—but they could start a family. Start fresh. Try again.

She loved the thought of that. Her hand went to his hair and she brushed it off his forehead with a loving touch. "Maybe we skip the condoms tonight, then."

Jonathan looked up at her in surprise. "Are you still on the pill?"

"I am. One step at a time. No baby yet, but . . . I want to feel all of you inside me." She wanted that bond that having his flesh against hers would bring them. The intimacy of knowing that nothing separated them from each other, that they'd made this commitment to each other's bodies.

"All right," Jonathan said softly, and his hand slid down to her panties again. This time, he pushed his fingers under the band and sought out her flesh underneath the fabric. "But I want your hands all over me, Violet. I want to feel every ounce of your skin against my own for every moment."

"I can do that," she told him in a low, sweet voice. "It'd be my pleasure." Her hand went to his cheek and she cupped his face as he placed his hand over her mound. He wanted her to touch him? She'd like nothing better. Her fingers trailed down his neck and over one muscular shoulder even as she felt his fingers push between the slick lips of her pussy, seeking out her deepest warmth.

He groaned at the feel of her. "God, you're dripping wet for me, Violet. I can't wait to get in there and drink you up. I want that sweet honey of yours coating my tongue."

She whimpered at his words. If that was true, then why were her panties still on? It was the last item of clothing she wore. He, meanwhile, was fully dressed. She dragged her fingers against the collar of his shirt in a silent plea. Skin. That was what she wanted. Hot, delicious, bronzed skin against hers.

His fingers pushed deeper, and she felt him sink one into her core. Violet moaned, bucking against his hand. "Oh, yes!"

"You're so wet and tight for me, Violet." He thrust his finger deep into her again and ground his palm against her clit in a motion that sent thrilling shock waves through her body. "God, I love how wet you get for me."

She moaned, pushing her hips against his hand. "Naked, Jonathan," she begged. "Want you naked."

"In a minute," he told her. "I can't wait any longer to taste you." His fingers slid from her warmth and she whimpered a protest. A moment later, his face was pressing between her legs, her panties bunching under his chin as he pushed his face down to lick her pussy. His hands framed her mound, pushing her panties back and pushing her lips wide, exposing her clit.

Then he leaned in and took a long, slow taste.

Violet nearly came off the bed with pleasure. "Oh!"

"I've missed this sweet taste," he murmured against her flesh. "I want this every day for the rest of my life. Morning, noon, and night."

She moaned when he tongued her clit again. "Jonathan, please."

"Please what, love?" Even his breath against her skin was driving her wild.

She sobbed at having to state it aloud. "Please make me come."

"Oh, I plan on it. I need more of this sweet juice to lick up." He dragged his tongue down her now-swollen folds, groaning with pleasure as he did. "I plan on making you come over and over again."

Violet arched against his mouth, trying to push her flesh against his tongue in suggestion. He continued to lick her, and every swipe and caress of his tongue was driving her maddeningly closer to the edge. Not quite over, but closer. Her fingers went to her nipples and she began to caress them in time with his tongue. "God, your mouth," she groaned.

"You're so lovely, Violet. So beautiful. I want you to come so hard for me. Come on my face so I can drink it down."

His words and her own teasing hands slammed her over the precipice; she came with a moan, her legs trembling as he continued to lick her with sure, slow strokes, lapping up every bit of wetness until she was shuddering with every lick as it sent aftershocks through her body.

Jonathan finally raised his mouth from her flesh, his lips gleaming wet, his eyes hot with passion. "Nothing tastes better than your come."

She stretched her arms over her head languidly, feeling delicious. "You're way too good at that."

He licked her pussy again, making her quiver all over. "It's my favorite thing in the world—seeing you lose control in my arms."

Violet tugged at the collar of his shirt again. "You know what would give me pleasure? You getting naked so I can put my hands all over you."

His eyes gleamed and he pressed one last kiss to her mound and sat up. "I can do that."

She propped herself up on her elbows and watched him as he stripped off his jacket and then his shirt, muscles flexing. She lifted her foot and pressed it against his lower abdomen as he reached for his pants. "Man, I don't know about you, but I've forgotten all about poetry."

"What poetry?" he asked, and gave her a wicked grin that made her shiver.

"My thoughts exactly," Violet murmured, pulling her foot back when he bent over to shuck his pants. A moment later, he stood upright and stepped out of his pants, and she gave a sigh of pure pleasure at the sight of him, naked and gorgeous. "That's much better." She sat up and began to run her hands down his chest, a little sigh of contentment escaping her. "You're so hard all over."

"I am," he said hoarsely. "You have no idea."

"Oh, I can tell." She reached down to his straining cock and took it in her hand. The length of him was rigid with arousal, the tip leaking beads of pre-cum. Her thumb found the wetness on the crown of him and rubbed it, circling on his skin. "All of this looks very hard and lonely to me."

"Lonely?" His voice was strained. His hands went to her

hair and he dug his fingers into it, tilting her head back and kissing her mouth.

"It looks like it wants to go home," she told him playfully. "I know just the spot for it, too." Her hand wrapped fully around his girth and she pumped him. "Someplace warm, and wet, and snug . . ."

He groaned against her mouth.

"Best of all, he doesn't need a raincoat," she told him, and then nipped at his lip. "Sound like your kind of place?"

"It does."

Violet wrapped her legs around his hips and pulled him closer. They kissed, and she could taste her own desire on his lips. Her hands smoothed up and down his back, and he groaned again. "I love your touch."

"I love touching you," she admitted. His skin felt hot against her own, and he smelled like a mixture of sweat and musk and Jonathan, and she couldn't get enough of him. She leaned forward and sat up, her nipples brushing against his chest, and sucked in a breath when he dragged her hips forward until her sex cradled his cock. Her body was pulled against his, and she sat on the edge of the bed while he stood, her limbs twined about him for support.

"I need to be inside you," he told her.

"I need you inside me," she countered, a faint smile playing on her lips. "What are you waiting for?"

His fingers curled in her hair and he tilted her head a little farther back, nipped at her mouth again, and then said, "I love you, Violet. With all my heart and soul."

And while her heart was fluttering at that intense, sincere admission, he pushed forward and seated himself deep inside her.

Violet gasped; she was always a little shocked at the feel of him when he pushed into her. The thickness of his cock, the sensation of him impaling her was always welcome but stunning. Today, it had the added sensation of his cock being bareback; she imagined she could feel every vein in his cock throbbing against her walls. "Oh, wow."

"God damn," Jonathan said hoarsely. "You without a rubber . . . Jesus."

"I know." Her hands caressed his chest. "I know."

"I'd forgotten how good it felt." He closed his eyes and pulled her tighter against him, burying his face in her neck. "I've never gone bare with anyone but you, you know."

"Really?" She swallowed. Why did that feel like such a meaningful thing?

"Really." His arms wrapped around her, holding her close, and then he gently lowered her backward onto the bed, dragging her forward as he climbed in with her. "You've been the only serious relationship I've ever had. The others were just . . . well, paid sex."

He'd mentioned that before, but it had never sunk in for her, not really. Now, the wonder of it truly hit her. There had never been anyone for him but her.

It was humbling.

Her hands smoothed over his shoulders. "Have I told you that I love you?"

He pulled back and then pushed into her with infinite slowness, her body still clasped against him with one arm, the other supporting his weight as he hovered over her. "You can tell me over and over again, and I will never tire of hearing it."

"That's good, because we have a lot of time to make up for," she told him in a soft voice. Her words broke off into a moan as he thrust into her again, so forcefully that their bodies slid up her sheets.

"I've heard make-up sex is the best."

She giggled at that, and her giggles turned into gasps when he began a steady rhythm, pounding into her with forceful thrusts. All lightheartedness left and she clung to him, digging her nails into his shoulders and moaning his name in time with his movements. Her heels dug into his ass, her hips lifting with each thrust. Each time their bodies rocked together, Violet felt her orgasm hover closer and closer, but she wanted to come with Jonathan. She'd already come once without him, and wanted to share this. She'd never felt closer to him than at this moment, and she clung to him as if he were a lifeline, feeling every thrust into her heart, her soul.

"I love you," she moaned as he began to pump harder.

"Keep telling me," he gritted. "I love hearing you say it."

"I love you," she repeated again, and gasped when he swiveled his hips against her own in a circular motion, making new nerve endings flare to attention. "Oh, God, Jonathan! I love you!"

"Again. Say it again."

She did. Over and over, with every pounding stroke, she told him she loved him, and it seemed to amp up his intensity. Within minutes, she was losing her mind with need, her voice raising into a shriek as he continued to pump harder and harder into her, driving her wild. "I love you! I love you!"

"You're mine, Violet."

"Yours!"

"And you're going to come for me again."

"Yes! Come with me!"

He tilted her hips to the side and pinned her by the hip, then began to hammer into her again. It totally changed the delicious friction and made things intensify by a thousand. Her orgasm roared to life, and, helpless to stop it, she began to come. Her legs tensed and she felt her pussy clench and tug around Jonathan's cock as waves of pleasure coursed through her. She gave a small scream—

And someone banged on the wall on the other side of the condo.

Violet's cry of pleasure turned into a horrified gasp. "Oh, my God—"

"Shhh," he told her. Jonathan's hand went over her mouth and he gave her a wild, almost feral grin. "I'm not done with you yet." And he began to drive into her harder, sending her shrieking right over the edge again, her screams drowned out by his hand. Even as she screamed and came, he came, too, a wash of heat bathing her insides and filling her with satisfaction as his face contorted with pleasure and his strokes slowed.

Eventually, he lifted his hand and grinned down at her, exhausted and sweaty but utterly pleased. He leaned in for one last kiss and then rolled to the side, panting.

She lay on her back, stunned, staring up at the ceiling.

His hand searched for hers and he twined his fingers with her own as they lay flat on their backs, and the small gesture made Violet's heart give a happy flop.

"I think we scared my neighbors," she whispered.

"I think you bit my hand," he teased.

She smothered a laugh.

He looked over at her. "So," he mused. "Do you love me, Violet?"

She peeked over at him through her lashes. "What, you couldn't tell? I think every neighbor in the building heard me shouting it."

He grinned. "How attached are you to this building, anyhow?"

"I don't know. Why?" Violet gave him a suspicious look.

He shrugged. "Was thinking about buying a condo of my own here in Detroit, though I'd probably get something bigger. What do you think?"

She considered this. "What neighborhood?"

"Whichever one you want."

Violet rolled over on her side, amused that his gaze followed her breasts as she did. "Are you asking me to move in with you, Jonathan?"

"I thought that was obvious. Wanna move in with me?"

She rolled onto her back again. "I'll consider it."

"Consider it?" Within seconds, Jonathan's larger body was on top of hers and pressing her against the mattress. "Do you need convincing? I'm pretty good at convincing."

She gave him a sly smile, her arousal rising again. Her fingers skated down his chest. "Maybe you show me a little of this convincing, then."

Neither of them got up from the bed for hours.

SIXTEEN

⌒

Two Weeks Later

"Y ou sure Violet won't mind if I drop in?" Cade Archer, ever solicitous, sounded concerned as the two men exited Jonathan's sports car and headed to the elevator in the parking garage.

"Of course not," Jonathan said, tucking his keys into his jacket pocket. "Besides, it gave me company on the red-eye back here to Detroit." He was glad for that, too. He'd been a little tired tonight, since he'd had to fly in to New York City earlier that day for business meetings, then stuck around for the weekly Brotherhood meeting. He'd considered staying in his Manhattan town house overnight, but the thought of getting back to Violet was a greater pull than sleep. "I called her earlier and she's fixing me a late dinner."

"So how are things between you two?" Cade asked.

Jonathan shot his friend a curious look. "Don't tell me you came all the way to Detroit just because you wanted to see how Violet and I were getting along?"

"Actually, no," Cade said, a wry smile curving his mouth. "I can see from the hickies on your neck how you two are getting along. I'm going to visit a friend here in Detroit tomorrow, and I thought I'd fly in with you just to say hi."

"Well, don't say hi for too long," Jonathan cautioned him. "I plan on dragging Violet into bed at the earliest opportunity."

"Bluntly put, sir," Cade said, unoffended. "I shall find myself a hotel posthaste."

"Well, you can at least have dinner," Jonathan said with a smirk. "But only dinner."

They headed up to the penthouse of the most expensive building in Detroit. It was farther away from the school than Violet liked, but she'd loved the apartment when they'd seen it. Jonathan had solved the distance problem for her by hiring her a driver so she could have someone else do the morning commute while she was still waking up and taking in her morning coffee. It was just one of the ways he got the opportunity to take care of her. Luckily, the building was close to his offices downtown, so by the time he left work, she was already home and grading papers for her students. He suspected his Detroit offices didn't know what to do now that he spent more time in Detroit than New York City, but they'd eventually come around. It allowed him the opportunity to observe the Detroit offices and management, since performances had been poorer than he would have liked last year. Really, this was a good thing all around.

Since they'd moved in together, Jonathan found Violet to be a joy. It was incredible to be able to wake up and find her in his bed every morning. Violet, it turned out, was a cuddler in her sleep, and she tended to cling to him, as if worried that she'd let go and he'd disappear. Thus, he tended to wake up with Violet's front pressed to his back and her cold feet pressed against his calves.

He fucking loved every moment of it.

They made love with abandon, talked about the future, and he didn't even care that she tended to throw her shoes off wherever it struck her, and he could follow a trail of dirty clothes back to the bedroom. After all, they could always hire a maid.

All that mattered was that when he climbed into bed at night, Violet's arms went around him. And when he woke up, he'd look over and see her lovely face on the pillow next to his.

Jonathan's heart had never been so full.

Cade kept up a stream of easygoing conversation as they headed down the hall toward Jonathan and Violet's new apartment, but Jonathan wasn't listening. He'd been gone from Violet for almost a full day; he'd left before dawn that morning and was getting back after two the next morning. This was the longest they'd been apart and he missed the hell out of her.

"You sure she's up?" Cade asked, stifling a yawn.

"She said she would be," Jonathan told him, and opened the heavy wooden door to the penthouse apartment. Immediately, the smell of a spicy stir-fry touched his nose, and his mouth watered. He loved Asian food; he'd developed a taste for it in his travels, and Violet had remembered that.

As if she knew he was thinking about her, Violet padded out of the kitchen, dressed in one of his old T-shirts and a pair of his baggy sleep pants that clung tightly to her generous curves. Her dark hair was rumpled and her eyes looked sleepy, but she held a spatula and beamed at him. "You made it home! I was worried about you." Her gaze went to Cade and warmed. "And you brought a friend. Hi, Cade! It's so good to see you."

"Violet," Cade said, striding forward to give her a quick hug. "You're looking lovely."

They hugged briefly and as soon as Cade released her, Jonathan dragged his beautiful woman into his arms, kissing her passionately. She returned his kisses breathlessly, then pulled away. "You're going to make me burn the food."

"You didn't have to cook," he told her in a low voice.

"I'm glad she did. It smells amazing," Cade said, leaning against one of the nearby counters.

Violet pulled away from Jonathan's arms with a blush and a quick look of longing, and then she turned back to the wok on the gas stove. "I needed to do something to stay awake while I waited for you. Coffee?" She gestured at the half-full coffeepot on the counter.

"I'm good," Cade said. "Can I look around while we wait for food?"

"Of course," Violet said, and winced. "Just . . . excuse the mess. I haven't picked up."

"I won't say a word," Cade said with a grin, and disappeared into the living room.

Immediately, Jonathan grabbed Violet and began to kiss her again, pressing her against a nearby counter and grinding his erection against the cradle of her hips. "God, I missed you."

Her return kisses were equally frantic, her hands clawing at his shirt. "Not half as much as I missed you."

His hand slid into the waistband of her pants and she whimpered, pulling at his hand. "No, Jonathan, wait—"

"I don't want to wait," he growled. He'd been waiting all day to touch her again. To feel that sweet slickness pool between her legs just for him. Twenty hours without Violet was too long. How had he ever gone ten years?

"Wow, the ceiling in here is enormous," Cade called from the living room. "Is the guest bathroom down the hall?"

"Y-yes," Violet called out, sounding breathless as Jonathan's fingers delved down the front of her sleep pants. She was pinned against the counter, but she wasn't fighting him. Instead, she clung to him, her hips pushing against his hand in a silent plea for more. Ah, there it was. Her clit was already poking out, stiff with need, and her wetness hit his fingers as soon as he touched her folds. God, she was always so wet for him. He began to rub and loved the little whimpers she gave even as she started to ride his hand.

Jonathan's mouth captured hers and he kissed her, hard and fierce, while he rubbed her to a quick, brutal orgasm. She came moments later, clinging to him for support, his palm flooding with her juices, her tiny scream smothered by his tongue. He loved the sight of that, and the glazed, exhausted, replete look she gave him when he pulled his hand away. She clung to him, tucking her head against his chest. "Mmm, I'm so glad you're home."

He chuckled and took the spatula from her hand and set it on the counter. The stir-fry was burning, so he turned off the stove even as she yawned and burrowed against him. "Let's get you to bed, love."

"What about food—" she began sleepily.

"I'll eat tomorrow."

"What about Cade—"

He swung her into his arms and began to carry her toward the bed. "He can go get a hotel room."

He thought Violet would protest, but she only buried her face in his neck and began to lick and suck on his skin there. He groaned with need. "Hurry up and kick him out, then," she murmured as he pushed open the door to the bedroom and laid her in the rumpled bed.

Jonathan pressed a kiss to Violet's forehead. "I won't be long."

He wasn't; Cade discreetly emerged from the back of the penthouse once Jonathan shut the bedroom door behind him and adjusted himself. "You know," Cade said, "I think I'll just head out, if it's the same to you."

"Perfect." Jonathan grinned at him in understanding. "You're a good friend."

"I might swing by the Lyons offices in a few days," he said thoughtfully. "Thinking about getting a customized car for a friend."

"It'll be on me," Jonathan said. *Just leave in the next few minutes.*

Cade nodded, seemingly distracted. "Catch you in a few

days, then, man." He clapped Jonathan on the shoulder. "Got keys I can borrow?"

"My roadster's keys are on the hook by the door. It's yours."

Cade grinned. "I'll see myself out, then. Tell Violet I said good night, and that it was lovely to see her."

"Will do," Jonathan said, and waited for Cade to leave. A few moments later, the blond man was gone and Jonathan went through the apartment, turning off lights and picking up Violet's shoes so she didn't trip over them in the morning. He tossed them into a nearby chair and then headed to the bedroom, stripping off his jacket.

Violet was already fast asleep, her cheek tucked into one palm. That was fine; he'd be perfectly happy cuddling his woman as she slept. Just touching her was pleasure enough. Jonathan stripped out of his clothes, turned off the lights, and climbed into bed.

Automatically, Violet turned toward him and he pulled her against his chest. She yawned when he pressed a kiss to her forehead and settled back into sleep.

At least, he thought she was asleep. A sleepy voice rose from the darkness. "This weekend, I think I want to visit my father's grave."

"Whatever you want," Jonathan told her, pulling her closer against him. He admitted to himself that he was curious about what was in the old man's grave, and if his treasured stele and Dr. DeWitt's journals were hidden there, great. But finding those had been less important than getting Violet back, and he was content to wait until she was ready to approach the task again.

Good things came to those who waited, and ten years of patience had won him the best prize of all. Kissing Violet's forehead again, he closed his own eyes, utterly content.

EPILOGUE

That Saturday, the skies were blue and the sun was out, the weather lovely. It was the kind of day that was made for picnics and walks in the park, not visiting a grave. But now that everything else in Violet's life had somehow lined up, this was the only question still unanswered, and Violet wanted closure.

Even if the prize at the end of this treasure hunt was just one of her father's silly notes or a research journal, at least she'd be able to move on from this. Hopefully, Jonathan's stele would be enclosed there, and he could move on, too. No more manipulation from Dr. DeWitt from beyond the grave. She liked the thought of that.

"You look lovely," Jonathan told her as she pulled on a plain black sweater.

Violet stepped into her black flats and gave him an odd look. She'd skipped makeup that morning, just in case she got emotional at her father's grave. On top of that, she was wearing all black. Her lips twitched with a nervous smile; God, why was she nervous? "Lovely, huh? Why is that?"

"Absolutely." He moved to her side, dressed in a black jacket. Instead of his normal T-shirt and jeans, he wore a collared black shirt and slacks out of respect for her father's grave. His hand tucked a lock of hair behind her ear and he gazed into her face. "It's the look on your face this morning. I can't take my eyes off of you. You're strong, and resolute, and every time you look at me, I see love in your eyes. You're the most beautiful woman I've ever seen."

An emotional knot threatened Violet's throat and she tilted her face back, silently asking for a kiss. For comfort.

He brushed his lips over hers. "Shall we get going?"

She nodded, not trusting her voice.

Hand in hand, they went out to the parking garage and Jonathan drove his roadster while Violet navigated with his tablet and a maps application. The graveyard was all the way across town, and they drove in relative silence, the only sounds Violet's quiet driving directions.

When Jonathan finally turned into a parking lot, Violet's heart gave a painful little clench. "We're here," Jonathan said quietly.

She nodded, frozen.

"Do you know where he's buried?"

She stared at the rows of gravestones and flowers, and then gave Jonathan a mutely pleading look.

He leaned over and kissed her cheek. "Wait here, love. I'll go ask."

She waited in the car, clutching the tablet PC to her chest. The day was a gorgeous one, and the cemetery quite pretty. In the distance, an elderly couple walked the rows. For some reason, it made Violet incredibly nervous. It wasn't death itself; her mother had passed when Violet was twenty-one, a miserable drunk to her very last moment.

Violet was terrified of what they'd find at her father's grave and at the end of the scavenger hunt.

She and Jonathan had lived in bliss for the past few

weeks. There was some schedule juggling, of course—they both had jobs. There were the usual growing pains of two people moving into a new place together. But God, she was happy. So, so happy. And she was terrified that whatever they found at her father's grave would somehow ruin this fragile happiness and destroy it forever.

She didn't count on anything less from Dr. Phineas DeWitt.

Her throat was dry when Jonathan left the on-site funeral home, hands in his pockets, and he came to her car door and opened it. "Shall we go?"

"Sure." She didn't sound sure, though. She sounded terrified. But when she got out of the car, Jonathan's fingers laced with her own and she felt a little better.

They walked through rows of gravestones, heading to the back of the cemetery. There, at the end of a row, close to a tree, was a long, narrow stone marker shaped like a famous obelisk—Cleopatra's Needle. Seeing that, Violet started to laugh. "You're kidding me."

Jonathan smiled at her. "Count on your father to go out in style. Look," he said, pointing at the top. "He's even got his name in a cartouche."

Sure enough, her father's name was spelled out in English, then below it, a cartouche with Egyptian hieroglyphs. "Aren't those only for royalty?" Violet asked, amused.

"Like that ever stopped your father?"

He had a point. If anyone thought he was entitled to everything the world had to offer, it was Dr. Phineas DeWitt. Smiling, Violet studied the front of the obelisk. It had his birth date and date of death, and instead of a family platitude, it read "The Garden of Love" poem again:

I went to the Garden of Love,
And saw what I never had seen:
A Chapel was built in the midst,
Where I used to play on the green.

And the gates of this Chapel were shut,
And Thou shalt not, writ over the door;
So I turn'd to the Garden of Love,
That so many sweet flowers bore.

And I saw it was filled with graves,
And tomb-stones where flowers should be:
And Priests in black gowns, were walking their
    rounds,
And binding with briars, my joys & desires.

"That must have had special meaning for him," Violet said softly.

Jonathan's hand squeezed hers in sympathy. "For all his faults, DeWitt had deeper waters than I think he ever liked to let on. He wanted everyone to think he was supremely in control of everything, but sometimes I wonder." He turned to Violet. "How are you feeling?"

She considered her father's headstone. It felt odd to think of him buried here. She hadn't even come to his funeral because she'd been so full of brimming resentment for him. Now, that seemed selfish. "I honestly don't know. Part of me still thinks he was a rotten man, and part of me . . ."

"Still loves him because he was your father?"

"I guess." Her voice was thick.

Jonathan wrapped an arm around her shoulders and hugged her close. "We can leave, you know. Whatever he's holding over our heads isn't worth it. We can turn around and get back in the car."

She buried her head against his chest, enjoying the warmth and strength that he offered. "But your stele? And the journals? I know you wanted both."

Violet felt him shrug. "There will be other steles, other journals."

They both knew that was a lie, but it was sweet of him to offer. She reluctantly pulled away from Jonathan's comforting embrace and shook her head. "We've come this far, haven't we? Might as well go the full distance."

He rubbed her back. "All right. Do you want to do the honors?"

"No. You can." She wasn't sure that she could. For some reason, she was feeling all emotional.

Jonathan gave her another squeeze, and then he walked to the back of her father's obelisk gravestone. He glanced around and gave her a rueful look. "Mind keeping a lookout? I'd hate to have someone come after me and wonder what I'm doing."

A hysterical giggle arose in Violet's throat at the thought of Jonathan being caught red-handed doing something to her father's grave. She obediently turned her back to him and scanned the area. There was no one nearby. A grounds-keeper was fussing with an edger in the distance, and the elderly couple she'd seen earlier was heading to the parking lot.

She heard Jonathan's clothing rustle and then he hummed under his breath. "There's a little ledge under the base here and I can feel a tiny lever."

A thrill raced through her. Not surprising, but still exciting. She glanced around, but there was no one close by, so she turned back to Jonathan and knelt next to him. His hands were running along the base of the obelisk. "Can you open it?"

"Yep. It's just got a lot of dirt crusted on it. Give me a moment . . . There." A loud click sounded and a tiny compartment shot out a half inch, then got stuck in the thick green grass. He groaned in dismay. "I guess he didn't think this whole secret compartment thing through all that well. I need to dig it out a little."

"Hurry," Violet whispered, glancing around. The cemetery was still empty, but her heart was fluttering wildly in her chest, as if they were in danger of being caught and chastised like naughty children.

"Almost have it," Jonathan murmured. He ripped up the grass at the base of the obelisk and dug his fingers into the soil until he could wiggle the small shelf forward a little more. The interior was a bright red, like a jewelry box, and she could see two creamy envelopes tucked inside a plastic bag.

Violet sucked in a breath. "There they are."

Jonathan wiped his hands on the grass and then reached for the plastic bag, taking it gently out of the secret compartment. He handed them to Violet, and slid his fingers into the compartment again. "Nothing else."

"No stele?" She felt a pang of disappointment. Poor Jonathan. He'd wanted that very badly, if for nothing else than to restore her father's name to the men he'd worked with for so long and ultimately betrayed.

"No stele," Jonathan said. "It doesn't matter."

She nodded absently and pulled the two envelopes from the protective bag into her lap. Both were sealed with her father's familiar wax symbol, and their names were on the front. Just like usual, except this time, Violet's envelope was thicker, as if it held multiple pieces of paper. She held Jonathan's out to him, fingers trembling. This was it. Unless her father was sending them on another wild-goose chase, this was the last communication she'd ever have from him.

The thought made her feel curiously hollow.

"Open yours first, love." Jonathan took his envelope and set it in his lap, waiting.

She nodded, breathless, and broke the seal. Inside were several sheets of handwritten lined paper. Unlike the notes from before that were sent on a thick, creamy vellum, this was pages of her father's loose, messy writing, torn from a notebook and folded over and over again until the paper was soft, as if he'd handled it repeatedly before lovingly placing it in the envelope for her to find after his death.

Violet unfolded it and began to read.

Darling Violet Isolde DeWitt,

I could start this out with a cliché and say that by the time you read this, I am dead. But I was never a man fond of the obvious, as you might have guessed now that you are reading this. I prefer to leave my mark with style. I'm thankful that you (and hopefully Jonathan) have followed my trail to my final resting place.

I know you've held resentment for me in your heart. There's been a lot of bad blood between us. And since it's impossible for us to talk without emotion and our past getting in the way of our words, I wanted to tell you everything from my perspective and hope that you could perhaps understand your dear old dad a little more.

Your mother and I should have never married. I was her teacher and she was my student, and we should have never been involved, but I couldn't resist her. I've never been able to resist her, really. I know that this is perhaps obvious as an adult, but I know it was hard on you as a child to have your parents be so at odds with each other. I have always been wrapped up in my work, and your mother was always looking for someone to save her from herself. I didn't realize that until it was too late, and then she was pregnant with you. We both wanted you—if nothing else to save our already failing relationship, and so we married. But I found that your mother wanted me to give up my work for her, and that there was no pleasing her. For the first few years, I truly did try. I stayed home from important digs, I made other arrangements, and I was at her side for every hour of the day that I was not working at the university. It still wasn't enough for her, and I began to realize that the black hole in your mother's soul that was sucking all happiness out of her was going to extend to me if I let it. I had to make a choice, and I chose my work since it was either that or for both of us to be eternally miserable.

I know that my choice wasn't the right one for you, but I didn't know what else to do. Half the time when I tried to come home, your mother would insist I stay away. I missed several of your birthdays, your kindergarten graduation . . . but I did it to try and please your mother. By the time I realized that there would never be any pleasing her, it was too late and you and I had grown so far apart that I felt there was an uncrossable gulf between us.

Violet swallowed hard. He'd stayed away while she was growing up because her mother had asked him to? She'd always thought he'd been too busy for her, too uninterested. To find out that her miserable mother had been equally responsible for Violet's loneliness wasn't surprising, but it was heartbreaking. How many times had she misunderstood old Phineas DeWitt, who knew how to handle a two-thousand-year-old vase with care, but didn't know how to spend time with his daughter or handle his too-young and too-unstable wife? Suddenly, things were no longer so black and white.

You were always the brightest little scrap, and even if I wasn't the best father, I was proud of you. You were smart and sensible where I wasn't, strong and independent where your mother was not. Both your mother and I were two really weak people at our core, but I like to think we created something special when we created you. When you graduated, I wanted you at my side for the summer in Akrotiri. Your mother didn't want you to go. She was jealous, I think, and lonely. I insisted, though. I loved having you there for the dig that summer. I know we didn't get to spend as much time as we'd wanted together, but I was so proud of you. I still am.

Now, you're probably wondering why I've dragged you all over the place and forced you together with

Jonathan Lyons once more. It has everything to do with Akrotiri, because that summer . . . I made a huge mistake.

It didn't take much digging to figure out the trouble you were in. Someone had overheard you telling Jonathan that you wanted to start a family, and one of the other girls that bunked with you confessed that you were crying a lot. It reminded me of how your mother and I got together, actually. I guessed that you were pregnant and trying to bring Jonathan home with you.

And I got selfish. I saw Jonathan as the son I never had, and the thought of him losing out on his dreams to go and raise a baby with you . . . it made me feel as if history was repeating itself. I was coming off of another bitter argument with your mother, and we were on the verge of making some really wonderful breakthroughs in Akrotiri, and my daughter wanted to take away my favorite assistant. So I acted selfishly, and when you left your letter for Jonathan, I took it and hid it.

He never got your message, Violet. That's my fault. It was clear he was in love with you, though. As soon as you left, he became a different person: morose, unhappy. It was like the light had gone out, and I knew the light was you. So I did my best to make him forget you so I could have my assistant back. I told him you'd married someone as soon as you returned home. It broke his heart, I think, but it did the job. He threw himself back into work, and I hid my guilt. I knew I had crushed your relationship, but I hoped, foolishly, it would end up being best for both of you. When I heard from your mother that you lost the baby, my guilt was overwhelming. By then, though, I'd chosen my course. You resented me for continuing to spend time with Jonathan, and I felt as if I'd lost every connection to my baby girl, and it was my own fault. I'd chosen archaeology over family for the last time, and I had nothing left but work . . . so

I worked. It wasn't something I could apologize for, so I tried to forget it ever happened.

Of course, it came back to bite me when I got too sick to work. By then, I'd chosen my path. There was no one to sit at a lonely old man's bedside and hold his hand and keep him company. I'd pushed everyone out of my life except for work colleagues, and if you can't work, you don't even have those.

I sent you on this long, crazy chase so you might remember me a bit more fondly over time. I've arranged this "scavenger hunt" in the hope that you will reconcile with Jonathan and at least part as friends. It was my fault that the two of you did not end up together ten years ago; the least I can do is bring you together upon my death.

You've probably wondered at the poetry, too. I remember my sweet Violet loved poetry once upon a time. It was a form of expression for someone who had a hard time expressing herself. I hope you enjoyed the pieces I picked. They spoke to me, and I thought the themes of love and loss were appropriate to how I felt, too. Perhaps you got your inability to express yourself from dear old dad, eh?

Please tell Jonathan that I stole the stele deliberately to force his hand. It's being held in a safety-deposit box at the Detroit Credit Union under your name and your date of birth is the passcode. I trashed my journals when I found out I was sick. Even this old bastard can keep a few secrets.

Most of all, I wanted you to know that even though I was a terrible and absent father, I still loved you with all the capacity of my small, selfish heart and I'm so proud of you.

> *Your father,*
> *Dr. Phineas DeWitt*

Tears blurred Violet's eyes. *I still loved you with all the capacity of my small, selfish heart and I'm so proud of you.* How many times had she wanted her father to say that to her as a young girl? And yet, if he'd approached her as an adult, she'd have turned away from him with scorn, her heart hardened by disappointment. She carefully refolded the letter, tears flowing down her cheeks. Then, she held it out to Jonathan so he could read it. He did, utterly silent as he paged through it, eyes scanning the words written in a shaky hand. She swiped at her tears with irritation, but they kept coming.

She was feeling so many things at this moment: sadness for her father, who'd died lonely and cut off, knowing that the choices he'd made in his relationships had condemned him; self-pity that she'd lost her father; helpless frustration at knowing her father's motives behind the choices that had screwed with her life. And a sad, sweet ache for the fact that she'd never gotten to tell her father that she'd always loved him, too, even if he disappointed her.

Most of all, she wept for the realization that she could have become her father.

She'd failed at relationship after relationship, not willing to open herself up to get hurt. Before Jonathan had pushed his way back into her life, she'd been alone, with friends at work but spending most weekends by herself and passing time by devoting herself to work. Just like her father.

Jonathan refolded the letter and tucked it back into the envelope. His gaze went to her. "Are you all right, Violet?"

She trembled, holding back her sobs. "I just . . . I was turning into him, you know? I've been holding on to grudges for so long that I refused to see him when he was sick. I almost pushed you away, too. And there would have been no letter after the fact to let you know that I still loved you, because it would have been too late." Her entire body quaked with suppressed sobs. "I wish I could have talked to him one more time."

Jonathan pulled her against him and held her while she cried, his hands soothing down her shoulders. "He understood, Violet. Your father knew you, and he knew you were hurt. I think that's why he sent you on this crazy letter hunt. That was the only way to break down your barriers. For what it's worth, I'm glad things turned out the way they did."

Her fingers plucked at the sleeve of his jacket as she sniffed. "Because we ended up together?"

"Because we ended up together," he agreed. "Everything else was worth it. All the heartaches, the misery, the lonely nights. If we could change anything, I still wouldn't, because it's allowed us to be here together, today."

She clung to him. "I love you."

"I love you, too."

Violet gave another watery sniff. "Did you open your envelope yet?"

"Not yet." With his arms still around her, he tore the seal with his fingers and shook out his letter.

A piece of yellowed notebook paper, folded into one of the intricate designs that Violet had learned in high school, fell onto the grass. It was sealed with a tiny Santorini postage stamp and said *TO JONATHAN—URGENT!!!* on the front cover.

Violet gasped at the sight of it. "That . . . that was my letter. About the baby."

"Still sealed," Jonathan said, the ache in his voice. His arms tightened around her. "Part of me wants to hate your father for that."

"And part of you feels sorry for him. I know," she murmured. She felt the same. "But we're together now."

He nodded.

"I guess we should go get your stele."

"Since I can't break it over anyone's head at the moment? Yes, I suppose we should."

Violet gave a shaky giggle at the mental image. "You wouldn't do that anyhow."

"Wouldn't I?" He pulled her away from his chest and gave her a serious look. "Violet, you realize you're everything to me, right? Nothing in this world matters to me more than you do. Nothing at all. I'd break every stele from here to the Smithsonian if it would make you happy."

"That would not make me happy," Violet said. "But it's sweet of you to offer."

"Then what would make you happy, Violet?"

She looked up at him, into his handsome, worried face. Worried for her. And she felt such an outpouring of love for this fierce, intense man. "I just want to be in your life. In every part of your life. Forever." She placed her cheek on his shoulder. "I have to warn you, I'm probably going to be an extremely clingy girlfriend."

"The thought of you being extremely clingy makes me extremely happy," Jonathan said. "Cling all you like. As for the rest of my life, it means nothing to me if you're not there at my side."

Violet sighed with utter contentment. She liked hearing that.

Jonathan kissed her temple, and then murmured, "Speaking of, what are you doing next Thursday? I'd like for you to fly with me to New York."

"Oh?"

"I have some friends I want you to meet."

That Thursday, Violet dashed out of Jonathan Lyons Middle School with the final bell. She swung her purse over her shoulder and rushed out the door with the students, as giddy and excited as they were to be out of class after a long day.

Parked in front of the school was a familiar form in a casual jacket and T-shirt, leaning against a shiny red Lyons roadster. Jonathan smiled at Violet as she rushed out the door and gave her a kiss as she came to his side. "Ready, love?"

"Ready."

He opened the car door for her, and she slipped inside the passenger seat. A moment later, they were blazing away from the school, heading toward a private airport where Jonathan's favorite turboprop Socata waited.

They flew into New York City just as the sun was setting, and Violet stifled a few yawns as Jonathan ushered her into a sedan and urged the driver toward an unfamiliar address.

When the driver parked on the street outside of a club, Violet gave Jonathan a curious look. This was the club he'd had "business" at before when he'd made her wait in the limo. Odd that they should come here again. She wasn't appropriately attired, either. She'd worn her normal school-teacher clothing—a pencil skirt and a high-necked blouse with long sleeves. "I'm not dressed for a night on the town, Jonathan."

"Don't worry," he assured her, moving to her side and sliding a possessive arm around her waist. "That's not our final destination."

Puzzled, Violet kept her thoughts to herself as Jonathan ushered her inside and through the club, then down a back hallway. There was a bodyguard in the hall, standing in front of a door, and Violet almost missed the bizarre hand gesture Jonathan gave him. The man grunted and moved aside, and Jonathan turned to look at her. "Promise me you'll share this with no one?"

"I promise," she told him, now more curious than tired.

He took her hand and kissed the back of it. Then, lacing his fingers with hers, he took the lead and descended the flight of stairs into the cellar of the club. Violet smelled cigars and heard the soft murmur of voices as the door closed behind them.

"Boys," Jonathan announced as he stepped down the stairs and into the room. "I've brought someone with me tonight."

Five sets of eyes stared at her in open surprise as Violet

entered the basement room with Jonathan. There was a large card table in the center, and five men sat around it, with one empty chair on the far end, no doubt waiting for Jonathan. Drinks and cards were scattered, and a cloud of cigar smoke hung in the air.

"Hi?" Violet said, looking at Jonathan curiously.

"I've brought Violet to meet my brothers," Jonathan said, a proud look on his face as he tugged Violet forward.

"Brothers?" she asked, curious. Jonathan didn't have any brothers, did he? She thought he'd had an older brother once, but he'd long since passed away. She gazed at the faces around the table and was surprised to see Cade Archer sitting amongst the men, a knowing grin on his face.

"Oh, shit," said a man with a goatee. "Here we go again."

Keep reading for a special excerpt from
the first book in the new
Billionaires and Bridesmaids series

THE BILLIONAIRE
and the VIRGIN

Coming soon from Berkley!

Marjorie Ivarsson adjusted the bow on her behind and craned her neck, trying to look in the mirror at the back of her dress. "How is this?"

"Fucking awful," said the redhead next to her in a similar dress. "We look more like cupcakes than bridesmaids."

"Do you guys really hate the dresses?" Brontë asked, wringing her hands as the women lined up and studied their reflections in the mirrors.

"Not at all," said Audrey, who Marjorie knew was the extremely pregnant, nice one. She elbowed the not-as-nice redhead next to her. "I think they're lovely dresses. What do you think, Marj?"

"I love it," Marjorie lied. Truth was, all that red and white made her look a bit like a barber pole with a bow, but Brontë had worked long and hard to pick out dresses and had paid for everything, so how on earth could Marjorie possibly complain? She'd seen the price tag for this thing. Apparently they'd been custom made by a fashion designer, and the price of just one dress cost more than Marjorie would make in months. Brontë was spending a lot on her wedding, and Marjorie didn't want to be the one to kick up a fuss.

So she adjusted the bow on her behind again and nodded. "It's beautiful. I feel like a princess."

"Oh, you're so full of shit," Gretchen began, only to be elbowed by the pregnant one again.

"I think I need this let out a bit more on the sides," Audrey said, waving over the dressmaker. "My hips keep spreading."

A woman ran over with pins in her mouth, kneeling at Audrey's side as Marjorie gazed at the line-up of Brontë's bridesmaids. There was herself, a six-foot-one Nordic blonde. There was Gretchen, a shorter, curvier woman with screamingly red hair that almost clashed with her dress, except for the fact that she was the maid of honor, so her mermaid-cut gown was more white than red. There was Gretchen's sister Audrey, who was a pale, freckled redhead and heavily pregnant. And sitting in a corner, beaming at them as if it were her own wedding, was a frizzy-headed blonde named Maylee who was currently being stitched into her bridesmaid dress. Apparently she was a last-minute addition to the wedding party, and so her dress had to be fitted on the fly.

Gretchen fussed with the swishing tulle gathered tight at the knees by decorative red lace. "My wedding is going to be in black and white, I swear to God, because this shit is ridicu—"

"So what made you decide to have a destination wedding, Bron?" Marjorie asked, trying to be the peacemaker. She was a little disturbed at Gretchen's rather vocal opinions about the dresses, and sought to change the subject.

Brontë beamed at Marj, looking a little like her old self. "This is where I met Logan, remember? We got stuck here when I won that trip from the radio and the hurricane hit." She grabbed Maylee's hands and helped the other woman to her feet as another tailor fussed over the hems. "Logan bought the island and decided to renovate the hotel. He pushed for them to have it done this week so we could get married here. Isn't that sweet?"

"Sweet," Marjorie echoed, adjusting the deep vee of her neckline. Truth be told, her brain had stopped processing once Brontë had said "bought the island." Marj was still weirded out by the fact that Brontë—quirky, philosophy quoting Brontë had dated a billionaire and now they were getting married. In her eyes, she always saw Brontë as a waitress, just like herself. They'd worked together at a 50s sock-hop diner for the last year or two . . . at least until Brontë had moved to New York City to be with Logan. It was something out of a fairy tale—or a movie, depending on which was your drug of choice. Either way, it didn't seem like something that happened to normal people. "You're so lucky, Brontë. I hope I can meet a guy as wonderful as Logan someday."

"Hope is a waking dream," Brontë said with a soft smile. "Aristotle."

Gretchen snorted, only to be thwapped by her sister again.

"Bless your heart, Brontë, for paying for everything so we could all be here with you," Maylee gushed, striding forward to line up with the other bridesmaids. "Look at us. We're all so lovely, aren't we?" She put a friendly arm around Marjorie's waist and beamed up at her. "Like a bunch of roses getting ready for the parade."

"I believe they are floats in a parade, Maylee," Gretchen said drily. "Which, now that you mention it—"

Marjorie giggled, unable to stifle the sound behind her hand.

"So who are we missing?" Audrey asked, counting heads. "I know Jonathan and Cade are also groomsmen, right? That's five groomsmen and I only count four bridesmaids here? What about Jonathan's ladylove? What's her name?"

"Violet," Brontë added. "And I offered for her to be in the wedding, but she declined since we're not familiar with each other, truly. Logan wanted me to add her to the bridesmaid lineup to make Jonathan happy, but Violet insisted on simply attending." She strode forward and adjusted the lace band under Marjorie's bust. "Does this look crooked to you? Anyhow, Angie's flying in but her kid was having dental surgery today, so she's not coming in until tomorrow."

Marjorie smiled at Brontë meekly. She'd feel a lot better when Angie was here. She, Brontë, and Angie had all waited tables together (along with Sharon, but no one liked Sharon) at the diner. Angie was in her forties, motherly, and wonderful to be around. They often went to bingo together.

Gretchen nudged Marjorie. "So do you have a date for the wedding? Bringing yourself a man in the hopes he'll catch the garter?"

"I do have a date," Marjorie said. "His name's Dewey. I met him playing shuffleboard."

"Dewey? He sounds ancient."

"I believe he's in his eighties," Marjorie said with a grin. "Very sweet man."

"Ah. I getcha." Gretchen gave Marjorie an exaggerated wink. "Sugar daddy, right?"

"What? No! Dewey's just nice. He's on vacation because his wife recently died and he needs a distraction. He seemed so lonely that I invited him to be my date at the wedding. Nothing more than that. He's a sweet man."

"Leave her alone, Gretchen," Brontë said, butting in. "Marjorie always finds herself a sweet old guy to dote on." Brontë gave her a speculative look. "I don't think I've ever seen her out with anyone under the age of seventy."

Brontë knew her well. Marjorie smiled at that. "I guess I'm pretty obvious. I just . . . you know. Have a lot more in common with guys like Dewey than most people."

It was true. She didn't really *date* older men. She just spent her time playing bingo with friends, and shuffleboard, and going to knitting circles and volunteering at the nursing home when she could. Her parents had died long before

Marjorie could remember their faces, and so she'd been raised by Grandma and Grandpa. Marjorie had grown up quilting, canning, watching *The Price Is Right*, and basically surrounded by people four times her age. It was something she never grew out of, either. Even at the age of twenty-four, she felt more comfortable with someone in their eighties than someone in their twenties. People her age never sat and relaxed on a Saturday morning with a cup of coffee and a crossword. They never just sat around and talked. They took selfies and got rip-roaring drunk and partied all night long.

And that just wasn't Marjorie. She was an old soul in a really long, lanky body.

That was another thing that the elderly never made her feel weird about—Marjorie was tall. At six foot one, she was taller than every woman and most men. No one wanted to date someone that tall, and most women looked at her like she was some sort of freak of nature. Not her Grandma and Grandpa. They'd always made her feel beautiful despite her height.

So, yeah. With the exception of Brontë, all of Marjorie's friends were living in retirement homes.

"Well, I think we're good on the fitting for now," Brontë said as the tailors finished their measurements. "Everyone out of their gowns. Go enjoy the day and I'll see you ladies tonight for the bachelorette party?"

Maylee giggled and Gretchen high-fived everyone. Audrey only patted her rounded belly. "Guess I'm the designated driver."

They shimmied carefully out of the fitted gowns and changed back into their clothing. Marjorie had brought her beachwear with her just in case, and changed into her polka-dotted one piece swimsuit, then wrapped a sarong around her hips, stuffing her clothing into a bag.

It was a lovely day for a walk on the beach, and she had a few hours before afternoon shuffleboard started up, anyhow.

———

"Look! Look! *Tits or GTFO*! Right?" The woman frolicking in the water near Robert Cannon's float pulled off her top and shook her extremely fake cans in his direction.

He raised his drink to her, inwardly wishing she'd go away and take her friend with her. He touched his bluetooth earpiece to remind her that he was on a conference call, despite floating in a raft on the beach, a mixed drink in hand. "What do you mean, ratings are down?"

"Just that," said his assistant. "Reports are in and despite the new shows, ratings are down for The Man Channel by two percentage points."

Rob swore and took another swig of his drink. Near his raft, one of the beach bunnies grabbed another tanned girl. Looking over at him, they began to make out in an attempt to try and get his attention.

Fucking typical.

"What about the new show?" Rob asked. Hell, if he was down two points despite the new show, he'd need a much stiffer drink. This one wasn't doing much to sustain his buzz.

"*Tits or GTFO*? Well, despite heavy marketing, it looks like we're not hitting that target 18-40 demographic as heavily as we'd like. I'm not sure what the deal is."

Robert swore again. "And advertisers?"

"Already making unhappy noises."

Great. That was just what he fucking needed. He swigged his drink, emptied the glass, and waved it at one of the beach bunnies. On cue, one of the women took it and headed to the shore to get him a refill, her tits bouncing in her tiny bikini. "I'll make some calls when I get back, all right? Just hold down the fort for this week while I take care of things down here."

"Any luck with Hawkings?"

"Not yet, but I'm hoping to make some progress," Rob

told him absently, watching the antics of the two women. They kissed again—and then looked over at him to see if he was paying attention. One of them waded back out to his raft, his drink in hand. Rob shook his head. Ridiculous creatures. He'd become jaded on people long ago, and these two weren't changing his mind, that was for damn sure. "I'll keep you posted. In the meantime, I want a full write-up of all the overnight ratings and a comparison of ad revenue. Have it to me by the morning."

"Will do."

"And find out at what point those ratings dropped. What's causing things to tank? Call me back."

"Will do."

He clicked off the phone and tilted his head back against the raft, letting the sun beat down through his Bugatti sunglasses. Fucking hell. With ratings down, he was going to have a hell of a time convincing Logan Hawkings that starting up a new cable channel aimed at white-collar businessmen and executives was going to be worth his while.

Not that Rob couldn't bankroll it himself. The billions in his bank account said differently. But he wanted Hawkings's stamp on it, because Hawkings knew everyone in New York City and had a lot of cachet that Rob didn't. People respected him and his business.

They didn't respect Rob's, no matter how much money it made him.

Most of the time he didn't give a shit. Notoriety had made him as much money as anything else. And if he'd made his fortune on capitalizing on cable channels and radio networks designed for the average Joe, so much the better. So some of his shows weren't exactly aboveboard. So what? *Tits or GTFO* was still popular. As long as there were girls with low self-esteem wanting to get on camera, they'd make money.

And he wouldn't feel bad about it.

It wrecked his social life, but he'd just cry into his piles of money. Every woman that was even halfway interested in him wanted his wallet, or to be on one of his shows. The only girls he seemed to attract anymore were vapid idiots like the two currently making out and cavorting in the water in front of him just to get his attention. Didn't care, really.

Rob took the drink that blonde number one offered him and sipped it. Strong, just the way he liked it. "Thanks, sugar."

"So," she said, giving her body a little wiggle to get his attention. "Think I've got what it takes to be on one of your shows?"

"Maybe," he said absently, taking a swig of his drink. Christ, that was strong. He took another swig, because why not? He needed to get good and drunk. Two fucking ratings points. Jesus.

The other girl swam up next to him. "I heard you did lines off of Tiffany West's stomach in Cannes," she said with a sultry smile.

"Did you? How nice," he said flatly. He didn't even know who Tiffany West was, and he sure as shit didn't do drugs. Alcohol was easy. Drugs just made you end up as someone's prison bitch.

"Wanna do lines off of my stomach?"

"I'm busy." Another call was due to come in any minute now.

He tossed down the rest of his drink and handed it off to one of the girls who watched him expectantly. When they didn't go away, he looked back over at them. "How about you and you," he said, pointing at both of them, "go do lines together and leave me the fuck alone?"

One of the blondes gave him a furious look and stormed away. The other wasn't quite so nice. She huffed up, her fake breasts rising, and then gave his raft a vicious shove.

Rob flipped over and landed in the water, head going under.

Fucking perfect. His head swam and he pushed his head

above the water, glaring at the women that left. One of those two was going to buy him a new Bluetooth headset, so help him—

One of his legs cramped up, shooting pain through his muscles. Rob went back under the water, thrashing. It was like his leg had locked up. Combine that with his spinning head, and he couldn't quite get his bearings. The current ripped at him, dragging him further away from the shore. Huh. Riptide. He thought you had to be further out for those sorts of things. His lungs were aching, and he tried to push his head back above the water, but it seemed further and further out of reach.

Goddamn it, was he going to drown on the beach of someplace named Seaturtle Cay? Really?

But he couldn't find air. Reflexively, his throat worked and salt water filled his lungs, his mouth, his nose. He choked, and the world started to go black. He was really, truly dying. His last thought was that he'd be in the tabloids for forever now—legendary for drowning in a few feet of water at the beach.

More blackness filled his vision, then red . . . and polka dots.

Polka dots?

A strong arm grabbed him, and suddenly Rob's face was hauled against a pair of breasts. Real breasts. He barely had time to process this before more darkness swam through his mind, and he followed it under.

"Breathe," a voice shouted in his ear, and then lips pressed against his mouth. Air pushed into his lungs—and fuck, that hurt like hell—and suddenly water was coming up out of his throat and his nose and he turned his head to the side, vomiting salt water. His head ached in the most blisteringly awful fashion, and those red polka dots were swimming in his vision again. But there was sand under his back, and slowly, blearily, he focused his eyes.

An angel bent over him on the beach. An angel with a faint peppering of freckles across her nose, a strong jaw and messy, wet blond hair, and dressed in the ugliest polka-dotted swimsuit he'd ever seen. And she was smiling down at him.

She'd saved him. And the look she gave him was so shy and proud all at once, that he felt his heart swell.

Well, damn. Rob was in love.

Jessica Clare

STRANDED
with a
BILLIONAIRE

A BILLIONAIRE BOYS CLUB NOVEL

With a visit to a private island resort in the Bahamas, billionaire Logan Hawkings has a chance to mend his broken heart. Then a hurricane, a misplaced passport, and a stalled elevator lead to an encounter with a most unusual woman.

Brontë Dawson is down-to-earth, incredibly sensual, and even quotes Plato. She also thinks Logan is simply the hotel's domineering yet sexy manager. And after several steamy island nights in his arms, Brontë's ready to give her heart to the man in charge. There's just more to Logan than he's told her—a billion times over.

jessica-clare.com
facebook.com/AuthorJessicaClare
facebook.com/LoveAlwaysBooks
penguin.com

M1478T0414

FROM *NEW YORK TIMES* BESTSELLING AUTHOR

JESSICA CLARE

BEAUTY
and the
BILLIONAIRE

A Billionaire Boys Club Novel

Real-estate tycoon Hunter Buchanan has a dark past that's left him scarred and living as a recluse on his family's palatial estate. Hunter is ready to give up on love—until he spots an enigmatic beauty and comes up with an elaborate scheme to meet her.

Gretchen Petty is in need of a paycheck—and a change. So when a job opportunity in an upstate New York mansion pops up, she accepts. And while she can overlook the oddities of her new job, she can't ignore her new boss's delectable body—or his barely leashed temper.

Hunter worries that his scheme might be unraveling before it's truly begun, but Gretchen is about to show him that life can be full of surprises…

jessica-clare.com
facebook.com/AuthorJessicaClare
facebook.com/LoveAlwaysBooks
penguin.com

"Clare's sizzling encounters in the great outdoors have definite forest-fire potential from the heat generated."
—*RT Book Reviews*

"A fun, cute, and sexy read . . . Miranda's character is genuine and easy to relate to, and Dane was oh so sexy! Great chemistry between these two that makes for a *hot* and steamy read, but also it is filled with humor and a great supporting cast."
—*Nocturne Romance Reads*

"If you like small-town settings with characters that are easy to fall in love with, this is the book for you."
—*Under the Covers Book Blog*

Praise for the Billionaire Boys Club novels

THE WRONG BILLIONAIRE'S BED

"Just thinking about it puts a smile on my face . . . In short, this is a really fun, entertaining, engaging book, and I can't wait to read (and reread) the other billionaires' stories."
—*Heroes and Heartbreakers*

"An awesome quick read that touched my heart and stirred my spirit. Buckle up and take the ride—you'll enjoy every peak, valley, twist, and turn."   —*Cocktails and Books*

BEAUTY AND THE BILLIONAIRE

"Clare really knocked it out of the park again . . . This series has been a pure and utter delight."   —*The Book Pushers*

"I am in love with this series."   —*Love to Read for Fun*

"Sexy and fun."   —*Smexy Books*

"I loved this book."   —*Heroes and Heartbreakers*

STRANDED WITH A BILLIONAIRE

"A cute, sweet romance . . . A fast, sexy read that transports you to the land of the rich and famous."   —*Fiction Vixen*

"[Clare's] writing is fun and sexy and flirty . . . *Stranded with a Billionaire* has reignited my love of the billionaire hero."   —*The Book Pushers*

"Clare's latest contemporary is gratifying for its likable but flawed hero and heroine, [and] sexy love scenes."
—*Library Journal*

continued . . .